The Switch

a novel

Heather Justesen

Other novels by Heather

The Ball's in Her Court
Rebound
Blank Slate
Family by Design

Novellas

Homecoming
Shear Luck

Short stories

Along no Longer
He doesn't Belong
Holding On

Non-fiction:

POD Like a Pro: An Author's Guide to Typesetting
and Formatting a book for print

The Switch

A novel

Jelly Bean Press
Fillmore, UT

Heather Justesen

ISBN: 978-0615632568

Published by Jelly Bean Press, 90 S Main, Fillmore, UT 84631

Dedication

For Gabby, keep writing, your dreams are closer than you think. Love you!

One

"Samantha, it's time for dinner. Get in here now!" Tia called to her five-year-old from the kitchen. It had already been a long day, and though she'd been running like crazy since before seven in the morning, Tia's to-do list didn't seem to be shrinking.

"I'm coming!" Samantha yelled, though she'd been saying that for ten minutes. "Be patient, Mom."

"Yeah, you tell *me* to be patient," Tia muttered under her breath as she buckled eighteen-month-old Tristi into the high chair. Her hands itched and felt swollen, but Tia blamed it on the fact that she'd been scratching them for at least half an hour. She must have rubbed up against something in the garden while picking the sage for the dish she was experimenting with for her cooking segment on the noon news.

"Here I am," Samantha said as she came into the room, her strawberry-blonde hair curling around her face and neck where it had fallen from her braid. "I was working on my story."

"I'm glad you're having fun with that, but I wish you wouldn't keep me waiting. Did you wash your hands?" Tia asked.

"Yeeeees." Samantha infused the word with the long-suffering tone first graders used so well.

Tia tamped back her irritation at her daughter's attitude and spooned the mac n' cheese onto her daughter's plate, along with a small spoonful of the pine nut and sundried tomato pasta she'd been tweaking. "Give it a try."

"You always make me try stuff." Samantha poked at the new dish with her fork before scooping up a bite and tasting it. She tipped her head to the side in boredom and swallowed before she pronounced, "It's okay."

"Okay, as in, you'd rather eat it than a pile of mushy canned spinach, or okay, as in, you kind of liked it?" Tia asked. Unlike most kids her age, Samantha was unusually laid back about trying new foods—which was good since Tia was always testing recipes.

Samantha pulled a face and turned to her mac n' cheese. "It didn't make me want to puke, but don't make me eat any more."

"Not your favorite then." Tia turned to Tristi and scooped some of the yellow pasta onto her younger daughter's high chair tray before putting some of the pine nut dish onto her own plate. She fussed over her daughters, making sure they had milk and corn—the only vegetable she could get Tristi to eat these days. "What's your story about?"

"I'm writing about a fire dog. He gets to ride on the truck and sniff out where fires start and stuff. Everyone loves him."

"I'll bet they do." Tia smiled despite her weariness and took her seat. Samantha had a fascination with all things fire. "I bet your story's great. Maybe after you help me with dishes you can read it to me."

"Okay." She dug into her dinner with more gusto this time.

Tia scooped up the new dish and tasted it. This version was better than the one she'd tried last week. After she swallowed, she tried another bite, savoring the flavor, analyzing it to see if there was anything else missing from the recipe. She jotted a quick note on the pad on the table beside her. A moment later she realized her throat began to feel tight.

Her next breath hurt as it rasped into her lungs and panic started to creep in. What was going on? The tightness increased and she looked at her hands which felt swollen and achy. Had her rash gotten worse? When breathing became more difficult, her panic increased and she stood to grab her cell phone. She froze when she realized it wasn't on the counter where she thought she had left it. Where was it? How could she call for help if she couldn't find it? Panic started to grow in her chest.

"Mom, what's wrong?" Samantha asked.

"Phone. I need an ambulance." Terror filled Tia as she fought for every breath. What was happening?

"Mom!" Samantha's voice was small and thready. She shot out of her seat and rushed to the living room. A moment later she returned, the phone to her ear. Her eyes were wide with terror as she sat in front of Tia, babbling, "My mom needs an ambulance. She can't breathe. We need help." All of the color had blanched from her usually rosy cheeks. "Please help."

Tia hoped Samantha had called 911 and not a friend. She leaned over and put both hands on the tabletop, fighting for breath and starting to feel light headed.

Samantha gave the address and talked to the person on the other end about what was going on. She turned to Tia, "Are you 'lergic to anything?"

"Must be. Tell them to hurry." Tia sat on the floor, afraid she was going to pass out. It seemed like forever before she heard the sirens approaching her apartment, but she knew it had probably only been a couple of minutes. They were quick. She was barely getting any air now, and shook all over.

Tia worried about the girls as Tristi cried in her high chair, smearing cheese sauce in her wispy red curls.

Samantha had tears pouring down her face, her white-knuckled fist still holding the phone to her ear. She ran to the door and unlocked it as the sirens stopped out front and she disappeared outside. "She's in the kitchen," her worried voice called.

Tia didn't even look up as two people approached her.

"Is this an allergy?" a male voice asked.

"Maybe. Can't breathe." The pressure on her chest was terrible as Tia gasped. As the edge of her vision began to turn dark and buzzing filled her ears, she felt a sharp pain on the side of her leg as the man hit it with the end of a long tube. He spoke to her in a soothing voice, but she couldn't understand his words. An oxygen mask covered her face, and when she felt the rush of cool air against her cheeks, she realized she'd been crying.

After a few seconds her lungs began to clear and she gulped in air gratefully. The fuzziness in her head started to dissipate and the voices began to make sense again. "That was fast." Relief filled her though adrenaline still pumped through her veins.

"That's a good thing. It's going to be all right." His voice was soothing, calming her speeding heart. "Breathe normally. In and out."

The panic receded and Tia looked up into eyes the color of the blue delft china she'd inherited from her grandmother. Several other people crowded around her, but Tia looked over to see a female EMT talking to the girls. She bounced Tristi on her lap and patted Samantha's arm. Tia felt sick at the worry she still saw in their faces and wondered if she'd scarred them for life. "My girls."

"They're fine. Tanya is taking care of them. We'll bring them to the hospital with us unless there's someone close by we can get for you."

"They're fine. Tanya is taking care of them. We'll bring them to the hospital with us unless there's someone close by we can get for you. Can we call your husband."

"He's dead. Go across the street in the blue house. Nichole."

He nodded and turned to a police officer, telling him. When the officer left, the paramedic turned back to her. "You must be feeling better."

"Much. That's never happened to me before." Tia never wanted it to happen again. Nothing had scared her like that, made her think she was going to die. She still felt an edge of panic, but it was much easier now. She was a little shaky, but otherwise fine.

"It can come on suddenly. Any idea what caused it? Was it something you ate?" Someone handed him a square of red gauze, which she recognized from giving blood.

"Maybe." She tried to think of what the dish had been again, but couldn't. "Can't remember what was in it. My brain's not working yet."

The blond man grabbed her hand and looked at the back of her wrist. She realized they'd put a rubber tie on her arm a few inches below her elbow. So they were going to poke her with a needle—not a thrilling thought, but better than what she'd just been through.

"That's okay. Give the adrenaline a moment to clear your system and you'll be able to think better." He swirled the iodine onto the back of her upper wrist. "I'm going to start an IV so we can get some fluids into you. Your blood pressure is still pretty low, but that's normal." He followed up with an alcohol wipe. "I'm Danny, by the way."

"Nice to meet you." Tia had a blood pressure cuff on her other arm and an oxygen sensor on her finger. How long had they been there? A glance at the numbers on the monitor displayed her blood pressure. It was much lower than usual. Maybe that was why she was still so muzzy.

"How are you feeling now?"

"Tired, shaky, a little like my brain went on vacation, but so much better."

"Hold on. Everything's going to be okay." He looked up into her eyes and she felt reassured. "There'll be a slight pinch now."

"That's what they always say." She gritted her teeth as he poked her skin. Though she wasn't a wimp about needles, she didn't have fond feelings for them, either. "How would you like it if it were me sticking needles in you?"

"Depends. Do you know what you're doing?"

"No."

His grin flashed as he focused on what he was doing. "Then I probably wouldn't like it very much."

"And if I did have training?"

He looked up to meet her gaze. "I probably still wouldn't enjoy it. It's not number one on my list of fun things to do."

Danny took something from a coworker and attached it to the tube in her arm, then screwed on some IV tubing. Once he'd taped it all down, he looked at her again. "You'll be better in no time. Let me help you stand and we'll slide the stretcher right over here so you can sit on it, okay?"

Tia took a deep breath and reached out. When she was on her feet, black spots appeared in her vision and the lightheadedness returned for a moment. She was grateful he had a good grip under her arm.

"Mom, are you still sick?" Samantha looked over at her as the man helped her sit down.

Nichole showed up at the door, worry on her face. "I came for the girls, are you okay?"

Tia smiled as relief that her girls would be taken care of flooded her. "I'll be fine. They're just going to take me in for tests and then I'll be back."

When the anxiety smoothed from Samantha's face, Tia's tension eased. Everything would be fine

They'd already been out on another medical run and dropped the patient off at the same hospital when Danny decided to check on his anaphylaxis patient. Though he sometimes checked in on patients when opportunity allowed, he felt an additional tug of interest in this one in particular. The two hysterical daughters had really gotten to him, but they were only a small part of it.

He found Tia sitting up in the bed talking on her cell phone and looking much better than she had last time he'd seen her. Her face color was good and she wore a pained expression. The wavy fall of red curls cascaded down her back and shoulders, begging to be touched, so he hooked his thumbs on his pockets.

She glanced up at him and smiled. "I'll call you back later, Mom. Someone's come in to talk to me. Don't worry, everything's fine. Of course. Love you, too."

Worry filled her eyes, and lines bracketed her mouth. The call had been stressful. Either that or she was still worked up from her ordeal.

"Parents are wonderful, aren't they?" he asked as he took the final steps to her bedside. "Even if they worry."

"Yes, and she's a champion worrier." Tia bunched the blanket between her fingers and met his gaze. "Thanks again. That was the scariest thing I've ever been through."

He wanted to touch her cheek, feel the warmth of her skin beneath his fingertips, but knew it was a bad idea. Even if he didn't already have a girlfriend, Tia was one of his patients, which made her off limits. "I'm glad I was able to help. Your daughter did well, giving dispatch all of the important information. Very impressive for a kid that age."

Tia smiled. "Yeah, she's a keeper."

The hospital would hold on to Tia for another few hours to make sure her symptoms didn't return. "Do you have any idea what caused the reaction?"

"It might have been the pine nuts. I started getting a rash after I chopped them." She shrugged and added a wry grin. "I've never heard of anyone having a pine nut allergy before."

"Not many people eat them often," he pointed out. "Have you been working on a recipe for your show?"

Her eyebrows shot up. "You recognized me?"

"Of course." He found her reaction refreshing, and a bit surprising—she was on television every day, after all, even if it was only for ten minutes on the noon news. "I've tried out some of the recipes on the guys at the station. They've been a hit. Will you still make the pine nut thing on your show?"

"Yes. I think the recipe is ready. It tasted fine in the seconds before it tried to kill me." She gave him a wry smile. "I'm not going to eat it again though; this was the end of all pine nuts for me."

"Sounds like a good idea." He glanced up and saw his partner, James, standing in the doorway. Time to leave. "I guess I better get back out there. I'll be watching your show tomorrow."

"It was good to meet you."

He smiled and walked out, waving goodbye.

Two

"You're awfully quiet," Laura said to Danny the next evening. He'd had the day off work, so he'd invited his childhood friend over for dinner.

"It's been a crazy couple of days." He'd just come off a forty-eight-hour shift with the fire department. "We had three auto accidents, a heart attack, an anaphylactic reaction, two family fights, and a call to a house where the guy had been dead for most of the night—and that doesn't include the easy stuff. I'm ready for a few days of peace." He flipped the steaks on the grill and watched her as she stuffed the deviled eggs.

"And you still invited me for dinner." She finished filling the last egg and reached for the paprika.

He'd prepared the yolk mixture for the eggs as he didn't trust her to cook anything herself. He stepped from his tiny patio back into the kitchen to take the spice from her and sprinkle it on instead.

"I can handle that," she protested, even as she moved away, pushing her straight brown hair away from of her oval face.

"So you say, but don't forget how long I've known you." He was amused by the irritation in her dark brown eyes.

She huffed but didn't argue the point. "Would you like me to mix lemonade or something?"

"There are sodas in the fridge if you want to get them. Set the table, would you?"

She rolled her eyes at him, but dutifully walked to the cupboard. "So what's Carrie doing today? I thought she'd be here."

"Last-minutes prep for her sister's wedding. She's been sucked in." As a rule, he didn't mind his girlfriends having plenty of outside interests—his job kept him busy—but he'd be glad when the wedding was over and Carrie returned to the fun companion she used to be instead of the list-carrying, anal retentive, obsessed woman she had been lately. Had she ever been the person he'd thought, or was this her true face? He didn't know anymore.

"Poor boy." Laura set down the plates in her hands and patted him on the head.

"Knock it off." He pushed her hand away, but found himself smiling anyway.

She chuckled and returned to the cupboards for more dishes.

He glanced over his shoulder. "Mom's been nagging me to go home for a visit. She said to bring you along." Their mothers were best friends, living half a block apart. He and Laura had been in and out of each other's houses since they were little—back when he still thought girls had cooties and she played dolls with his sister Janie.

"I'm sure she has." Laura moved to grab the sodas from the fridge. "My mom's been pushy too. It *has* been several months since either of us visited. It'll have to wait a bit though. School's out Tuesday, but I have that women's retreat to St. Louis—we're going to the symphony. Then there are football games and homecoming preparations—I'm on the committee for the fund-raising dinner in a couple of weeks." Working as the high school secretary kept her deeply involved.

Danny walked to the calendar hanging on the wall and checked. "How does October third and fourth sound? I'll have the weekend off."

She pulled out her cell phone to check her own calendar. "Perfect." She typed for a minute, then stuck the phone back in her pocket. "I miss home."

He stepped back out to check on the steaks, smiling when they looked perfect. He scooped them onto a plate and brought them to the table. "I miss your mom's cinnamon rolls, warm and dripping with cream cheese frosting."

"Don't mention her cinnamon rolls. I swear I put on two pounds just thinking about them." Still, a look of bliss crossed her face.

"That's physically impossible, and your weight's fine." He gave her a sidelong glance. "But you know you can work out with me anytime you want." This was an invitation he'd made several times. He knew she'd never get up early enough to join him.

"Forget it. I'm on my feet enough as it is without getting up before the crack of dawn to look like a wimp running with you."

He chuckled and reached for the soda she'd set in front of his plate. There was nothing like spending a couple hours with Laura when he needed some downtime.

I love my mother. I love my mother. I love my mother. Tia hoped if she kept repeating the mantra she would be able to hold her tongue until she was alone. She looked over at where her mother was poking through the kitchen cupboards and then away again. She plunged her hands into the dish water to keep from grabbing the cans on the cupboard and putting them back.

Mona Baumgartner had been searching for anything containing allergens in her daughter's house. She was determined to remove all such foods before she returned home to St. Joseph. "What if Samantha hadn't been able to call? Or what if she hadn't been here?" She plunked a jar of peanut butter onto the growing stack. "You would be dead."

"Mom, I'm fine. The girls are fine. We'll avoid pine nuts from now on." These encounters with her mother always left Tia emotionally exhausted. Drama queen didn't even begin to cover it.

"Not good enough. And I was thinking, if you needed a blood transfusion, they would need to know what your blood type was. What if they didn't have any O blood and you were unconscious? How are they supposed to know?" She whirled around, her black-colored bob flaring out with the centrifugal force. "Have you had the car seats checked lately? Is the baby seat in tight? You know they say something like half of all baby seats are improperly installed in cars."

"Yes, I went to one of those classes before we had Samantha, remember? Everything's nice and tight." Tia tried to hold onto her calm expression even as her mother pushed her toward her limits. She rinsed the pan from dinner and set it on the towel to dry.

Mona moved to the next cupboard and began rooting around, pulling out two cans of mushrooms. "Nasty stuff, mushrooms. I never trust fungi." She set them with the peanut butter and canned clams.

Samantha ran in with a drawing to show to them. "Look what I drew!" She held it up, displaying a crayon depiction of an ambulance complete with a gurney and stick figure people who were obviously supposed to be EMTs. "That's Mom!" She pointed to the body-less head on the gurney.

"See, even your daughter is worried about you. I swear I'm going to have those medical alert bracelets made up for everyone with your blood types on them." Mona's hand fluttered over her heart. "It'll give me peace of mind."

And Tia would feel obligated to wear it because Samantha might let it slip if they only wore it when Mona was around. And that would cause hurt feelings. Tia tried to ignore her growing headache. "Whatever you want, Mom." She was relieved when her brother-in-law, Garrett, walked in to pick up Samantha to go out for ice cream.

"Hey, Mrs. B. Good to see you." His brown hair flopped over his eyes and a scruff of beard attested to his disdain for razors. He scooped up Samantha, tickling her armpits before turning to Tia. "Feeling better?"

"Much. Thanks for agreeing to take the girls for a few hours. I really do need to get out tonight."

Mona plopped a can of cream of mushroom soup on the counter with the other food.

"We're not allergic to any of those things," Tia protested.

"It's better to be safe than sorry." Mona closed the last cupboard door. "I suppose that's my cue to leave. I'll throw these out on my way."

"Mom," Tia reached out and put a restraining hand on her mother's arm. "I'll take care of it. I appreciate your help and concern." If appreciate wasn't quite the word that came to mind, she didn't have to admit it.

"You're sure?"

"Yes, I can handle it. Anyway, I need to get ready. A couple of ladies from my neighborhood are going out for dinner and a movie together. Just the girls." It would be heaven to get out for a while.

"Okay, dear. I'll call you tomorrow. Take care of yourself." Mona hugged Tia briefly, then kissed each of her granddaughters on the cheek before hurrying out the door.

Tia helped move the car seat and booster to Garrett's car, giving the seat belts an extra tug in defiance of her mom's suggestion that she didn't know what she was doing. She kissed the girls goodbye, and returned to the kitchen to put the food back in the cupboards.

Her mom had these dramatic life-or-death reactions to things two or three times a year. They rarely lasted for more than a few weeks and fighting Mona always made things worse. Tia had long-ago learned to go along, or at least pretend to, in the interest of family harmony. Hopefully this one would be short lived and the bracelets would never surface.

She put it out of her mind. Tia had fifteen minutes to freshen up her makeup before Nichole picked her up for their girl's night.

Three

Danny was relaxing at home Tuesday night, listening to the news while he stretched out on the sofa. He'd spent the afternoon teaching a CPR/First Aid class to pre-teens at the community center and was ready for some downtime. He listened to news about upcoming elections, then swiveled his head to stare at the screen when the anchor announced they had received word of a major bus accident near Independence.

"Reports say a white van rolled across the median and into a large charter bus heading west along I-35. Information is still coming in and we'll give you updates throughout the evening as we learn more."

Danny switched his pager so he could listen to radio traffic. His cell phone rang. "Tullis," he answered.

"It's Stu. Can you come in and cover at the station?" his commander asked. "We're sending some units and extra hands to the bus accident. Have you heard about it?"

"It just hit the news." Danny stepped into the bedroom to grab a clean uniform. "I'm on my way." Bus accidents were an emergency worker's worst nightmare. Injuries could include anything from cuts and scrapes all the way to deaths and major injuries—and on a massive scale. The weather was wet and miserable, which wouldn't help any, but at least it wasn't winter yet.

The pager squawked and hummed between reports coming in from police and emergency workers on the scene. By the time he reached the station, the news rolling in wasn't good. At least four dead, several others in critical condition. Hospitals in a sixty-mile radius were bound to find their emergency departments crowded and the next six to twelve hours would be sleepless for most everyone involved.

An hour passed, then two, as the guys at the station listened to updates coming through. They went on a couple of runs and returned. Danny didn't start to worry until the television station reported that the bus had been carrying a group of women on a retreat to St. Louis.

Remembering his conversation with Laura the previous week about her trip to the symphony, he snatched his phone from his front pocket and speed-dialed her number. Surely she was fine. Her phone rang several times and went to voice mail. He thought about calling her family to find out if they'd heard anything. She could be in a hospital being treated. But he thought better of it. If she was fine and her phone was lost or her batteries dead, he didn't want to freak out her parents.

Then again, he knew if it was her bus and she was all right she would've let him know somehow. She would've called him by now, aware he'd know about the accident.

He tried calling again. And again. Then he finally left a message. "Laura, you better call me now. I need to know you're all right. I don't care how late it is."

He responded to an accident a few blocks away and took a patient to the hospital. A stroke victim. A possible drug overdose. The shift change came and the other guys went home, but Danny was on the schedule for the next twenty-four hours, so he inventoried all the supplies on the rig. They went on a call for a broken femur, and when they got back, he power-washed the outside of the rig and started detailing it. He should sleep while he had the chance, but he was too restless.

As he vacuumed the carpet in the cab of the rig, he hit his head on the steering wheel and had to clench his jaw to keep from cursing.

He needed to calm down and take it easy; letting himself get worked up wasn't helping. But he couldn't stop thinking about the bus accident. Why hadn't Laura called him back? Dread tightened in his gut and he reminded himself it could just be the phone. She might be fine. Nothing could have happened to her.

Part of his mind wouldn't let go of the truth: every day he helped people who thought that their emergency would never happen, wasn't possible. He knew better than to think anyone was exempt from trouble.

Then his commander, Stu, approached him. "Danny, come on back to the office."

"What's up?" Danny didn't like the grim set of his boss's jaw, or being pulled aside. Had he screwed up something in their run earlier? He was more than a little distracted. He couldn't think of anything he'd done wrong, though.

Stu didn't answer, just ushered Danny into his office and shut the door behind them. He fidgeted with a pen from the desk for a moment, then looked Danny in the eyes. "I received a phone call a few minutes ago. You mentioned earlier that you're worried about a friend of yours who might have been on the bus."

"Yes. Have you heard something?" Danny's stomach clenched, his heart rate picked up and he tightened his hands into fists as he fought to control the wild possibilities that ran through his head. Stu looked too serious for the news to be good.

"I just spoke with your parents. Laura's injuries from the accident were extensive." He paused for a few seconds and when he spoke again his voice was tight with emotion. "I'm sorry, she didn't make it." Tears swam in the man's eyes. Laura had come by the station many times, joined them for meals, chatted and laughed and brought cookies to the guys.

Danny gulped in air, feeling like he was drowning. His throat started closing up and he shook his head. "No. No, it isn't true. She can't . . . " His stomach turned and tears filled his eyes, then

16

overflowed. Surely not. It couldn't. No, no, no. He shook as he tried to deny what he was hearing but he could no longer deny what he'd feared.

All Danny could think was that others had been there when Laura died. They'd been on scene, and Danny hadn't. He hadn't been there for her when she needed him most. He could see her, crying out in the night, her body wracked with pain, and not getting the help she needed.

Images of the horrific things he'd seen in his job came back to him, and he saw her with broken bones and struggling to breath. He set his face in his hands, trying to calm the sobs that stole over him.

"I'm sorry, Danny." Stu touched Danny's arm. "I already called someone to cover the rest of your shift. Mike will be here in a few minutes."

"Mike was out all night." At the accident scene.

"He's coming in anyway."

"Do you know what her injuries were?" He fought for control, but couldn't get it; his chest heaved from the emotion.

"No. Your parents said it was quick. She didn't suffer, at least not for long."

Danny's sobs increased and Stu squeezed his shoulder, then got up and left him to grieve alone.

When Danny came out of the office later, he had no idea how much time had passed, but Mike was already there. The guys gave their condolences, but he was glad to get away without having to discuss it.

Tia hoped she'd heard the end of the blood-type issue until she received an email from her mom the next day.

Honey, please check to see what blood type you and your girls are so I can order those bracelets. They should be here in a couple of weeks. It would so ease my mind.

Mom

The problem with ordering them was her mother would expect them to be worn at all times, which was ridiculous. Maybe when the shock of worry thinned out Tia would be able to calm Mona so they wouldn't have to use the things. In the meantime, it was easier to humor her.

She made a note to check the file of medical records that night and send the information along.

The next morning when she checked her email again, however, she had a new note from her mother.

Tia, don't be ridiculous, did you even check the records? You can't be B+. Your father is A- and I'm A+. Go find your files. And double-check the girls, while you're at it.

She had checked her records, and she was B+. Her mother must have been mistaken about her ex-husband's blood type—not a surprise when they'd been divorced for twelve years. Rather than responding, Tia opted to let the email sit for a couple of days.

When the thought that he might not be her dad crossed her mind, Tia brushed it off. Her mom wouldn't push the subject if that was a possibility.

The drive home to Junction City passed in a blur as Danny remembered the hundred little things he and Laura had done together over the years. He'd been asked to be a pall bearer at the funeral and the date had been set for Saturday.

Though he'd been putting off the call to Carrie for several hours—yard work had kept him moving, even if he'd had far too much time to think—he decided it was time to let her know what was going on. He had called the previous day saying that Laura had died and he was going home for a few days, but the conversation had been short. He hated the thought of disappointing Carrie, and his news was not going to please her.

After getting a glass of water, he pulled out his cell phone and dialed Carrie's number. "Hey babe," he greeted when she picked up. "How are things going for the wedding?"

"Great. We picked up the dresses this morning, the bridal photos are gorgeous, and the wedding favors are all ready to go. I hope things are okay at home. When are you getting back? Don't say Saturday morning; I can just see you coming in late and out of breath."

Guilt ate at Danny and he rubbed his shoulder muscles. "Actually, the funeral has been set for Saturday, so I'm not going to be able to make the wedding."

"What do you mean you aren't going to make it?"

Danny had to move his cell phone away from his ear to prevent damage from Carrie's screaming. He gritted his teeth and repeated himself, "The funeral is set for Saturday morning. I can't be at your sister's wedding and Laura's funeral at the same time. I'm sorry I'm not going to be there for you."

"But this is an important day for me. I'm the maid of honor, I have responsibilities. I need you there." Her voice took on a wail. "I can't go dateless!"

He wanted to end the call and forget it, but he'd been taught better. "I'm sorry I'm not going to be there for you, really I am," *Even though I didn't want to attend the wedding in the first place.* "I need to be here though. You know she's—was," he swallowed hard as a knot of emotions clogged his throat when he used the past tense, "my best friend."

"Are you sure that's all she was to you?" Carrie's voice snapped across the line. "I could swear sometimes she was more important to you than I am. How can we have a relationship if you put her first—she's not even here anymore and you're still putting her first."

Danny had about lost all patience with Carrie. It had been an awful twenty-four hours and the next few days didn't look promising. He understood her sister's wedding was important to her. He wasn't asking her to miss it to support him. Was it too much to ask that she understand his grief?

A hand touched his shoulder and he turned to see his father standing behind him, lending support. Danny returned his attention to his call. "You know you're not being fair, Carrie. I hope the wedding goes beautifully, and I'm sorry I won't be able to see you in your new dress. You'll have to show me the pictures, and maybe I can arrange a special night so you can wear it again soon." It was as close to conciliatory as he was going to get in his current mood.

There was a short pause, then a hefty sigh. "Okay." Another pause. "I'm sorry about Laura and everything. I know this hasn't been easy for you. I just reacted badly to the surprise about the schedule change. I ought to go, my boss doesn't like me taking personal calls while I'm at work."

"Yeah. Bye." Danny wanted to rub his face, his tired, burning eyes, but didn't want to lose control in front of his parents. He turned back to his dad. "What's going on?"

"Your mom's got lunch ready. Come on in and get some food into your bottomless pit." He hooked an arm around his son's shoulders, though he was several inches shorter. "Woman trouble?"

"What other kind is there?" Danny got his reward when his father cracked a smile for the first time since Danny had been home.

Four

Danny needed something to distract him, to fill his time and get him back into normal life once the funeral was over. He returned to Kansas City the day after the burial and threw himself into preparations for National Fire Prevention Week festivities. His next date with Carrie went badly as she watched every nuance of his actions. She pouted when he picked up an extra shift for one of the guys at the station, fussed when he was busy with the annual activities, and rolled her eyes if he so much as brought up Laura's name in conversation.

The final straw came when she was at Danny's place for dinner. He was pulling chicken off the grill and plating their meals when he saw her pick up the picture of him, his sister Janie, and Laura at a Christmas activity several years earlier—they were crammed in close together so they'd all fit in the shot. She gave the photo a moue of distaste, then set it face down on the end table.

"Put it back up, please." Danny continued to dish out the potato salad beside the meat, trying not to grind his teeth.

"It's not healthy to hold on to all of her pictures and memories."

"It's barely been two weeks since she died and I don't appreciate you making this even harder on me." He fought to keep his voice even, knowing he was more irritable than usual.

"I don't appreciate coming in second all the time." Carrie put her hands on her hips and tossed her shoulder-length, bottle-blonde hair.

Surely she hadn't been so self-absorbed when they first started dating, had she? He slammed the plate back on the counter, loud enough to express his roiling emotions. "Then you can go home."

She crossed her arms over her chest, her eyes narrowed. "If I leave now, we're through."

"Fine by me." Danny watched her huff, snatch up her purse, and hurry out the door, slamming it behind her. He rubbed his neck and slid the plate across the counter. He wasn't hungry anymore.

He let the meat cool, then wrapped it all up and put it away, cleaning the kitchen. It wasn't like he'd lost much in ending their relationship. Not when Carrie obviously didn't understand him—and didn't care enough to try. They hadn't dated long. Still, he'd miss the companionship, and they'd had a good time together.

He didn't want to think about all of the empty days ahead of him, so he finished the kitchen and grabbed his gym bag. He'd go work out at the station. Maybe he'd feel like eating when he returned.

Danny and James didn't work on the day of the station's celebration for National Fire Safety Week. Instead of going into the station, they spent the day visiting elementary and middle schools, doing assemblies where they spoke to the students about fires. They passed out fliers, shook hands, and talked to dozens of children. It wasn't until the last group though, that Danny found himself face-to-face with Tia's little girl. He couldn't remember her name right away, but he recognized her the moment he saw her.

"Hello," she said as she stepped closer to greet him. "You came to my house."

He grinned and knelt on one knee so he could look into her eyes. "I sure did. How's your mom?"

"She's better. She says you saved her life." She put her hand on his arm. "Do you like saving lives?"

"Firefighters and paramedics all like saving lives. It's why we're there. You were very brave when your mom was sick."

Her eyes cut away from him and she frowned slightly. "No I wasn't, I was scared."

The child-like honesty warmed him as nothing had since Laura's accident. "It's okay to be scared. You know, sometimes I'm scared too. Being brave means we do things that need to be done even when we're scared."

She nodded her acceptance. "I'm going to bring my mom and sister to the firehouse tonight. I want to ride in the fire truck." Enthusiasm shined in her green eyes.

"I'll watch for you then." He looked at the little towhead with the pale red highlights. "What was your name again?"

"Samantha. What's yours?"

"Danny." He saw her glance back at a class lined up at the door. The teacher gave them an exasperated look. "I think your class is waiting for you. You tell your mom hi for me."

"I will." She waved over her shoulder as she hurried back to join her class.

"She looks familiar," James said as he joined Danny.

"Remember the pine nut allergy. That was her mom." Danny stood again, feeling lighter than he had in weeks.

"Right. She's a good kid." He tipped his head toward the door. "You about ready to go then? Lots to do back at the station before all the munchkins start to show up."

"I'm all set." He grabbed his gear.

Danny had been helping children and a few curious parents on and off the rigs in front of the fire station when they stopped to change passengers on the fire trucks. It had already been a long day, first the school assemblies, then setting up for the open house. This had always been one of the yearly events he'd most enjoyed, but this time he'd thrown himself into it like a lifeline.

Has it already been over two weeks since Laura's funeral? It was still too painful to think about, so he buried it in the back of his mind. Another truck pulled in and he smiled brightly at the kids as they climbed out. "How did it go?" he asked a boy of about seven or eight.

"It was so cool! Can I go again?"

Danny laughed. "Maybe a bit later. We still have a lot of kids who haven't had a chance. Did you see the booth where they're giving out tattoos?" He lifted the sleeve of his T-shirt to show off the rub-on tattoo he'd applied before everyone started to arrive. It had the firefighter crest and his station's identification on it.

The boy's eyes widened with excitement. "Awesome. Where are they?"

Danny pointed him in the right direction and the kid tore off for the table.

He helped several more children onto the truck, then turned back to find Tia, her girls, and another little girl Samantha's age were next in line. "Hi, there. You're looking well." Tia looked terrific, actually. Better in real life than on television despite the minimal makeup and her hair pulled back from her face in a ponytail.

"Thanks. I'm feeling much better. No new problems." Her smile was slightly embarrassed. "Samantha was so excited to come tonight. She loves fire trucks."

"What a coincidence, so do I." He crouched down to Samantha's level. "I see you managed to bring your mom and sister. Who's this?" He pointed to the dark-haired girl beside her.

"She's my best friend, Casey. She lives across the street from me."

"Hello, Casey." He extended his hand and smiled when the girl slid her tiny hand into his for a shake. "I'm pleased to meet you."

"Me too," Casey said in a shy voice.

He stood and looked back at Tia. "I have a couple seats left in the rig. Or if you want to ride with the kids, you can wait until the next load."

Samantha tugged on one leg of his protective firefighter clothing. "Yes?"

"Is he going to make lots of noise?"

"Who?"

"Him." She pointed at James, who was getting out of the driver's seat. The little girl's eyes widened as he came over to stand beside Danny. Even Danny couldn't blame her; James was six foot five and built like a tanker truck. He was also a natural with kids, which made him a great partner when they treated younger patients.

"Do you want him to make lots of noise?" Danny asked, thinking he already knew the answer.

"Yeah!" Her whole face lit up. "I like the sirens. Can I wear a helmet?"

"We'll see." He laughed and itched to reach out and tousle her hair, but didn't want to worry Tia by acting too familiar when they barely knew each other. He looked at Tia again and smiled. "I caught today's cooking segment. I see you must have let everyone else enjoy the pine nuts, since you're not in the hospital."

"Yes. It was hit with everyone who tried it." Her blush was visible in the dusky light. "I wore gloves when I prepared it so I wouldn't get a rash again."

"Good idea."

James slapped Danny on the shoulder. "He tests a lot of your recipes on us, they're all really delicious. You must give good directions. He hasn't poisoned anyone yet." He turned to Danny, "Hey, want to take the next bunch? I need a break before my hearing goes. I'll be back in a few minutes."

"Sure. You two girls going up?"

"I want to ride in the back," Casey said.

"Is there room for me?" Samantha asked.

Danny lifted Casey onto the back of the truck and one of the other guys helped buckle her in, then he turned to Tia. "If you don't mind, I'll take Samantha up front. I can show her how to use the siren."

"Yay!" Samantha jumped up and down.

Tia looked amused. "Just down the street, right?"

"Around the block, then back. It'll only be a few minutes."

She glanced at her bouncing little girl. "Samantha won't be a problem up front?"

"No, loads of kids have sat there tonight. I promise to take good care of her."

"That should be fine."

Five

Through the open driver's door, Tia watched Danny lift her daughter into the passenger side of the truck, and show her some things on the dash. Samantha pushed at a button with a tentative finger, then jumped, laughing, when the siren started to wail. When her finger moved away, the siren wound down, then started up again at her command. After a moment, Danny said something to her and she slid back onto the seat.

He handed her the seatbelt and walked around the front of the truck to climb in while Samantha buckled up. He slid his own seat belt on, then called back to the kids to hold on tight and with a wave to Tia, the truck pulled onto the road.

As she watched him go, Tia thought about him watching her cooking show—that larger than life, over-confident, totally gorgeous man. It seemed so odd considering her first impression.

"He's a hunk, isn't he? Those fire trousers, suspenders, and a tight T-shirt." Nichole sighed. "It ought to be against the law to be so good looking."

Though she agreed whole-heartedly, Tia turned to see Nichole at her shoulder and shrugged. "He is good looking, I suppose." She glanced at the infants in Nichole's double stroller. "Manage both diapers already?" After five years of trying to conceive following her first daughter's birth, Nichole had come across a pregnant teenager who wanted to give up her baby for adoption. The week before the baby was born, she realized she was three months along with her own miracle baby.

"Nice and easy. Kim's a jewel, always lays still. Kael is another issue, but he did well this time." She pushed the chin-length fall of hair behind her ear. "So, back to the hunk—did you get a name? I saw the way he looked at you."

"You couldn't possibly have seen his expression from the parking lot." The line of kids was growing behind them, so Tia gestured to a spot farther away and led Nichole there.

"Who said I was in the parking lot the whole time?" Nichole wiggled her eyebrows.

Tia reminded herself Nichole was her best friend and deserved to have her pushiness overlooked. "He's one of the guys who gave me the ambulance ride. He's just being friendly. Don't read too much into it." But the thought of him actually being interested in her made her heart speed up a little.

"Lee's been gone almost two years." Nichole reminded her. "You're still young—live a little, will you?"

Tia held back her eye roll. It was far from the first time Nichole had said something similar. "Move on to a new subject?" Tristi started crying, so Tia fished out a cracker for her daughter. "Do you dare risk the hotdogs?"

"I don't see them using extinguishers to keep the flames under control," Nichole said dryly as she looked at the large slow cooker the dogs were floating in at the Coca-cola truck. "I'm guessing they're nonpoisonous, anyway, since no one appears to be sick. Besides, Casey will throw a tantrum if I don't let her have her hotdog."

Tia held back a laugh at her friend's put-upon expression. Nichole wasn't much of a meat eater, and really, *really* not into processed meats. Still, she allowed her kids some here and there, and hoped they'd follow her own philosophy someday. "Dream on," she muttered.

They could hear the fire truck returning from more than a block away. The siren blared and Tia wondered if her daughter had managed to sweet talk her way out of her seatbelt to run it, or if her baby blues had mesmerized the handsome driver into ruining his own ear drums. It wouldn't surprise her if they were all deaf when they returned.

After coming to a stop, Danny hopped from the truck and headed around to the other side to help Samantha out. After noticing her daughter removing her seat belt—which meant Samantha's eye-fluttering powers were still in good working order—Tia thought again about the firefighter. His suave self-confidence bothered her and his flirting unnerved her. She wondered if it ever got him into trouble on the job.

Samantha ran back over and wrapped her arms around her mom's legs. "I pushed the siren, and Danny ran it for me a lot."

"I heard, sweetheart. I think the whole state heard, actually." She tapped a finger on her daughter's nose.

"He said if I'm good I can try on his fire hat."

"Did he?" Tia didn't have a chance to decide how she felt about it before he was in front of them.

Danny grinned and crouched so his face was even with Samantha's. "I'm glad you helped me tonight. Maybe you could bring your mom and sister and help again sometime. I can show you the cool stuff we have inside the ambulance." He glanced back into Tia's face and she felt her cheeks flame. "Not while strapped into the gurney this time."

"I think that's a great idea," Nichole said, extending a hand in greeting. "Hi, I'm Nichole Baugh, Tia's friend, and you are?"

"Danny Tullis." He angled a glance at Tia's face. "And very glad you all came tonight." He turned and beckoned to someone behind them, then returned his gaze to the ladies. "I did promise Samantha a chance to try on my helmet tonight. Do you have a few minutes?"

Tia's chest constricted and she became self-conscious about what she said around him. Why was he paying so much attention to her? She'd been out on a date or two since Lee died, but none of the men really flirted with her. She got the feeling, however, that flirting was second nature to Danny, so she tried not to make anything of it. "That will be fine."

Since Nichole agreed, and the girls bubbled over with excitement, they all headed for the building. Danny stopped to talk to another firefighter, a woman with pale golden hair falling halfway down her back, and ask her to drive the truck full of kids until James returned. Then he led them through the building.

"My locker's back here." He stopped at one and twisted the combination lock until it popped open. First, he pulled out his firefighter's helmet and set it on Samantha's head.

"It smells like smoke," she said, wrinkling her nose.

Danny laughed. "Fires do tend to smell like smoke." He pulled out a heavy yellow set of protective clothing like Tia had seen on television and movies. "These are my turnouts, they protect me when I'm doing my job. I have different sets depending on the type of call I go on. This is for fires." He briefly described how they protected him from getting burned and gave each of the girls a chance to wear the jacket so they could feel how heavy it was.

He returned it and the fire helmet, which Samantha seemed done with for the moment, to his locker and removed a lighter black outfit. "These are extrication turnouts. I wear them when I'm not worried about fires, but if we're opening up a car so people who are trapped inside can get out. It protects me from glass and other sharp objects. I wear this when I go to accidents on the ambulance, too." He let them all finger the heavy material and briefly talked about the equipment they used.

"How cool." Samantha said. "I want to help people when I grow up!"

Tia could see how Samantha's charm and hero worship were wrapping Danny around her little finger. When he reached out and touched the girl's shoulder, Tia thought of Lee, and of the way her husband had loved their daughter. She missed the way he'd come in from work and scoop Samantha into his arms, listening to her chatter and grinning at her boundless enthusiasm.

Samantha had cried often, missing her daddy when he shipped out to Afghanistan. It got worse after the funeral when Tia had to tell her Lee wasn't ever coming home. Two years later Samantha didn't cry much anymore, but she was starved for male attention, despite Garrett's best efforts to be there for his dead brother's family. Tia's throat felt tight and she had to take a measured breath to hold back emotions that always hit her at the worst moments.

When Danny met her gaze, she saw something flicker there. "I better get back to my post," he said after a moment. "But you're welcome to stop in some day for the ambulance tour. Call ahead to see if I'm here and I'll squeeze in time for you." Though his words had included everyone, his eyes ended on Tia. "It was a pleasure meeting you all."

He left them at the table where they were doing rub-on tattoos, and Tia watched him return to duty at the line of kids.

"Samantha, put down the fire truck and get over here and eat your breakfast. You're going to be late." Tia growled under her breath and handed Tristi a second sippy cup of juice. The first was still spread across the kitchen floor from when Tristi had "dropped" it. That game was getting awfully old.

"I'll be there in a minute, Mom," Samantha called from the living room. She moved the truck slowly into place beside the rest of her collection, making beeping noises as she backed it in.

"Now, Samantha Marie, or you'll be missing out on breakfast entirely!"

Samantha slouched across the room to the table. "I had to put the truck back. They have to be washed and returned to the firehouse after every time you take them out, so they'll be ready for next time." She left the implied 'duh' off the end of her sentence. "Danny

31

wouldn't want me to be irrsponsble." She struggled through the last word.

Danny had been the main topic of the five-year-old's interest since leaving the fire station the previous evening. Tia blamed Lee, who had been so sure he was going to have a boy, he'd cleaned out all of the Tonka trucks and Matchbox cars at local yard sales before the birth. Their daughter had been in love with them since she was able to focus on what he had placed in her hand. After all, he'd said, he wasn't raising his girl to be a sissy who only played with dolls.

The memory made Tia smile, even as an ache pierced her chest again. It seemed Lee was always on her thoughts—more often lately as the second anniversary of his death approached. "It *is* important to be responsible," she told her daughter as she put away the extra bread and eggs. "But school is your most important job right now, so you need to take it seriously—even more than you do your fire trucks."

Samantha huffed, but dutifully forked up some scrambled eggs.

Tristi began to call loudly, signaling she was done and wanted out, so Tia unbelted the toddler—who without the belt, would have been face first on the floor minutes after being placed in the high chair—and hauled her over to the sink to clean her sticky hands and face.

The tune to "We Are Family" by Sister Sledge started to chime, and she sighed. It was her mother's cell phone ring. Tia didn't have time for hysterics right now, but if she didn't answer, her mom would keep calling back, certain they had all died of carbon monoxide poisoning or something. Then the police would end up at her house on a courtesy call—again—to make sure she was all right.

Still carrying around a sticky daughter, Tia dried her wet hand on her pants and reached into her front pocket for the phone. She maneuvered it open one-handed and tucked it into the crook of her shoulder. "Hello, Mom." It used to be so much easier when the phones were like bricks instead of credit-card thin, she thought as she adjusted its position again.

"I still haven't gotten those blood types from you."

"I double-checked last night," Tia said. It had been a couple of weeks since the conversation first came up. She had hoped her mom would have let it go for a more pressing imaginary emergency. "I was right the first time."

"Tia. This is a serious matter. Are you sure you weren't looking at Lee's paperwork?"

"Mom, I checked, all right. You must be mistaken about Dad." She pressed her fingers to the bridge of her nose.

"I'm not. Call him and ask. Your paperwork must be wrong. You should have your blood typed again to see what it really is."

"Fine, Mom. I'm sure you're right." *Except you're not.* "I'll check my other papers and get myself retyped if you want."

When she finally hung up the phone, Tia felt a headache building behind her eyes. She was already seeing spots and wavy lines—the aura that was always a precursor to her migraines. She hurried to the medicine cabinet and downed a migraine pill, praying it would kick the thing before she had to run Samantha to school. Tia really didn't have time to deal with a migraine when she had to film her cooking segment in less than four hours.

Six

October seemed to slip away in a blink and was more than half over. Tia could hardly believe Samantha was turning six already. Six. It was mind boggling. It also meant a family birthday party with both of Tia's parents. There were few things Tia found less soothing than any celebration including the warring factions. She knew having her grandmother as well as Lee's brother and parents in attendance wouldn't stop hers from snipping at each other. Thankfully Nichole's family was joining them and she would help keep things moving along.

The event started off predictably with Mona coming into the house, an enormous package in her arms which was covered in pink metallic wrapping and liberally decorated with beads and shiny ribbons. She greeted both her granddaughters with kisses and hugs, cooed and fussed, then proceeded to give Tia a rundown of everything that had gone wrong—real and imagined—over the past two days.

Tia's father, Ron, was far more level headed, though he also brought an over-sized gift, if not as flashily wrapped as his ex. He was tall and broad shouldered, thin faced with a full head of hair which had once been dark, but now was liberally sprinkled with white. He had a cheery grin and plenty of hugs and kisses for them all. "How are we doing this evening?" he asked as he helped his mother to a seat in the lounge chair.

"Great, Dad. Everything's ready, and Samantha loves her cake."

"It's a fire truck. It's so cool. Come see it!" Samantha grabbed her grandpa's hand and dragged him into the kitchen to see the confection Tia had created for her.

Glena chuckled as she watched it all. "I declare, that girl's got more enthusiasm than a cheerleading competition."

"At least." Tia took a moment to sit in the chair beside her grandmother. "How are things going?"

"Right as rain, child. I suppose your mother's still as crazy as ever. Something wrong with them genes of hers."

"Jeans?" Tia intentionally misunderstood, furrowing her brow—it was a familiar refrain. "But she's wearing slacks tonight." Ron wasn't the only one who didn't get along with his ex-wife, though he usually managed to keep himself aloof, while Glena dished out as much ill will as Mona.

"That's a terrible pun, honey, but I'll be good. Promise." She pursed her lips and mimicked locking her mouth.

The rest of the group trickled in over the next fifteen minutes. As long as Mona fussed with the food and drinks, she seemed more or less happy. Ron kept his distance, and Tia tried not to let her imagination convince her the walls were closing in.

When the evening was nearly over and Tia started to think they would get away without a single argument between her parents, her mom entered the living room wielding a dripping dish rag. "You still haven't gotten your blood types to me yet."

Tia plastered on her smile and kept her voice low. "Mom, I've already told you what our blood types are. I have two records agreeing with what I told you."

"Why does she need to know?" her father asked.

Mona, of course, had to explain it all, which only increased her agitation.

"So why don't you believe her when she told you her blood type?" Ron asked, his hands on his hips. "And it's not like they need to carry around medical bracelets. You're so overprotective. Quit smothering the girl."

Mona slapped the wet rag onto the coffee table. "And now you'll probably agree with her and say yours is different just to show me up!"

"I'm A-negative. I don't see how it has anything to do with this." He scooped up the wash rag and carried it back into the kitchen.

Nichole distracted the kids, while shooting concerned looks in Tia's direction. Her husband, Gary, was outside with Wes and Garrett, but Lee's parents watched the proceedings, nonplussed. Tia thought they really ought to be getting used to the frequent spats her parents held every time they all got together.

"See, he even agrees with me. You better go get tested again," Mona said to Tia.

Ron's eyes swiveled to Tia. "What are you?"

"Does it matter?" She seriously wished they would let the whole thing drop. She could see the spots appearing in the periphery of her vision. A migraine was coming, but if she could calm the conversation and get her parents out quickly, maybe she'd be lucky and keep it down.

Ron sent a sidelong glare at his ex-wife. "Yes, it matters. What's your blood type?"

What was with him? "B-positive."

The room grew silent except for the kids giggling and chattering.

"Impossible," Ron said after several seconds passed by. His expression was dark as a night with cloud cover.

"That's what I keep telling her, but she won't listen," Mona complained. "They sent her the wrong records or something."

"I have the test results. One of you must be wrong." Tia scooped up the dirty plates from the coffee table and set them into the kitchen sink.

"We're not wrong." Ron turned to his ex-wife and glowered silently. Tia was shocked since he generally managed to stay civil with Mona, even when she didn't deserve it.

Mona's face turned red, but she lifted a finger and shook it in his face. "Don't you glare at me like that. You're wrong."

Lee's parents looked distinctly uncomfortable at this point, but it was all Tia could manage to send them apologetic smiles.

"Exactly how early in our marriage did you start cheating on me?" Ron's voice was hard.

Tia's gasp was echoed by others in the room, though it was Mona who spoke up. "You promised never to bring that up."

Tia felt her stomach plummet to her feet. She did *not* just hear what she thought she heard. She couldn't have.

"How early?"

"Chuck was the first and only," Mona protested.

"How can I be sure?" Ron asked. "She can't be my daughter—"

"It's not true. I wasn't with anyone else." Tears flooded Mona's eyes and poured down her cheeks "She's yours, and I can't believe you would mention it after all these years." She stood and stalked out of the house.

Silence filled the room. Tia felt like history was being rewritten. How could they have kept such a secret from her? She felt lightheaded from shock and pain teased at the edges of her senses. She could tell she would be sick soon. Relief poured through her when her in-laws stood in concert and gave hugs and kisses to the kids, slipping out in seconds. Wes followed. The traitor.

Nichole came over, looking closely at Tia's face. "You're getting a migraine."

"Yes." Tia rubbed her temples, knowing this was going to be a doozy.

Nichole gave Tia's arm a quick squeeze, then picked up Tristi and herded Samantha back to her room to change for bed. Tia figured her friend deserved sainthood and made a promise to herself to take over some cookies or a cake the next day.

When Gary took his kids home for bed, Tia turned to her father. "Thanks for coming tonight, Dad." She wasn't sure what to say to him. Her parents had never told her the reason they'd split up, saying they'd decided they couldn't live together anymore. How had he managed all those years knowing his wife had cheated on him?

"I'm sorry, sweetheart. I didn't mean to cause a scene. I was so surprised by the topic." He took her in his arms, but though his voice had been strong, he trembled as he held her to him.

"Do you really think I'm not your daughter?" The thought made her heart sore. Hadn't she endured enough already? How could this be happening?

He was quiet for a long moment, then shifted back from her so he could look her in the eye. "I don't care who your biological father is. You're my daughter."

That soothed part of her pain away, but inflamed the rest of her worry. He really *didn't* think he was her father. He thought her mother had stepped out on him. Of course, Mona had apparently given him reason to doubt her word, she admitted to herself. Still.

"I better let you get to bed before you become sick." He pressed a kiss to her forehead. "I love you, honey."

"I love you too, Dad." Tears flooded Tia's eyes and she fought to stay in control. She watched her dad walk out into the night, pulling the door closed behind him. Tia took something for her head, then moved to put the dirty dishes in the dishwasher, wrap what remained of the fire truck cake she had made, and prepare for bed. She moved in a haze, the pain and shock slowing her movements. Her stomach rolled and her head pounded and she could still see lines and squiggles in her vision, but she pressed on—someone had to.

Nichole came out of the girls' room and joined Tia in the living room. "I don't know how long they'll stay there, but they're asleep for now."

"Thanks." Tia fought to stay upright. "I appreciate it. I better get to bed before I puke."

"All right. Let me know if you need anything else," Nichole said before leaving.

She was such a lifesaver, Tia thought as she slid into bed a minute later, praying the girls would sleep through the night, and she'd feel better in the morning.

Seven

The phone rang again, but noticing her mother's number, Tia ignored it and guided the stroller around the emergency preparedness fair. She was not taking Mona's calls. Not right now when she needed strength and endurance. She texted her mom saying she wanted time to think, and please not to call anymore.

The struggle with the truth—her parents had split up because mother had cheated on her father, and Ron may not be her biological father—was more than Tia could bear. Then an evil little voice whispered that Mona could be telling the truth. If she was, did it mean Tia wasn't their child at all? She pushed the thought away as soon as it came, not wanting to consider the possibility. It was so far-fetched.

Instead she'd moved through the day taking care of other things. Tomorrow would be soon enough to face her questions.

Tristi spilled juice down the front of her shirt and started to fuss, Samantha tripped over a cord that had been taped down on the floor. But she popped back up, her eyes still wide with excitement at all of the booths around her. She had a butterfly painted around her right eye and a purple balloon on a string as they wended their way through the crowd from booth to booth, picking up tips for severe weather safety.

"Look, Mom," Samantha said, pointing. "The ambulances and fire trucks!"

Tia smiled wanly, already wishing they were done for the day and she could take a nap. "Let's go check them out."

They peeked into the back of a truck marked "Tender" when Tia saw movement and looked up to see Danny stop beside her, wearing his uniform. "Hi," he greeted her. "I hoped I'd see you here today."

"Hello." Tia felt a small flutter in her chest at his smile. She noticed Samantha glance up and catch sight of him, the look of hero worship clear in her face. She waved from Tia's other side and he greeted her.

"You never came by to check out the ambulance," he whispered to Tia.

"We've been really busy."

"I'm sure you have." He stuffed his hands in his back pockets. "You look tired."

That's because I haven't slept much in three days. She wasn't about to say it, though. It would only encourage him to ask more questions. "Thanks. I love it when people tell me I look awful."

"That's not what I meant. You couldn't look awful if you tried."

Despite herself, she felt her face grow warm. She'd never gone in for the smooth type before, the guys with the golden tongue. Or maybe it was more accurate to say none of them had ever taken an interest in her. Still, she couldn't help but be intrigued by Danny. The tug of attraction she'd felt for him the first day they met increased every time they spoke.

"Are you having a good time?" he asked Samantha, though his glance back at Tia included her.

"Yes, it's fun here. Do you like my butterfly?" Samantha grinned. "I got to be fingerprinted earlier." She held up her hands, which were still a little grubby from the ink.

"Fun. Let's hope we never need them." He helped her onto the back of the fire truck and explained everything there, drawing out their time together and answering Samantha's questions with endless patience.

When they were done, Danny set Samantha on the floor again and turned to Tia. "I wondered if you'd be interested in coming over for dinner at my place? I have some chicken in the freezer I could pop on the grill. Doubtless you have some recipe you need to test on a guinea pig." His lips turned up in a flirtatious smile.

"Yeah, Mom, can we?" Samantha asked.

"I don't know." Tia wanted to say yes, felt the tug of excitement at his offer, but at the same time, she hardly knew him. They'd only met a few times. "The girls will tear your place apart."

"I'm not worried about a little cleanup, but if you'd prefer, you can invite me to your place. I think I could find it again." His easy grin was disarming.

"Please, please, please, Mom!"

"Pease, pease," Tristi chimed in, though Tia doubted she had the first clue what Samantha wanted. She just liked to do and say the same things as her sister. And she was too darn cute to turn down.

Tia was afraid her mother would 'drop by' to talk things out that evening, so though she wasn't sure the visit was a great idea, she looked up into Danny's eyes again and found herself nodding. "If you're sure."

"I am." He pulled out a scrap of paper from his pocket and wrote a hasty note. "My apartment's pretty easy to find."

She glanced at the address and directions. She knew the area. "That'll be fine. Five o'clock and I'll bring dessert?"

"Perfect." He set a hand on Samantha's shoulder and gave it a squeeze. "I'll see you ladies then."

Tia found her stomach tightening in knots as she approached Danny's apartment building. The past few days had been a real rollercoaster and she wasn't sure dinner with him was a wise idea. On the other hand, Mona had left several messages on Tia's phone after being told not to call. She'd threatened to visit if she didn't hear back soon. Tia had sent her mom a text, saying she was taking the kids somewhere for the evening and would call the next day. She hoped to discourage Mona from popping by unannounced, but doubted it worked.

"Are we there yet?" Samantha asked as they pulled into the parking lot at Danny's.

"Yes, we're here." Tia refused to let herself second guess the decision to come to dinner, even though a hundred scenarios for how the evening could go had run through her head on the drive—all of them ending badly.

She handed the pie to Samantha and released Tristi from her car seat, then plastered on a smile.

Danny's grin flashed when he opened the door. "Welcome to my small, and humble abode." He tweaked Samantha's hair as she walked past, "I see you brought a pie. What kind?"

"Apple. It's yummy!" Samantha answered.

He shut the door behind Tia and turned back to Samantha. "I can't wait, but what are the rest of you going to eat while I eat this?" Danny took the pie and unpackaged it, sucking a deep, exaggerated sniff.

Samantha put her hands on her hips and gave him an annoyed look. "It's not only for you. You have to *share*."

"I do?" His eyes landed on Tia's face. "You brought something this delicious and you're going to make me share?"

"I'm afraid so." She set Tristi on the carpet. "This is a different variation than I've tried before. You'll have to tell me what you think of it."

She took a surreptitious look around the scrupulously clean apartment. It was sparsely furnished, but a few pictures on the wall turned the décor from bland to personal. She liked the picture of him standing in front of a fire truck in full turnouts, his helmet tucked under his arm and his face black with soot. Other pictures were of friends and family and one of him and a dark-haired woman sat on the entertainment center. Several of him and the woman were scattered around the space, she realized after a moment, though many held other people as well. She caught him watching her as she looked at the photos, but he didn't explain. She didn't ask.

"It smells awesome, so I know it'll be good." He set the pie on the counter and turned back to the pasta salad, giving it a final stir and launching into questions about how she managed to land the cooking show.

Conversation meandered from topic to topic as he finished putting together dinner—refusing all assistance from Tia—and keeping an eye on the chicken on the grill. To her surprise, Tia found herself relaxing in his presence. He was good with the kids, cooked competently, and kept the conversation lively.

After dinner was done, dessert was a memory, and the girls sat in front of a kids' movie Tia had brought—just in case—Tia and Danny settled comfortably in his living room.

"I have to admit, I didn't expect to have such a good time tonight," Tia said as she kicked off her shoes and tucked her feet under her on the sofa. It was even more comfortable than it looked.

"You underestimated my charm?" His grin was teasing and nearly irresistible.

"On the contrary, I wondered if there was anything *under* all of your charm. All too often charm is just smoke and mirrors to cover up an empty shell." She winced inwardly after she spoke. Did she just insinuate she'd thought he'd be shallow?

"And you came anyway?" He looked amused rather than offended, giving her the courage to explain.

"Promise not to hate me?" When he nodded, she plowed ahead, "I'm trying to avoid my mom, and the best way is to be out of the house and turn off the phone. You were a good excuse."

He covered his chest with one hand. "I'm wounded." His amused expression said otherwise. "What's the deal with your mom, if you don't mind my asking?"

Tia paused to consider her words. This was extremely personal, but she felt like she could talk to him. He was a much better listener than most men, and since she'd already admitted to more or less using him, not giving him some kind of explanation wouldn't be fair. "I found out a few days ago that my parents divorced because she cheated on my dad. Now we think he may not be my dad at all."

Danny didn't give her the pity she dreaded, just sympathetic understanding. "Wow. How long have your parents been divorced?"

"Sixteen years. All this time they've been saying it was a personality conflict, and they decided they'd be happier apart. My dad never even hinted at my mom's infidelity." It was just like her dad—who while not exactly self-effacing, did at least tend to put his kids' best interest first. Her mom certainly wouldn't have done the same if the roles had been reversed.

"Did your mom marry the guy she cheated with?" Danny reached up and touched one of her auburn curls, wrapping it around his finger.

"No. She has married and divorced again since then, but she met the second husband years after the divorce finalized. I keep asking myself if I was really so naïve I had no idea what was going on in our home." Tears prickled Tia's eyes and she willed them away. She was tired and vulnerable, which meant it was time to leave. "I better take the girls home." She stood and Danny joined her, stopping her with a light touch to her shoulder before she could move to the kitchen to collect her things.

"I'm glad you came over." Danny searched her face. "I'd like to see you again sometime."

Her heart fluttered again at his words, part of her longing to shout out her agreement. The rest of her wasn't ready to get involved with someone. She really liked him and wasn't sure they could keep it casual. The emotions he stirred up in her definitely weren't platonic. "I don't know if that's a good idea."

"Why not? Didn't you have a good time? The girls seem content." His eyes switched to flit over them before returning to her face, a smile growing on his mouth. "Besides, you need to give me a chance to weasel the pie recipe out of you."

Tia chuckled. "You don't have to spend time with me to manage that. Watch my show on Thursday and you'll get it all step by step."

"That's something anyway," Danny murmured low so she doubted Samantha could hear him. "But it's not quite enough."

His request was more tempting than she wanted to admit. "I think I've got plenty going on right now without throwing a relationship into the mix."

"Maybe you're right." But he didn't look convinced. Danny moved to the kitchen and picked up her pie plate with the two remaining pieces. "I make a great friend. If you change your mind, you know how to reach me."

Tia seriously doubted he'd be contented with friendship for long. Or that she would. "You can keep those last two pieces if you like. I do need the dish back, though."

With a grin he pulled a plate from the cupboard and slid the rest of the pie onto it. "If you insist, who am I to argue?" He washed the pie pan and Tia moved to gather their things.

As she pulled out of his parking lot a few minutes later, Tia told herself she'd made the right decision, even though she couldn't help wondering what might have happened if she'd agreed to go out with him.

Eight

Tia arrived home to find Mona on her doorstep, tapping her toes. Though she wanted to snarl, Tia composed herself and greeted pleasantly, "Hello, Mom."

"Where have you been?" When Tia didn't respond, Mona asked, "Are you going to let me hold my grandbaby?"

Glad to put the confrontation off for a few more minutes when she still had Danny's smile lingering in her mind, Tia passed Tristi to Mona.

They went through the evening routine, getting the girls through baths, stories, prayers, and into bed. Tia was amazed Mona managed to hold her tongue until the girls were tucked in for the night.

When they sat in the living room afterward, however, the politeness came to an end. "Where were you? I waited for over an hour," Mona complained.

"I told you I had plans." Tia fidgeted with a bottle of water from the fridge, grateful to have something to hold.

"I thought you made that up." Mona's eyes narrowed, studying her.

Irritation rushed through Tia. "You were wrong."

Mona clasped her hands on her lap in the way she always did when she was tired of being put off. "Where were you? I called Nichole and she said you weren't over there."

"I wasn't."

"Obviously. You wouldn't have driven across the street."

Tia didn't feel like explaining her actions. Telling Mona that she had enjoyed dinner with a handsome man would only prolong the conversation. "I was going to call you tomorrow."

"I know you were, but you know as well as I do, you won't be able to see my face over the phone, so you won't believe me when I tell you the truth."

Surprised at her mother's comment, and thinking she was probably right, Tia nodded. Though she was not entirely sure she was ready for the answer, she asked, "What is the truth?"

Mona played with her own bottled water, but her eyes stayed steady on her daughter. "I made a mistake when you were eleven. A huge mistake which cost me my marriage. It was the first time I made that mistake, though. I swear I wasn't involved with anyone else when I got pregnant with you."

Tia studied her mother's face and decided Mona had been right. If she'd told Tia over the phone, doubt would have lingered. She knew all of her mother's tells, though, and Mona was being truthful. It was a relief to know, though it brought on more questions than it answered. Her gut twisted as she tried to deal with the possibilities. "What do you mean? How else could I be B-positive?"

"I don't know. I wish I did."

Tia took a few sips of her water, then sighed. The thought had crossed her mind repeatedly since the big revelation, but she'd hoped not to have to pursue it. "I guess the most obvious place to start is with a DNA test."

Mona nodded. "I'm sure your father would appreciate it."

Though she hesitated to push it, Tia decided it was necessary. "I mean for both of you, Mom." Nervous, she clasped her hands on her lap so she wouldn't fidget.

Mona looked shocked, then offended. "Both of us? Are you saying you don't believe I would know my own child?"

It seemed far-fetched to Tia too, but she wanted to cover all the bases. "The fact is, something doesn't fit here, and if you're sure you didn't step out on Dad, then it follows that the problem could be something else." Tia didn't want to think about it, but knew she couldn't ignore the possibility forever. Better to eliminate it right off rather than letting the possibility haunt her.

"What a ridiculous suggestion." Mona folded her arms over her chest and harrumphed. "Of course you're my daughter. How could you not be?"

"Then the tests should prove what you know is true—I had a mix up somewhere else and got the wrong blood results." Tia paused, choosing her words carefully. "If things don't come out the way we want them to, however, I need to know what happened." She stared out the window at the darkness and tried not to let herself believe it could be true.

Though Mona insisted it was a waste of money, she agreed to go along with the test.

The next day after work Tia met with her father for a late lunch. He took time away from the office and she left Tristi in daycare for an extra hour.

"Hey, hon." Ron wrapped her in a hug outside the restaurant. "I wondered if you were going to call me, or if I'd have to contact you first."

She felt a pang of guilt. "Sorry. I've been all tied up about everything."

"That's understandable," Ron said. They went inside and by mutual consent, waited to be seated before broaching the subject. Once their orders were placed and drinks sat in front of them, however, he didn't waste any time.

"Have you spoken with your mother?" He played with the straw wrapper.

"Yes, she showed up last night and we talked through things." She fiddled with her fork, not wanting to meet her father's eyes.

"And?"

"She said she wasn't . . . she didn't . . . " Tia was acutely aware of the other patrons around them, but knew he understood—which was good, because it was too awkward to say out loud. "I believe her." She glanced up at him to catch his reaction.

His eyes flashed at hers, widening. "Then how does she explain the blood typing?"

She knew her father thought she had bought into a lie. "She can't."

He lifted his brows in derision. "How convenient."

Tia dropped her hands to play with her napkin on her lap. "I did some research last night on DNA tests. If I ordered the kits today, we could have results by the end of next week."

Ron shifted back in his seat. His face was impassive, but his voice held an edge of pain. "So you're going to test to make sure I'm your father? I thought you believed her."

This was where it got sticky, because she really didn't know what to think or believe anymore. Thinking about it made her stomach hurt, but she couldn't keep her mind off of it. "I do. But I need answers, for my peace of mind. You know you'll always be my dad, no matter what happens."

Though his eyes spoke his relief, his brow furrowed. "So what are you suggesting?"

"If she insists I'm your daughter, but evidence indicates otherwise, I thought maybe we should check both of your DNA against mine." Tia prepared herself for anger or irritation at the suggestion.

He sat in stunned silence for a moment. "Do you think it's possible?"

"Highly unlikely, actually. But I'd rather know absolutely than wonder." If she was only tested against her dad and the test came back negative, that would only make the rift between her parents worse. If they both came back negative, though . . . she pushed away the thought for now.

Ron nodded, and they sat in private contemplation for several minutes, which was broken only by the arrival of their meals. When the waitress left again, he began salting his food—before tasting it, as he always did. "I think that's a good idea," he started as if there hadn't been a pause in the conversation. "It's best to make sure it's all clear. Tell me where you order the kits and I'll pay for the tests. I'm sure they're not cheap, and I know you don't have a lot of extra money."

Tia felt gratitude swamp her at his acceptance—and the offer to purchase the tests when her budget was extremely tight was an added bonus. "Thanks, Dad."

He reached across the table and set a hand over hers. "I meant what I said. I'm doing the tests because I need to know, and I know you won't be able to rest until you have answers, but you are my daughter, regardless of what the tests show."

Tia had to swallow hard to hold back the tears. "Love you, Dad."

"I love you, sweetie." He squeezed her hand before returning to his meal.

Nine

"What's going on?' Danny asked as he entered the station for work. James held a clipboard, making notes as he began the daily shift inspection on their ambulance.

"They say it's been quiet since three." James popped the hood and set down the clipboard to check the fluids.

"So we're due something soon." Danny dropped his gear and grabbed a pressure gauge, calling out greetings to the rest of the guys while he checked the tires. A week had passed since he'd had Tia and the girls over for dinner. He was feeling at loose ends again. He'd thought—more than once—about popping by Tia's to see how things were going, but didn't think dropping in would go over very well. She'd been friendly, but not encouraging—to his great regret. Something about her called to him.

He and James finished the vehicle check and moved to the break room for a start-of-shift meeting.

"All right, guys, I know you're anxious to get to important things like video games." Stu looked pointedly at Chris, who smiled back cheekily, "but we have a challenge from station C. They think they can raise more money for burn camp than we can. Each shift at the station has to come up with a way to raise money. Any ideas?"

"You mean like accosting people on the street and holding them hostage until they ante up?" Chris joked.

"This is the real world, Chris, not a video game." James threw something at Chris.

"I think we should stick with our strengths," Danny said.

"A kissing booth?" Larry joked and got an elbow in his ribs.

Pager tones sounded and the men all stood and hurried to the rigs to respond to the car accident. The discussion would have to be tabled for a while.

As they cleaned up from the run, Danny mulled over the challenge his commander had posed an hour earlier. What were they good at? What would earn money? He was still considering it when he found James hunched over a bowl of chili and Dan Wells' latest horror novel. "Found the perfect chili yet?" Danny dished himself some from the slow cooker.

"Nah, it's good, but not quite right." James took another bite, then flipped the page of his book.

James' quest for the perfect chili would never end. Danny spooned some up from his bowl and savored it. He paused, his hand halfway to his mouth with another bite. "That could be it."

"No, the spices aren't quite right."

Danny set his spoon back in the bowl and grabbed a cornbread muffin as Stu came in.

"Is it any good?" Stu asked.

"Better than most." Danny took another bite of chili. "I was thinking. What if we had a chili cook-off here to raise money? We could get people to make the best chili and cornbread, then make the winning entries' recipes available online." He smiled as a thought occurred to him. "Maybe bring in a local celebrity as a judge."

"Who do you have in mind?" James asked.

"Tia Riverton from the noon news cooking segment. We responded to her house a few weeks back. She might be willing to help out as a thank you." And it would provide him with plenty of excuses to contact her over the next few weeks—he'd take what he could get.

James' smile widened. "I knew you had a thing for her."

"She . . . intrigues me." Danny split the muffin and spread margarine over it. "I've run into her a few times since then and we've talked. I'll be happy to approach her, if you'd like."

The metal feet of the chair next to Danny scraped across the tiles as Stu pulled it out. "When the other guys get in here, we'll ask them what they think, but it'll do fine. I know some newspaper reporters too, so we should be able to get good coverage."

The other guys came in and before Danny finished his second helping of chili, the basic details were in place. He smiled to himself and scraped out the bottom of his bowl, knowing exactly how to approach Tia. He washed his bowl and turned the channel to Tia's station to watch her demonstrate the apple pie.

The days Tia had waited for the DNA test kits to arrive had seemed endless. Mona had left numerous phone messages, but Tia had avoided speaking with her, finding excuses to cut calls short and missing as many as she dared without bringing on her mom's wrath. She really didn't know what to think about the whole mess and didn't want to hash it all out while she waited for answers.

Now that the kits had arrived, Tia looked at the package in her hands and wondered how she was going to do this. Was she ready for the possibility that one or both could turn out negative?

There was a knock at the front door and Tia stashed the box on the fridge.

Danny was the last person Tia expected to find on her doorstep. Both surprise and a glow of happiness slid into her when she saw him. She had told him a relationship was a bad idea right now, not that she was disinterested. Considering the alternative, his interruption was anything but unwelcome. "Hi."

"Hey, I've been wondering how you're doing." He hooked his thumbs in the back pocket of his jeans. "You were a little upset last time I saw you."

Tia wasn't sure how to answer. It hadn't been the most amazing week of her life. "I'm keeping afloat." She debated for only a moment before stepping back and gesturing for him to enter. "Would you like to come in?"

"I would." He stepped inside and shut the door behind him, then took a look around the room. "It's amazing how few details you notice when you're on an ambulance call once you've done the initial room check." His gaze seemed to linger on the family portrait of Tia, Samantha and Lee, before Lee had been deployed, though Danny didn't comment on it. Finally he met her gaze. "Your place is nice."

"Thanks. I do my best." She felt her cheeks heat slightly, knowing he was being generous. The apartment was comfortable, but not fancy. The neighborhood was safe and the building in good repair, but her income wasn't very big, and after paying off the most pressing bills, the remaining life insurance had been socked away into a college savings account for her daughters. If it weren't for the government social security payments in Lee's name for the girls, they would never make it financially.

"Mommy, who's there?" Samantha's voice entered the room only an instant before she did. Her face brightened when she saw Danny and she ran to him, opening her arms for a hug as he scooped her up. "Danny!"

"Hey, kiddo." He held her only for a moment, then set her down and crouched to her level. "You haven't come by the ambulance shed so I can show you around."

"I keep asking Mom, but she always says there's no time." She pulled a face. "There's never any time."

Danny looked up at Tia, who fought the urge to look away even as she made her lame excuse, "We've been busy. We'll make it before too much longer." When his brows lifted slightly, she felt a funny twist in her stomach, wondering if she were as transparent as she felt.

He just nodded, then turned his attention back to Samantha, who was already chattering about school and her friends. Danny listened attentively for several minutes, letting her wind down before giving her a pat on the shoulder and standing again. "Good. Sounds like you're having fun. Hey, can you do me a favor?"

"Sure!"

"I need to talk to your mom for a little bit. Could you give us a minute?"

Samantha's face fell. "You're sending me to my room?"

Amusement tugged at his face. "Isn't that where you were before I got here?'

"Well, yes." Samantha scuffed her shoes across the carpet. "Do you want to stay for dinner? 'Cause if you do, maybe she won't make me eat Brussels sprouts."

Danny's lips quirked, but he managed to hold back the smile that made his eyes glitter. "I'll see what I can do about it."

Samantha's face brightened and she waved goodbye, rushing to her room. When the door slammed behind her, Tia winced. It was time for Tristi to get up from her nap, but slamming doors didn't usually result in happy awakenings.

"You don't have to invite me to dinner, if you don't want to," Danny said, studying Tia.

She instantly felt bad that he'd misinterpreted her expression. "Sorry, the face wasn't for you. I'm listening for the wails of an angry toddler." When a few seconds passed and none came, she let out a breath of relief and put it out of her mind. "Now, what was it you wanted to talk to me about?" She led him to the sofa set and took a chair for herself. Asking him to stay for dinner was tempting, but she hesitated, afraid acting on her attraction would be a mistake.

"Have you ever heard of burn camp?" Danny sat, leaning forward and placing his elbows on his knees, all of his attention riveted on her.

"Is that where firefighters go learn how to burn things more efficiently?"

He chuckled. "No, that's called Boy Scout camp. Don't tell the leaders though, they generally discourage it. No, in this case it's a camp for youngsters who've been badly burned in fires. They usually have extensive skin grafts or serious disfigurements. It gives them a chance to be with other kids who've been through the same difficulties and creates bonds. I helped out at the camp last summer for a couple of days. It's incredible what they're doing there. These kids just need a place where others don't stare, or treat them different. And a lot of the kids stay in touch, forming lasting friendships."

Tia felt her heart melt. "It sounds great. I bet the kids and their families really appreciate it."

"Yes." He swallowed, but didn't look away as he plunged ahead. "Well, there are lots of kids who need to go, and too many families who can't afford the cost of sending their child. Because of this, the fire department is raising money to send children to burn camp."

Tia marveled at the light of excitement in his eyes. "Are you looking for donations, because I've got to tell you, I don't have a lot left over in my budget." She might be able to scrounge something, though.

He chuckled. "No, I'm not looking for a donation—we'd never turn one down if you felt so inclined—but what I want from you is your help. If you're willing."

That intrigued her. "What can I do?"

"Each of the departments in the area is putting together fund raisers for the burn camp, and my shift decided to do a chili cook off. The thing is, we need to get some celebrity judges, and since you're pretty well known around here, and food is kind of your thing . . . " His lifted his brows, his face hopeful.

56

"That's like saying fire and bloody accidents are *kind of your thing*," she pointed out, unable to help being amused.

He grinned. "Yeah, so I'm good at understatement."

Tia couldn't help herself, his smile was infectious. "All right, so you're looking for a judge. It sounds like a great cause. When's the event?" She tried to figure how far out they would need to plan to get the word out, and wondered if he was looking at Christmas or early January.

"Saturday the twenty-seventh."

She goggled. "That's less than a month away. You're going to have your hands full to pull it off so fast."

"I know, but we'll handle it. I have a lot of free time I can devote to it on my days off, and we'll all work together. Firefighters are good at teamwork, and the other guys at our station will help."

"You're like a family." She'd noticed the camaraderie between him and the other firemen when she'd seen them all together.

"Of course."

Tristi started crying from the other room and Tia stood. "Hold on a moment while I get her."

Danny nodded and she hurried to check on her toddler. The event and benefitting program were good, very laudable, and she'd be happy to be involved, but she needed a moment away from his mesmerizing blue eyes and captivating smile to think clearly. She could not let herself be sucked in by him, so some time to reflect was definitely required.

Her racing heart attested to how susceptible she was to his charm. And when she thought about spending more time with him, she had to admit the thought appealed. Tia wasn't sure she could handle the ups and downs of a relationship with everything else going on, though. She scooped Tristi from the crib and snuggled her close. "Hey, babycakes. It's okay, settled down. Shhhh." She bounced slightly and pressed Tristi's soft hair back from her face and skimmed a kiss to her forehead. "You hungry, sweetie?"

"Yes." She sniffled and wiped her face with a fist.

"All right. Let's go get you a little snack. We'll have dinner soon."

"K." Tristi burrowed her head under Tia's chin, a warm bundle of love.

Tia smiled, unable to help enjoying the complete trust of her little girl. It was truly sweet being a mother at times like this. She returned to the living room and found Danny with a picture in his hand. It was of Lee holding Samantha on the day she was born. Love and joy radiated from his face as he looked at his daughter. The memory brought an ache to Tia's chest, a sweet warmth at how much he'd loved their daughter. Over two years after his death and she still missed him every day. She wondered what he would think of how their girls were growing.

Danny looked over his shoulder at her and their eyes met, lingering before she glanced away. He set the picture frame down. "Is this your husband?"

"Yes, with Samantha. He was deployed before we found out I was pregnant with Tristi. He never saw her." That thought always made a lump rise to her throat. Seeing Danny with Lee's picture in his hand made her feel guilty. Lee was gone, and though he'd told her that if something happened to him, that he wanted her to remarry, discussing him with another man was awkward. Though she'd had a couple of dates in the past year, she hadn't been really interested in either of the guys. Danny was another story entirely.

She knew it was stupid and forced the thought away for the time being.

"I'm sorry. It must have been horrible for you." He watched her, studying her reaction, but didn't move closer—which she appreciated.

She nodded, unable to form words about how difficult it had been to finish her pregnancy with Tristi after burying her husband. Danny didn't need to know everything, anyway. "It wasn't exactly a high point in my life."

"If you ever want to talk about it . . . " He left it open ended, obviously sensing that she didn't want to at the moment.

"Thanks. I'll remember that." *I won't talk to you about it, though.* How could she? She decided to change the subject. "You're welcome to join us for dinner. I'm testing out a new pasta dish tonight."

"But with no pine nuts, I'd guess," he teased.

"Right," she nodded. "There are no pine nuts in this house. Peanut butter on the other hand—we go through tons of that. But not tonight."

"Sounds great. Could you use an extra pair of hands in the kitchen?"

Tia released the tension in her shoulders and put him to work. Everything was going to be okay.

Ten

It was so not okay. She had already swabbed her own cheeks and gotten her father to do the same. Now she waited impatiently for her mother to show up and do the test. In the morning Tia would send the test kit back and within a week she could have an answer to everyone's questions.

If her mother would show up.

Mona had insisted she would come over to do the test, there was no reason for Tia to make the drive, and besides, it would give her a chance to spend time with her grandbabies. Of course she hadn't had time to stop and chat when she arrived to get the girls.

Tia appreciated her mother's willingness to take Samantha and Tristi out for a couple of hours. It was amazing how much she'd managed to get done without the constant distractions, but it was long past time for her mother to get back so Tia could tuck the girls into bed. What was keeping them?

She stalked across the living room again and tried not to look at the clock—it would only irritate her. Had they been in an accident? Tia wanted to call, but last time her mother had taken the girls, she'd thrown a fit about Tia checking up on them. A glance at the clock urged Tia to pull out her cell phone anyway. She waited impatiently for the ringing, then gritted her teeth when it went to voice mail.

What was going on? Tia sighed in relief as the doorbell rang, then nearly growled when she opened the door to find Nichole standing there instead of Mona.

"Wow, what's wrong?" Nichole asked.

"My mom has the girls. Still. And she should have been home half an hour ago. And she isn't answering her phone." She led Nichole into the room and they sat on the sofa.

"Odd."

"Not for my mother, it isn't."

"Yet you're still upset."

"Irritated, yes." It finally occurred to her to wonder what Nichole was doing there so late. "Sorry. What's going on?"

"I could see you pacing and thought maybe you could use a sympathetic ear."

Nichole lived across the street, and when both had their drapes open, they could look right into each other's homes.

"Thanks. She was supposed to do the DNA swab tonight, then offered to make it grandma time, and she rushed the girls out so fast we didn't get the swab done. Now she's late coming back and it feels like she's dragging her feet. I want this over and done with. I wish she'd come last night instead. Then they'd already be in the mail." The tension of not knowing made a hard ball of worry tighten in her stomach.

"Yes, but then she would have given you the third degree about Danny stopping by for dinner." Nichole's eyes twinkled at her.

"How did you know?" A ridiculous hint of embarrassment slid into her, even as she felt herself blush with the memory of their time together. She liked Danny more every time she spoke with him.

"I live across the street, remember? Besides, Casey mentioned Samantha went on and on about it."

Tia blushed. "He came to ask me to judge a chili-cook off his department is holding for a fund-raiser. He didn't come with the intention of joining us for dinner."

"Sure he didn't." Nichole chuckled. "That's why he waited until nearly six to pop by. He had the whole day off, you'd been home for hours . . ."

61

"You're delusional if you think I'm going to get involved with a guy right now when everything else is up in the air." She only had so much room for change in her life before she went on overload.

Nichole sent her a piercing stare. "It's been nearly two years since Lee died. You deserve to be involved with a nice guy who cares about you. It would be a shame to miss out because you're scared."

The words made Tia's throat ache. She was about to change the subject when there was another knock at the door. "That better be my mom, or she's so dead."

Samantha's excited voice from the other side of the door put Tia at ease before she got close enough to unlock it. There was a flurry of excited hugs and chatter as the girls told her about what they'd done, and Mona made small talk with Nichole.

As Tia took her yawning toddler from her mother's arms, she looked at Nichole and mouthed, "Don't let her get away."

Nichole nodded and gave her the thumbs up signal.

Glad for the backup, Tia made her excuses and whisked the girls off to put them into pajamas. The bedtime routine lasted longer than usual; Samantha couldn't keep the toothbrush in her mouth for more than five seconds without thinking of something else she wanted to say.

Finally Tia tucked them into bed and returned to the living room. Nichole stood firmly in front of the door, talking about something that had happened at a school activity. Mona looked mutinous at the blockade. "I really do have to go," she said.

"Oh, but here's Tia. Now you can say a proper goodbye." Nichole peeked over Mona's shoulder. "It was good chatting with you again, Tia. Play date tomorrow afternoon?"

"Yes, thanks." Tia hoped her smile conveyed her appreciation as she took her mother by the elbow and led her to the sofa. "Don't you have a few minutes, Mom? We need to talk."

"It's pretty late, much later than I'd planned on staying," Mona protested.

"Well this won't take long." Tia heard the front door close behind Nichole and was grateful again she'd popped by. If Mona had gotten away tonight without swabbing her cheeks, Tia would have had to chase her down the next day and she didn't need the aggravation.

"I'm already running behind."

"That's because you stayed out late. Don't worry. The swabs don't hurt and it'll be done in a few minutes." Tia grabbed the package with the swabs and pulled it open.

"Sweetheart, are you sure about this? I mean, there's no real reason to have me tested. I know my own daughter!"

"Mom, I thought we already covered this. It's just for form's sake. Besides, the test kit came with swabs for both parents, and it's better to clear away any questions before they arise, don't you think?" She handed the first cotton swab to her mom. "Now, rub this pretty firmly against the inside of your cheek, remembering to get along the gumline as well. It has to get skin cells in it, not just saliva, so twist it as you go to ensure plenty of skin cells are all over it."

"But honey—"

Tia wanted to scream. Couldn't anything about this be easy? "Mom, please do it for me, okay? Please? This is such a simple thing and Dad's already paid for the test kit."

Her comment seemed to have the desired effect because Mona started swabbing like mad. "I could have paid for the kit. I'm perfectly capable on my own. I don't know why you insist on letting him pay for everything."

Tia held back a smile and timed her mom, then switched swabs and put the used one in the provided pouch.

"This is so unnecessary," Mona said as she handed the second swab back after finishing with it.

"Thanks for humoring me." Tia passed over the final test and sighed in relief as her mother took care of it.

"I don't understand why you're making such a big deal about this," Mona protested.

"You're the one making a big production out of it." Tia took the final specimen and sealed it in the package. "If everything comes back on this like you expect, then there's no harm done. The only reason you should be upset is if you believe the results will be negative." She eyed her mother, wondering again if there was more going on than she would admit. But if Mona had suspected something, she would never have opened this can of worms by insisting the blood type was wrong.

"My heavens, a mother knows her own baby! The problem is you don't trust me. If you did, you wouldn't have put us through this ordeal."

Tia decided it was too late to argue now. She was tired and had another full day ahead of her. "Thanks for taking the girls tonight, Mom. They had fun and I appreciated the break. I got a lot done."

"I remember what it was like to have young ones at home and how hard it was to get anything accomplished." Mona kissed her cheek. "Take care, and make sure you let me know when the results get back."

"I will." Tia was grateful for the momentary reprieve from hostility. All she could do now was wait for the results.

Eleven

The next week passed entirely too slowly. Tia had spoken with Danny on the phone a couple of times about the chili cook-off, and they had submitted info about the event to her supervisor at work. The station manager thought it a great publicity opportunity for Tia and the station, as well as good for the charity. Samantha was still poking at her to go to the fire shed to see Danny and the ambulance, and Mona had started calling, asking about updates on the DNA test before the envelope could have even arrived at the company that would run the tests.

The days seemed to stretch, lasting far longer than they should have. Finally Tia sat at the computer, logged onto the website and checked her results.

She stared at the screen for a long moment, stunned.

There was no biological relationship between her and *either* of her parents. Though she'd had a niggling thought about this, she hadn't really believed it. How could it be possible? She couldn't have been adopted, or her parents would've told her when all of this came up—beside that, she had pictures of her mom, dad, uncle, and grandmother all holding her in the hospital, and she had her bracelet from her birth tucked into a scrapbook. Hers and her mother's hospital bracelets, in fact.

Tia stood and walked away from the computer, then turned and paced back again. Emotions roiled in her: worry, loss, sadness, and concern for the future. Tears poured down her face as she tried to understand everything. Hadn't she been through enough with Lee dying? Did this have to happen too?

Now she had the answers she'd looked for, she didn't know what to do about it. She had to tell her parents, of course, but she could already see the recriminations, hard feelings, and finger pointing—and that was just her mother. Samantha ran into the apartment with Casey hot on her heels. "Mom, can we go see Danny now? Pleeeease? We're bored!"

Tia's first instinct was to say no, then retreat to her room to curl up in the fetal position. She followed her second instinct, which was to avoid thinking about it entirely. She dabbed at her eyes, trying to keep Samantha from seeing her face clearly. "What a great idea, honey. I'll call Nichole to see if Casey can go with us."

She grabbed her cell phone and headed for the bathroom to check her makeup. She had no idea if Danny was working that day or not—his schedule seemed sporadic and she hadn't asked about it. Once she had permission from Nichole, she stared at the phone, then called Danny to see if now was a good time.

"Hi, Tia," he answered before she could introduce herself. "How are you doing?"

"I'm well." *Not.* "Hey, Samantha wondered if now would be a good time for us to swing by the fire station for the ambulance tour you mentioned. If it's not, we can arrange another time."

"Now would be great. We're all cleaned up from the last run. With any luck we'll have a break before the pagers go off again."

"We'll see you in a bit." She ended the call and touched up her makeup, though she had to pause for a moment to get her emotions back under control. "Nothing has changed. Everything's exactly the same as it was an hour ago. You just know about it now," she reminded herself. She didn't really believe it. Everything seemed different.

Danny looked forward to seeing Tia and the girls again. He'd been tempted to swing by and visit them during the week, but decided he'd need to take things a little more slowly with Tia. She was a bit skittish.

He'd had his hands full with preparations for the chili cook-off, anyway. Most of the other guys at the station had families or second jobs, so he'd taken on the lion's share of the planning and organizing—which was fine by him since it kept his mind off other things.

The sound of little voices wafted through the open garage door and Danny saw Samantha and Casey enter with Tia following behind, Tristi in her arms.

"Don't touch anything unless Danny says it's okay, all right?" Tia told them.

"We won't." Samantha's voice carried across the ambulance bay and she waved wildly when she saw him. "Hi, Danny. We've come to see you!"

"So I see." He leaned over and hugged her, then set a hand on Casey's shoulder and gave it a squeeze. He could sense Casey was still trying to make up her mind about him, and he didn't want to make her uncomfortable by hugging her. Then he looked into Tia's eyes, his smile widening. "I'm glad you finally brought them." He noticed the strain around her mouth, and the slight redness in her eyes, but decided not to comment on it.

"Thanks for being willing to see us on such short notice."

"Anytime." Feeling the distance she projected, he turned back to the girls and began talking about the ambulance and the kinds of calls they went out on. He took them into the ambulance and pointed out the supplies and equipment and explained what they were all used for. Samantha's fascination seemed to increase the longer they talked. Casey was not quite as enthusiastic, though she didn't appear bored, either.

Next he took them through the building and showed them the bedroom and exercise equipment, then back through the kitchen, introducing them to everyone they passed. Tia hardly spoke a word the whole time, and though he thought she was interested in what he was saying, there were times when her attention wandered and she appeared upset.

When they finished the tour, he sat the girls at the kitchen table with some popsicles he'd dug out of the freezer—he had no idea where they'd come from, but they'd been there long enough no one would miss them. "Hey, James, can you keep an eye on these ladies for a few minutes while I talk with Tia?"

James was doing a crossword puzzle and smiled up at him. "Sure. No problem." He winked and Danny hoped Tia hadn't seen. The man seriously had no subtlety.

"It's okay, I don't want them to be a burden," Tia protested.

"It's really all right. They'll take a few minutes with the popsicles anyway," James insisted.

"Come on," Danny grabbed her wrist and gave it a gentle tug. She sent one more worried look at the girls, then followed him out. "Don't worry about them," Danny said. "James has a couple kids of his own. He's great with children."

"What did you want to talk about? If it's about the chili cook-off we could have talked as easily in front of the girls." She kept her arms crossed over her stomach and didn't meet his gaze.

"It's not." He stopped her in sight of the kitchen doorway so she'd be comfortable about leaving the girls there, but far enough away to have a private conversation. He looked her in the face. "What's wrong?"

"Nothing," she denied without hesitation.

"Tia. I can see something's bothering you. You're distracted and upset." He reached out and set a hand on her shoulder. It was as far as he dared go. "Tell me."

Tears started to fall and she wiped at them, looking mortified, but she seemed unable to speak.

Danny sighed. He'd had a girl for a best friend, so tears were nothing new to him. He didn't have to like them much, though. He felt an ache of empathy in his chest and pulled her close, tucking her head against him and wrapping one arm around her back. "Hey, let it all out."

"This is so embarrassing," she stuttered between hiccups. "I'll get makeup on your shirt."

"Don't worry about it. My shirt will wash and I have a spare." He ran a hand along the silky strands of her hair, giving her a moment to weep before asking again, "What's going on? Can I help somehow?"

She shook her head against his shoulder. "Stupid of me. Not important." But her renewed sobbing contradicted her words.

Danny glanced back at the kitchen in time to see James come to the door and look out. Danny waved to him, then maneuvered Tia further away so she wouldn't upset the girls. Another minute passed and she started to calm. He tried again. "Okay, can you tell me what's got you so worked up?"

She took a deep, hitching breath, and let it out, then pulled away from him. He released her with some reluctance. Her lashes sparkled slightly with dampness and mascara was smeared on her cheeks and his shoulder, but he didn't care.

Tia took one more slow, deep breath, this time much calmer than before. "I told you I recently found out my mom had cheated on my dad and that's why they divorced? It all came out because of an argument over blood types and my mom finding out I was the wrong type, which had my dad thinking she'd been cheating on him when I was conceived. It escalated into this big mess where we had DNA tests."

"I'm sure it was hard, but the peace of mind will be worth it." He pressed her hair back from her face. "Did you get the results?"

"Yeah. Turns out neither of them are my biological parents." She stumbled over the last few words, barely getting them out.

That must have been a shock. He thought she would start sobbing again, but soon she seemed to get it back under control. When he was sure she could answer him, he asked, "Were you adopted?"

"Don't you think they would've told me if I was adopted?" She hit him in the chest with her fist, but if she was trying to hurt him, it was a pretty lame attempt. "Wouldn't they have stopped and explained before we sent in cheek swabs?" she continued.

"Hey, I'm only eliminating the most obvious possibilities." She was right, of course they would have told her. He just hated seeing her torn apart like this. "I'm sorry. I can understand why you're so upset. It must be overwhelming." He took her hand and gave it a squeeze. "What did your parents say?"

She sniffed. "I haven't told them yet. I found out just before I called you. My mom will have a come-apart. The worst thing is I don't know what to do. Do I try to find out what happened? Where do I look? Is it going to open a can of worms that will mess up a lot more lives?"

A couple more tears fell, but she didn't dissolve into sobs again, so Danny figured it was a step in the right direction. He picked up a lock of her curly hair and played with it. He loved the way it curled around his finger, so soft and shiny. "Don't think you have to have the answers all right now. You just found out. Give it a day or two to settle before you decide anything." He settled his hands on her shoulders and pressed a kiss to her forehead. Her skin was soft and her hair held a light floral scent that went straight to his gut.

"Mom, where are you?" Samantha's voice rang through the building.

Tia furiously wiped at her face, smearing the makeup worse. "I'm a mess."

"Here, let me show you the bathroom. You can clean up there." Danny took her around the corner to the bathroom and then walked back to Samantha. "Hey there, girlie. Your mom had to take a pit stop. Are you about ready to go home?" He hated the thought of sending Tia home upset, but it was almost dinnertime and he knew she'd want to get away. She was probably kicking herself for telling him anything in the first place.

"Yeah, unless you'll let me ride on the ambulance with you." She looked hopeful.

"Sorry, squirt. You're a little too short, yet. Maybe when you get a bit bigger." He ruffled her hair and smiled. He loved the hero-worship in her eyes when she looked at him and never wanted it to fade away. She was such an open book, so friendly and trusting, so excited about the world around her. It was refreshing.

"I'm always too little. I don't get to do anything." Her bottom lip popped out as she pouted.

Danny held in a laugh, remembering Laura taking a similar stance many times over the years. He felt a sharp ache in his chest when he thought of his friend, but swallowed it back, pushed it away. The loss was there all the time, but now was not the time to think about it.

He could hear Tristi fussing before he reached the kitchen door, so his first move was to swing her into his arms and tickle and tease her back into a good mood. It was no mean feat considering what she really wanted was her mom. Danny had the feeling Tia was going to be a few minutes, though, so he took the girls over to one of the fire trucks and boosted them in, explaining what all of the knobs and buttons were for.

When Tia re-emerged, she looked quite a bit better, definitely more in control. "Girls, are you ready to go?"

Tristi immediately stretched out her arms and slid into her mother's embrace. She began babbling. Danny only understood a few words, but Tia seemed to catch far more of her chatter.

"Mom, can we come back some time?" Samantha asked.

Tia met Danny's gaze and her mouth curved slightly. "I'm sure we'll be back sometime. In fact, I'm judging a chili cook-off in the parking lot next door in a couple of weeks."

"Yay!" Samantha jumped up and down. Casey looked pleased, but wasn't as enthusiastic.

It only took a few minutes for Tia to herd the kids back out to the car and get them buckled in. Before she opened her own door, she looked back at Danny. "Thanks for putting up with my tears. I appreciate it. I guess I really needed to get all of it off my chest."

"I have broad shoulders. Feel free anytime." When he realized his eyes had strayed to her mouth, and he was wondering what it would be like to kiss her, he stepped back and shoved his hands in his pockets. This was not the right time. Not yet. "I'll be in touch."

"I'm sure you will." She smiled weakly, then got in the car.

He watched her pull out of the parking lot, then turned and walked back into the station, determined to keep in touch—and he intended that literally.

Twelve

While Tia was making dinner the next night, she called her father and left a message, asking him to pop by when he had a chance. Then she called her mom's cell—using a code to bypass the call so it would go directly to voice mail. She didn't want to face a barrage of questions over the phone. She anticipated seeing both of them that evening, but she was still surprised to have her mom show up on her doorstep before dinner was over.

Mona stood in the doorway, her eyes worried, her face pale, as if she already knew the answer. Still, Tia managed to get her to help ready the girls for bed and tuck them in. Before Tia had said goodnight to Samantha, though, the doorbell rang again and Mona let Ron in.

Both of her parents at once. Tia wasn't sure if she was glad she'd get it over in one swoop, or if she was worried about the reactions if they were both in the same room. Would the kids actually fall asleep or would the tears and recriminations get too loud and keep them up? She said a quick prayer for strength and returned to the living room.

She took the chair opposite them and clasped her hands on her lap, unsure what to say or how to explain.

Mona broke the silence. "Well, you didn't have to bring me here to say he's your father. I told you, I didn't step out on him."

"Then," Ron clarified.

Mona blushed beneath her makeup, but gave a stiff nod of acknowledgment.

"Actually," Tia said, fisting her hands together on her lap. "The test proved something else entirely. It showed . . . neither of you are my biological parents."

Tia closed her eyes against the noise of her mother's loud protests. She felt her father take her hand in his large, calloused one and squeeze it. Tristi start to whine down the hall and Samantha asked what was wrong as Mona continued to argue and wail.

Tia opened her eyes, tears rimming her lashes, to find her father looking steadily at her. He squeezed her hand again, his face sad, but tearless. He laid his other hand on Mona's shoulder and told her to settle down. His voice was soft, filled with authority. He released Tia's hand. "Go check on your girls."

Tia rose automatically and did as he said. Soon Mona's protests calmed to a murmur, and Tia was able to settle both girls back into bed. When she returned to the living room, she found Mona leaning against Ron's shoulder, crying softly. It was a big improvement in her behavior, and odd seeing them like that after all the years of bickering.

Tia sat and said nothing. She was exhausted, confused, and wanted a few hours to herself to let her mind wander.

"All right," Ron started after a moment. "So now we know."

"Do we? Maybe they mixed up the results." Mona wiped at her face with a damp tissue, smearing the makeup worse. "We should have the tests done again."

"That won't change anything," Tia said. Not that it hadn't crossed her mind to double-check, but she'd suspected what the results would be, so there was no point in trying again.

"So where do we go from here?" Ron asked.

Tia deliberated. She'd been thinking about it for more than a day now. "Do we assume the switch was made in the hospital? Could it have happened later?"

Ron shook his head. "No. If you were switched, it had to be right after you were born. In the first six hours, most likely, when we'd barely gotten a look at you. We would have realized if it had happened later. I'm surprised we didn't anyway."

Mona's wails grew louder again.

"All right." Tia's stomach felt tied up in knots. Part of her wanted to pretend none of this had happened and she was still blissfully unaware. The other part of her wanted to know what happened, not because she was looking for something more or better, but because she needed answers. "Then I guess I start with the hospital." She wondered, with the HIPAA laws, if she would be able to get any information about other females born the same day she was.

"What can I do to help?" Ron asked.

"You're going to look for your real family? We're not good enough for you?" Mona asked, her voice growing in pitch every few words.

Tia rubbed her forehead. A headache had been growing all afternoon, so she was grateful there were no signs of migraine this time. "Mom, this isn't about being good enough. The fact is, there's another family out there in the same situation as us. I want to know who they are."

"And then you'll destroy their lives by telling them about this. Why rock the boat, Tia? Why bring the extra pain on them too?" Mona sobbed out her objections.

Tia wet her lips as she considered her mother's point. Did she have a right to mix up another family? She didn't know, and once she had answers about who they were, maybe she would choose to leave things alone.

Maybe.

"I don't know if I will yet, or if I will even be able to find the family. We'll have to see what happens." She would know what to do when she met them—she hoped.

Danny drove to the television station and parked in front of the four-story building. He hadn't told Tia he was coming, but she would start cooking soon, and he hoped he could talk his way into the studio. Even if he had to wait until her segment was over, he wanted to be there, to see her, look in her eyes so he could tell if she'd been sleeping or not.

She hadn't been far from his mind since her visit earlier that week. Memory of her sad blue eyes haunted him.

The man at the front desk asked him for ID, then called back to the studio to find out if Tia knew him. A few minutes later a woman came through a set of nearby doors and smiled at him. "You must be Danny. You should've seen the way Tia brightened up when she heard you were here." She offered her hand and he took it.

"I'm glad to hear it. I'm Danny Tullis."

"Marilyn Novak." She picked up a guest pass from the guard and handed it to Danny. "Come with me. Tia's busy doing her last-minute prep, but I can take you in to talk to her for a few minutes."

"Thanks." Danny was fascinated by the low buzz of talk around them as they walked down a few hallways and into the studio. The news anchors were huddled around some papers on set, three men spoke by one of the big cameras and people rushed past. Marilyn led him to the other corner of the set where the tiny kitchen was arranged. Tia scooped flour into a small glass bowl on the counter and lined it up with several other bowls. She glanced up at them and a smile bloomed across her face. "This is a nice surprise. What's going on?" she asked when Danny got close enough to hear.

"I stopped in to say hi, and to see how things are going." He studied her. Through all of her stage makeup it was hard to tell if she had dark shadows under her eyes. Had she slept better? She didn't look tired. He glanced at Marilyn, who smiled in understanding and made her excuses before retreating.

"I'm all set up here for noon." Tia stopped to check the oven and nodded. "Right on schedule. I have a few minutes." She led him out of the kitchen area to a corner, releasing her hair from the elastic which held it away from her face.

"Good. Sorry to drop in on you. I wasn't sure if you'd have time to talk with me." He brushed a lock of her curly red hair back from her cheek. "I've been wondering how you were dealing with everything."

Tia nodded. "I told my parents last night. They were shocked."

"That was probably an understatement."

"Yeah." Her lips twisted in a parody of a smile. "As far as we can tell, the switch must have happened in the first four to six hours after I was born, otherwise they probably would have realized I wasn't their baby. Now I have to figure out who else had baby girls during that window, and then try to track them down."

"And then what?"

She blew out a long breath. "I don't know. Even if I find the family, do I disturb their lives by telling them the truth? The other woman, the one my mom gave birth to, has she lived a happy life? Who switched us? Why would they? How did they manage? Didn't they put tags on us before we ever left our mother's sides? There are too many unanswered questions."

She twisted her hands together. "And then there's my brother, Wes. He knows why my parents split up. In fact, I have the feeling he knew even before Samantha's party, though he never breathed a word of it to me." Her brow furrowed in irritation at this. "We haven't discussed any of it with him. Or at least, I haven't. What is he going to think about it?"

Danny set his hands on Tia's shoulders. "Give it time. First things first. We'll find out about your other family, see what we can learn, and go from there."

"We?" She smiled at him, curiosity sliding into her eyes. "Since when did this become *we*?"

He chuckled. "Wishful thinking on my part?"

"You don't even know me."

He thought he probably understood her better than she realized. "I'd like to."

"I see." Several seconds passed as she absorbed his comment. "I think I'd like that too."

Danny wanted to do a fist pump, but managed to keep from making a fool of himself. That was definite progress.

The producer called out a five-minute warning until the show started.

Tia sighed. "You better go up to the control room to watch. They don't like visitors on set during filming."

"Would it be okay for me to hang around until you're finished?" *Say yes.*

She smiled. "I'd like that. Then you can taste today's dish."

"My mouth is already watering." To kiss her, but he managed to keep his hands and lips to himself.

Tia laughed, then motioned to a man with shaggy black hair. "Hey, Tom, can you take Danny up to the control booth to watch the filming?"

"Sure."

"See ya." Danny cocked a grin at Tia and followed the man upstairs.

Watching the maneuvers behind the scene was an education. Danny studied the way people moved in the room, who did what, and wished he could ask Tia about each job. He watched her pull the pan out of the oven and test it, then set it on a tray out of the way.

Soon the camera moved to her and she began her cooking segment. She did the first part of the show, then they broke for commercials. She rushed through mixing, then moved the last few ingredients closer. When they came back to her, she finished the dish, then pulled out the pre-baked version and sliced a piece. From the sound booth he was unable to smell the food, but the look of it alone—not to mention the memory of how delicious it had been the previous weekend—made him eager to taste it. He was impressed as always by her calm friendliness on camera, the way she rarely stumbled over her words or showed the least discomfort.

She was made for television.

Finally the entire show wrapped up and he was allowed back on the stage. She pulled the second pan out of the oven and dished it up for the rest of the crew. When Danny reached her, she looked over and smiled. "I've been saving some for you."

"Good. It smells terrific."

"And it tastes as great." She handed him a sample before turning to take care of a few other crew members.

Another half hour passed as she finished clean up, and he lent a hand where he could. When he finally walked her out of the building, he wondered why he hadn't realized how much work her cooking segment was. It was amazing she managed to keep up with the schedule. "You do that every day?"

"Yep. It can get a bit crazy, and searching for different recipes five days a week is a challenge, but I enjoy it."

He nodded. "It's easier to do a challenging job you enjoy than an easy one you hate."

"Isn't that the truth!"

He walked her to her car and leaned one hip against the hood. "So is there anything I can do to help with your search?"

She swallowed hard as she met his gaze. "Not right now. Actually, I'm still trying to figure out where to start. Hospital records are private, so how do I find out about the other girls born that day? I don't want to alert anyone to what happened until I know how I'm going to deal with it. I'm not sure if there's any other way, though."

He thought for a long moment, considering and rejecting several ideas until his thoughts snagged on something that might be useful. "What about birth announcements in the paper."

"Birth announcements?" Her brow furrowed. "I suppose one or two may have paid for an ad."

"No, I mean the bare-bones listings hospitals used to put in the papers. 'Baby girl to Joe and Jane Smith of Olathe.' " He remembered seeing one of those for his cousin's baby before the privacy laws changed.

She clearly hadn't thought of that. "Oh, I could check to see if the hospital did those. I can't remember how much information was in them, but it's a good place to start. If I can find any listings."

"Where were you born?"

"Here in Kansas City, on the Kansas side. St. Mark's Hospital." Tia checked her watch. "I need to pick up Tristi from daycare, and I have some errands to run before Samantha gets out of school."

He wanted a few more minutes alone with her, but conceded. "All right, then. How about if I come over for dinner and afterward we can search online?"

She tilted her head and a light furrow developed between her brows. "Are you serious? Why would you want to get mixed up in this?"

He picked up a lock of her wild hair and curled the silkiness around his finger. "I told you, I want to get to know you better." He smiled as a sweet ache entered his chest. "Besides, my best friend long ago told me I have a white knight complex. I can't seem to help myself." He missed Laura.

Tia looked amused. "You do know I'm not a damsel in distress, right? I can take care of this alone."

"That doesn't mean you have to." He released her hair with reluctance and moved back. "I like how you're strong and independent. Oh, and did I mention beautiful? It's a killer combination."

Her eyes narrowed slightly. "I can't quite figure you out."

"Another reason to spend more time together." Though he didn't want to leave her, he knew he needed to let her go. "But it will have to wait until this evening. I'll see what I can find out online before we meet." He shifted out of the way so she could open her car door.

"Six o'clock," she told him.

"I'll be there."

Thirteen

Tia checked the chicken enchiladas in the oven and nodded in satisfaction. They smelled good—now she hoped they tasted as good as she thought they would. The trials of testing new recipes weren't limited to anaphylaxis—adding the wrong ingredient or too much of it while trying a new twist was a very real possibility. Thankfully she did that far less often now that she had more experience. She glanced back at the bubbling butter in a pan and began whisking in flour to make a roux.

The doorbell rang and she glanced at the stove clock. "Right on time." She liked that about Danny. Promptness was a big plus in her book.

"I'll get it!" Samantha called as she ran down the hall and stormed the front door. There wasn't a direct line of sight to the door from the kitchen, but Tia heard the locks snick and the door squeak slightly as it opened. "Danny!"

"Hey, kiddo. How are you doing?"

"Great. Mom made enchiladas." Her voice dropped slightly in decibels, but was still clearly audible, "It smells good, so maybe it won't be yucky!"

"Samantha!" Tia called out, only mildly scandalized by her daughter's pronouncement. She was getting used to being embarrassed by similar comments.

"Mom, it's true! Oh, those are pretty."

"Don't worry; I have a much more sophisticated pallet than the average six-year-old." Danny said as he entered the kitchen, holding a bouquet of bright wildflowers. He glanced at them. "I saw these and thought of you."

"Oh, you *are* a charmer." Tia wasn't sure how to feel about it, but it seemed he had no plans to go away, and she liked him too much to shut him out.

"I try." He handed the bouquet to Samantha and asked her, "Have you got a vase around here?"

"Yes. In the cupboard." She pointed to the tiny one above the fridge—the safest place in the house for breakables, since neither girl could reach it. Danny, however, had no trouble at all. He didn't need Tia's step-stool, or even to go up on his toes.

Tia watched his jeans stretch across his perfect backside, bit her lip, and turned away. Was she attracted? Oh yeah. Times ten. Was it a good idea to let him get close? The jury was still out, but she decided to take her chances. After she added the rest of the ingredients and turned off the heat, she turned back to where he was cutting the stems and putting them into the vase of water. "Where did you learn to do that?"

He smiled at the flowers, a far-away look coming into his eyes. "My second mother—my friend's mother—always made Laura and I help her in the garden, then trim back the stems and make bouquets for her to take to her church group or to people in the neighborhood who needed a bit of cheer."

"And you didn't duck out of it?" The thought made her feel all warm and gooey inside.

"I tried. She wouldn't let me." He set the last stem in the vase and fiddled with them a little. Obviously he didn't have any natural talent for arranging them, but it was sweet anyway. "She said it would impress girls someday." He glanced up at Tia. "Was she telling the truth?"

"You appear to have gotten a pretty thorough education in impressing females." Should she be more coy? Less coy? Tia didn't know; it had been too long since she'd played the dating game.

"I like 'em!" Samantha grabbed his hand and tugged him toward the living room. "Come play fire station with me."

When he looked at Tia for confirmation, she waved him away. "Go ahead. I'll put this in the oven when the other is done in a few minutes, and then we can sit down to eat."

He winked as Samantha pulled him from the room.

After they'd eaten and all the dishes were washed and put away, Tia sent Samantha to change into pajamas and brush her teeth. Though she grumbled, Samantha followed orders. Once she was out of the way, Tia turned back to Danny. "So did you find anything this afternoon?"

"I made a few calls and found out which paper used to run birth announcements from St. Mark's Hospital twenty-seven years ago. They don't have any of those papers archived online, however, so we'll have to dig through their hard copies. It could take a few hours to find the listing, and then you'll have to start researching the families. I have no idea how many babies were born there each day then. Hopefully there will only be a few options."

"The thought of trying to find someone all of these years later is overwhelming." Tia still wasn't sure if she *wanted* all the answers.

He took her hand in his, toying with her fingers. "I know. There's no rush, though. You have plenty of time to poke around and see what's out there."

"Which is good, since I don't know what I want to do about it. I'm going to do the research, but do I mess up their lives by telling them what happened?" She sighed, already weary of the confusion. "Do I owe them the truth, or will it do more harm than good?"

"I'm sure you'll make the right choice when the time comes." His voice was low and soothing, lending strength and conviction.

"Thanks." She wasn't certain why she was talking to him about all of this—how had he wormed his way into it, anyway?

"I don't go back into work until Friday," he said. "If you'd like an extra set of eyes, I'd be happy to go along with you."

Tia had mixed feelings about his offer. "I should be able to handle it myself. I'll have to rearrange my schedule to get over there and I don't know when I'll make it."

"All right." He ran his thumb along her knuckles, raising goosebumps on her arm. "Open invitation, though. Let me know if you need anything."

After he left, she thought she might take him up on his offer. If she needed anything.

Fourteen

It was the following week before Tia was able to squeeze in time to go to the newspaper office. She dropped Tristi off at daycare a couple of hours early and had her ingredients prepped the night before so she could take more time if she needed to.

She arrived at the newspaper and a young blonde led her through the busy newsroom and back to archives—a room smaller than some people's closets—full of huge books holding every newspaper the company had ever printed. Tia looked at the shelves and shelves of books and hoped they were filed chronologically. It took several minutes of poking around before they found the book that started shortly before she was born.

Tia flipped through the pages to her birth date and studied the headlines. It was interesting to learn what had been going on in the area and in the country on that day. After finishing the paper, she leaned back and settled in for the duration, knowing the right issue might be dated weeks later.

"What are you looking for, exactly?" the young woman asked.

"Birth announcements. I'm told they used to run them periodically." Tia paused when she came across a big section of announcements listed by hospital, organized by date, and comprised solely of the baby's gender, followed by the parents' names and city. Unfortunately, her hospital was not listed.

"Why do you want to know how many babies were born twenty-seven years ago?"

"It's research." Tia continued onward through the pages.

"Like for a book or an article?"

"Something like that." No need to be too forthcoming just to satisfy the girl's curiosity. The banal chatter was irritating, and Tia wasn't finding what she needed, which only irritated her more.

"You know, you look familiar."

"I have one of those faces."

"But I could swear I've seen you somewhere before."

Tia fought the urge to roll her eyes, "Probably on TV. I work for PGRE news." She flipped the newssheet and scanned the next page, then flipped again.

"Really? Oh my! I'd love to get into television news! I totally took a double major in journalism and theater. I'm an intern here, because it's so hard to get an internship at a television station, and—wow! I can't believe I'm meeting a real television news reporter!" the intern gushed, perky enthusiasm in every word.

Tia wanted to smack her forehead on the table, anything to get the young woman to shut up. "I'm not actually a reporter."

"Oh, well, quit being so humble. I remember you now. Didn't you report about the big drug bust a few weeks ago?" She continued prattling on while Tia wondered if she would get a chance to refute the woman's words.

In the meantime, Tia didn't take her eyes from the newspapers in front of her. She finished the book and closed it. "Can you show me the next one?"

"What?" the intern stopped mid-stream. "Oh, yeah. Here, let me put this away." She lugged the book over to the shelf where it had been before, and muscled out the volume next to it. It hit the table with a thud, and to her relief, the dates on the cover were right.

"Thanks." Tia opened the book and began paging through it.

"So what degree did you get?"

"What?" Tia hadn't been listening.

"In school, to get your reporting job. What degree did you get? And how did you get hired on?"

"I went to The Culinary Center of Kansas City. I do the cooking segment every weekday." She stopped at yet another list of birth announcements and grinned when she hit pay dirt.

"You're a cook? You aren't a news reporter?" Disappointment filled her voice.

"Right." Tia pulled out her notebook even as she scanned the page to her birth date, then sighed when she found six other couples who had given birth to a girl that day. Seriously? Then, only remembering her mother had stated she was born in the middle of the night, and not remembering what time, she wrote down the parents who were listed for the day before and the day after. Fourteen possible names, but some of them would be eliminated, most likely, depending on when she was born.

"So how did you get the job?" The intern eyed her warily.

"I applied and got a lucky break." Tia snapped her notebook shut. "Thanks for your help." As she left, her mind buzzed with everything she needed to do, the searches she would have to make. Would any of these people still live in the area? And how many duplicate names would she have to pick through?

Tia wasn't even out to her car before she speed dialed her mother.

"Hey, Mom, what time of day was I born?"

When she got off the phone a few minutes later, she crossed all of the births the day after hers off the list. Down to ten.

Fifteen

A few hours later Tia answered the phone to find Danny on the line. "That was a nice mention of our cook-off today," he said after they exchanged greetings.

"I'm glad you liked it. Did it bring any attention? Any sign-ups? My boss loved the idea of featuring the winner and their recipe on the show." She pulled into the parking lot at Samantha's school. Sometimes she thought she didn't do anything but cook and chase kids all day.

"About ten more teams signed up. We now have eighteen."

"Great! I had the web gal add a note about it on the web page where they feature my recipes. It'll run until the competition. The station is behind you guys, one-hundred percent!"

"And we appreciate it." There was a small pause. "I wondered if I could take you out to say thank you."

"I know Samantha would love to see you again," Tia maneuvered into a prime spot and did a little dance in her seat at the location. Her mind was still half on her search and what lay ahead of her.

"Actually, I meant just you."

Tia turned her full attention on him as she processed what he'd said. Though she was cautious, she also felt a little trill of excitement at his invitation. "You mean like a date?"

"Yes, exactly like a date. I thought you might talk Nichole into taking the girls for a couple of hours. We can grab some dinner where the conversation doesn't revolve around what the other kids did on the playground."

"I thought you liked my girls." Had his interest in them been feigned? Had they been obnoxious? Samantha did have a habit of monopolizing him.

"I do like them. Samantha has me completely wrapped around her finger and Tristi's a joy, but I still want to spend more time alone with their mother." Loud beeping came over the line and he muttered something. "Sorry, I've got to go. Ambulance pager. I'll call back later. Will you think about it?"

"Yeah. I will." She sighed as he hung up. There was no question of what she wanted—she wanted to get to know him better. So why was she hesitating? It wasn't like they hadn't been alone before. Some of their time together had been very date-like.

She smiled and waved when she caught sight of Samantha barreling toward her car. There would be time to worry about Danny's invitation later, and she had no good reason not to take a chance with him. She thought the excitement of the relationship might be worth any trouble or struggles it brought her.

A few days rushed by as Tia tried to keep up with her normal life. Danny called and they set a date for Saturday night. Samantha had dance classes and piano lessons and Tia let the information she'd gathered from her visit to the newspaper collate in her mind before rushing out to do anything with it.

Thursday after the kids went down for bed, Tia turned on her computer and began a search on the other families. She had ten families to research, and she wasn't sure how much she could find online. She didn't have any of the names of the other women who were born when she was, so she would have to start with the parents. The question was whether or not she'd be able to narrow down the possibilities. She may come up with multiple couples with the same names, or she might find nothing at all on some of them. If the parents had been divorced like hers, that would add even more difficulties to the search.

The first names were Robert and Janice Monroe. She pulled out a notebook and began taking notes. After an hour she'd verified there were three couples with those names. One couple was too old to be a likely choice, and Janice had passed away the previous year.

Another couple had only boys—according to a short bio on Robert. She couldn't completely rule them out. If their daughter had died young, she wasn't likely to be mentioned in the bio. The third one actually brought up a family picture—they and their two children all had very dark hair, and shared a remarkable family resemblance. With a little more digging she was able to find the names of the daughters. An hour later she verified one of them was born in Kansas City the same year as Tia.

Though she couldn't cross the other names off the list entirely, she put a note next to the family's info, marked them as unlikely swaps, and closed up for the night.

"So how's the search going?" Danny asked Tia as they sat across from each other in the Mexican restaurant. He had started to wonder if he'd ever get her there, between haggling over a night they could both go, and the list of do's and don't's for the babysitter.

"Slow." Tia dipped a tortilla chip into the salsa in front of her, playing with it. "I've researched a couple names. I'm fairly certain I found the right family for the Monroes, but the Ibsons are more elusive."

"It's not easy, is it?"

"No. I hadn't thought of all the MySpace and Facebook accounts I'd have to sort through. Then there are the death notices, news articles, and school athletics scores." She ate the chip and swallowed before going on. "Every name has to be followed until I verify whether or not they could possibly be right. Thankfully Ibson isn't very common, but I still can't pin down one group of names as the most likely family."

"You need some help?"

"If I had some idea what I was going to do once I found the answers, I'd be in a hurry to find them." She shrugged apologetically. "Since I don't, I'll handle it myself for a little longer."

He took her hand, stopping it halfway to the bowl of chips so he could get her full attention. "You know I'm happy to help if you'd like some company." She looked tired, vulnerable, and as usual, his instinct was to comfort.

"I appreciate the offer. Really." She turned her hand over in his and gave it a squeeze. "Mostly I'm glad to have someone to talk to who isn't going to freak out on me."

He threaded their fingers together, loving how soft her skin was. "Are your parents making things difficult?"

Tia sighed. "My dad's trying to be understanding and supportive. Whatever happens, I'm sure things between us will work out fine in the end. My mom is another issue. She's always been high strung and demanding, but is making an art form out of it now."

He chuckled. "I know people like that. I'm sure she's uncertain of her place in your life now. Stand by her and eventually she'll stop freaking out."

"Easy for you to say." She used her free hand to pick up another chip. "And then there's my brother, Wes. I still haven't talked to him about everything, but he didn't seem amazed about the reason for the divorce or that I might not have been my father's child. He was so detached. I'm not sure if he doesn't care, or if he's trying to protect himself."

Danny squeezed her hand, sensing she just needed him to listen. A few seconds passed before he brought up the other issue plaguing him. "Do you mind if I ask what happened to your husband? Tristi's not very old."

The frustration in her eyes melted into sadness. "I got pregnant just before he shipped out. I didn't even know until after he left." She brushed the hair back from her face, and kept her eyes glued to the food in front of them. "It's been nearly two years since he was killed in Afghanistan. A car bomb went off as he and some of the other soldiers walked past. He was the only American death, but five Afghanis died in the blast as well. I heard about the bombing on television the day before the military caught up with me." She wet her lips.

"It must have been an awful couple of years."

"It's been tough." She took a deep breath and met his gaze. "But things are going well for me. It's not easy being a single parent, but my girls are pretty good and I have Nichole to help out and talk with. Lee's family's been great, as well. They love the girls and make every effort to spend time with them."

"That's good. We all need support when we lose a loved one." He felt his throat close off and heard his voice go husky on the end of his statement. He had not planned to bring Laura up, and hoped Tia didn't comment on what he'd said.

She must have noticed, because she looked up at him as the server brought their meals. "Are you speaking from personal experience, then?"

Danny waited until the waitress left. "It's not the same, but I'm sure you heard about the bus crash a couple months back."

"The women's retreat?" Though it was a question, Tia nodded in acknowledgement. "It would be hard to miss considering where I work."

"Of course." Danny tried to smile, but knew he failed miserably. "One of my childhood friends was on the bus." He cleared his throat, trying to dislodge the lump in it. "She didn't make it home."

Sympathy softened her expression. "Were you close?"

"The closest. She'd been over to my place for dinner only days before the accident. We'd made plans to go home and see our parents—our moms were both hassling us about not visiting often enough." And now it was too late for her to visit her family.

Tia squeezed his hand. "I'm sorry."

"Me too." But he couldn't talk about it right now without getting too emotional, so he pushed back the pain. "Now, maybe we should both eat, and find an easier subject."

She smiled and withdrew her hand. "Okay. Do you suppose they have any hot sauce around here?"

Danny thought it was precisely the sort of question Laura would have asked. He smiled and motioned to the waitress to request a bottle.

Sixteen

With the upcoming chili cook-off, Thanksgiving, and life in general, Tia only had time to search for two more families the next week. Luckily she was able to find couples who were the likely parents, and cross them off her list. Thanks to Facebook, she was even able to verify one of the women was born the same day she was, but again, there was no family resemblance to Mona or Ron, and plenty with the woman's parents. That one got marked as an unlikely swap.

Tia reached the firehouse early on Saturday, grateful Lee's brother had agreed to take the girls for a few hours, and to bring them by for some chili after the judging was over. She was amazed to see how organized everything was. There was a school next door to the firehouse and the guys had gotten permission to set up in the parking lot, to keep their emergency vehicles unimpeded for quick response.

There were tents and tables, plenty of chairs, and everything was roped off so people who wanted to shell out a donation for the charity had to come past the entrance.

She hadn't known what to expect, but not having asked about the sign-ups lately, Tia found nearly thirty competitors for the title of best chili recipe. She didn't know how she was going to manage. Even if she only took a bite of each dish she'd be sick by the time she reached the end.

Danny met her at the entrance to the roped off area. "Hey, Tia!" He slung an arm around her shoulder and led her back to the tents where the contestants were set up. They had spoken on the phone several times during the week, and she had brought over a few pies to the firehouse for the guys' Thanksgiving dinner, since he had been working. "All set to test these recipes? We have thirty-two."

"How did we ever manage to get so many contestants?" It was terrific, a great show of support for the fire department, but way more than she had expected.

"Are you kidding? We had another three people call yesterday and ask if they could still sign up. We had to turn them away."

"Holy crow." She liked chili as well as the next person, but that was a whole lot of chili. "The camera crew should be here any minute."

"Good. James is collecting samples from each of the pots now. As you asked, each bowl will have an index card attached with the list of ingredients and an entry number on it." He led her into a smaller tent with its side flaps down.

On the table inside, she found nearly two dozen Styrofoam bowls lined up side by side. "All right. First we need to see if there are different categories." She glanced at all of the ingredient lists and started sorting them by traditional and white bean. There weren't enough other variations to make subgroups.

James brought in another tray full and announced it was the last of them.

Another minute of sorting and she was done.

"You're not going to sort out the turkey from the beef too?" Danny teased her.

"No." She bumped him with her elbow. "This will be fine." She had opted not to meet the chefs until after she tasted the chili—she didn't want some cute kid or grumpy old man's attitude to influence the scores on their food.

The camera crew arrived and took a shot at the bowls lined up on the table before she started to taste them. The reporter asked Tia a few questions about the event, the charity, and how she got involved.

She put on her camera persona and gave the requisite sound bites, but was relieved when the crew left her tent so she could begin the judging. The other judges, a local restaurant owner and the fire chief, approved of her organizational efforts and they began their taste tests.

They didn't agree on the merits of all of the dishes, but they checked their score sheets, taking time to discuss why they each preferred their top three. Another taste test of the best dishes and they were able to narrow down a winner in each of the categories, plus a grand master. Another three people judged the corn bread competition, and had nearly as much trouble with their selections—though they weren't nearly as numerous.

Finally Tia was able to go out and meet the chefs. It took nearly two hours to make the rounds, stopping to answer questions and shake hands, and she didn't get to speak with any of them for long. They stopped midway through her rounds to announce the contest winners, then continued meeting the chefs.

The crowds who came to eat the chili and support the burn center and burn camp swelled to over five hundred at noon, and stayed steady until nearly two o'clock. Tia was glad everyone brought gigantic vats of their chili and huge trays of cornbread. They ran out of food before people stopped coming, but the donations continued to pour in.

Samantha and Tristi arrived with their uncle and spent an hour wandering around, sampling the various dishes, and Samantha chattered with school friends.

Six hours after Tia had reached the firehouse, she sat with the guys in the tiny kitchen. The tents were down, the chairs and tables put away, and Danny and James were counting donations. In addition to the forty-three blankets they had collected for the burn center patients, the cash donations came out to over eight-thousand dollars.

"Wow. That was seriously impressive!" Danny said when the last of the money had been double checked.

"You guys put on a mean party," Tia said. She was exhausted, but felt good about what they'd accomplished. No doubt Lee's brother was more than ready for her to pick up the girls, but Tia wasn't sure she had the strength to get them through their evening routines.

Danny grinned. "Unless someone else has seriously good luck, this should easily put us in first place for fundraising in the city."

"You guys and your competitiveness. It's not about winning; it's about the kids—isn't it?" Tia asked, lifting her brows.

"Of course it is," James rushed to agree. "Winning the competition is icing on the cake."

Tia shook her head and held back a chuckle. She was a big believer in healthy competition, as long as it didn't turn cutthroat. Seeing the merriment in Danny's eyes told her it was all in good fun. And how could that be bad? "I ought to be going. The girls have to be getting on Garrett's nerves by now. Besides, I need to take them shopping so Samantha can get a couple of Christmas presents."

Danny reached over and took her hand, standing and helping her onto her feet. "Let me walk you to your car."

It was nice having a man hold her hand and feeling comfortable with him. The tiny thrill of excitement when she saw the tenderness in his gaze was an extra bonus. She thought for a minute that he might ask to join them in their shopping trip, but he didn't. Instead he brought up the fire station's annual Christmas party. "It's the sixteenth. Do you think you can come?"

She gave him a sideways glance. "You mean as a date?"

He turned her as they reached her car and backed her against her door. "Yeah. And I'd like to see you before then, too." He leaned toward her.

Tia allowed herself to show the flirty smile she felt blossoming inside. "You're seeing me now."

"Tomorrow," he said. "Come to dinner tomorrow. You can bring dessert again. I'll throw something together for the meal." He tugged away a lock of hair that had blown in her face. "It'll be nice."

She felt her heart pick up speed. "I'm sure it will. And what about the girls?"

"Sunday dinners are for everyone." He set one hand on her shoulder, and teased the side of her neck with his index finger. "We'll arrange a date for the two of us later."

Tia felt a shiver of excitement race across her skin as he leaned closer. It hadn't been a date—but much of the day had a somewhat date-like quality to it. He rarely left her side, ushering her around, making sure she met everyone. Still, he might kiss her.

His eyes said he wanted to kiss her, but instead of leaning down to take her mouth, he brushed his lips across her forehead. "You're exhausted. Go home and try to rest for a while. I'll see you tomorrow."

She wished he hadn't restrained himself, even as she was glad he was taking things slow. "Six o'clock?"

"That'll be perfect."

Seventeen

"Okay, try this one." Danny fed Tia something off the Thai platter sitting between them. He smiled as her eyes popped, either because she liked the taste, or it was burning her from the inside out. He hadn't been to this restaurant since Laura died—a shame, he thought as a smile spread over Tia's face. How was it she'd never eaten Thai before?

Her mouth was still full, but she covered it with her hand. "Oh, wow, this is so hot! But delicious." She chewed the food some more and swallowed. "What's it called?"

"No idea. We'll have to ask the waiter when he comes by again." A couple dates a week were all he'd been able to talk her into, including the Sunday night dinner with the girls. Every minute he spent with Tia, though, convinced him more that she was special—really special. He'd dated plenty of women, but none of them made him feel like she did.

He picked up some crispy noodle shrimp and ate it himself, then shared a bit with her. Tia was so warm and fun, she was open to new experiences and had this zest for food that fascinated him. "So do you think you'll be adding some of their dishes to your lineup next year?"

"Definitely. I may bump one into line before New Year's, in fact. I'll have to do some research."

Ah, an opening of sorts. "Speaking of research. How's it coming?" He'd been dying to ask, but hadn't wanted her to feel like he was grilling her by bringing it up earlier.

She shrugged one shoulder, playing with the red chicken curry on her plate. "It's moving right along. I think I've identified all of the families, though I'm still not sure about the Lowells. I'll have to do a little more digging on that one. But it can wait a few weeks. My days are filling up fast."

"I bet. I hope some of those blocks of time are reserved for me." The table where they sat was small, cozy, and tucked into a private booth. It was easy to pick up her hand and bring it to his mouth. He pressed a kiss to the inside of her fingers, and then to catch her reaction, to her palm. He saw the blush rise to her cheeks and had to smile. Yes, there was something very special about this woman. The fact such a simple gesture could bring on a blush only made him like her more.

"A few Sunday dinners at least," she teased.

"And more, I hope."

"And more." She popped another crispy wonton into her mouth.

"Good." Her response filled him with relief.

"Well, isn't this cute?" The voice came from the doorway to their booth and was edged with ice.

Danny looked up to see Carrie standing beside the table. He wanted to groan at the sight of his ex-girlfriend, but forced himself to keep a pleasant smile instead, even as he dreaded the encounter. "I'm sure you find it nauseating. Let me introduce my date. Carrie, this is Tia Riverton. Tia, Carrie Lockley."

"We used to date—before I gave up on ever becoming a priority in his life." Carrie leaned over the table, her shoulder-length brown hair coming between him and her as she spoke to Tia. "Take it from me—his priorities are his dead *non*-girlfriend, his work, and somewhere around twelfth or thirteenth place, he'll squeeze you in. He's not the marrying kind."

Tia's brows lifted and she gave Carrie a bland smile. "Since I'm not expecting a marriage proposal anytime soon, I guess we'll be fine."

Danny didn't have time to decide if Tia honestly didn't think the relationship was going anywhere, or if she was just spectacular at the cool-cucumber attitude. They were a long way off from making a commitment, but he definitely felt more for her than anyone else he'd dated. He only glanced her way before turning his attention back to his ex-girlfriend. "It was nice to see you again, Carrie."

"Spare me." She turned on her five-inch stilettos and walked off.

"She's bound to twist an ankle in those things," Tia said as she lifted her drink for a sip.

Danny didn't know where to begin his apologies. Experience with other women indicated said apologies would be manifold, and he was better off starting out right away. "I'm sorry."

"Don't worry about it. She's an ex-girlfriend who obviously had issues about your friendship with Laura." A smile teased Tia's mouth. "It's perfectly understandable. What girlfriend wouldn't wonder about their boyfriend's relationship with another woman? Carrie strikes me as the kind who wouldn't like to share."

He took Tia's hand in his. She really wasn't going to make him pay for the almost-scene? Carrie would have had a fit in her place. "You nailed it. The relationship with Carrie was a mistake for both of us—we weren't really suited for each other."

She nodded and took another bite of dinner. The conversation was closed when she switched to another subject, but Danny couldn't help but wonder if the encounter would come up again.

As Danny walked Tia to her front door a couple of hours later, she wondered when she'd last had such a great date. It had been too long, that was for sure. She held his hand as they sauntered up the sidewalk. After the incredible meal, he'd taken her to a magic show, which had been light and fun and so different from what she'd expected when he'd asked her out.

She wondered if she would ever get a handle on the real Danny.

They walked in and Tia paid her babysitter, then sent the neighbor girl home to sleep. As the front door closed, she turned back to Danny. "I had a great evening."

He stepped close enough that he could easily reach out and tangle her curly red hair in his fingers. "I'm glad. It was fun watching you have a great evening."

"I don't think I'll ever figure you out." She shivered slightly as the backs of his finger brushed her cheek and chin in his casual, yet deliberate way. His cologne seemed to swirl in the air around them, musky and familiar.

A smile spread across his mouth as it lowered toward hers and his voice grew husky. "Good. When you figure me out, things might start to get boring."

Tia tilted her chin up to him, leaning in as he covered her lips. She felt his arm come around her back even as she threaded hers around his neck and moved closer. She'd missed kissing, missed the closeness and taste and touch. When he tilted his head to improve the angle, she followed suit as his mouth moved across hers tenderly. Her chest flooded with warmth and a sweet ache. She felt him tug lightly on her hair and tilted her head back even more for a long moment before she made herself pull away. He let her go. When she opened her eyes, she found him already watching her.

"Go out with me Saturday," he asked.

"The girls."

He stepped back, releasing her, but caught her hand. His voice returned to normal. "We'll all go somewhere. We'll catch the latest Christmas flick at the theater and grab some burgers or something. Then we can see Christmas lights around town, make the girls smile."

"It sounds great." She was already looking forward to it. "I thought you meant for us to go alone."

His familiar, teasing grin appeared. "And then we'll put the girls to bed and stay up talking or arguing over a board game. Or something." He brushed his thumb over her bottom lip.

Her stomach quivered at the look in his clear blue eyes. "That sounds pretty wonderful."

"Good." He leaned down and brushed his lips over hers one more time, lingering for a few seconds until her mind blurred at the edges. "I better go," he said when he finally pulled away. "I have to be at the station early tomorrow. I'm on for forty-eight."

She was both disappointed to have him go, and a little relieved. This was progressing faster than she'd expected and she needed to step back and rearrange her vision of the world. Tia had three days to get her bearings and adjust, because she didn't think this was a road she was going to take a detour off of anytime soon.

A few minutes later as she watched his car pull out of the drive, she couldn't wait for Saturday.

Eighteen

Danny hung his fire turnouts back on their hook and headed for the shower. It wasn't going to be a very merry Christmas for the family whose home had just burned out. Three crews had been working on it for the past two hours. The brick façade might be salvageable, he thought, but the rest of it was a bust. Why was it fires seemed to multiply during the holidays?

He loved being a firefighter even more than his paramedic shifts. He loved to watch the flames roar, to hold the hose as water rushed through it, onto the blaze. There was magic in fire, in the way it moved across floors and walls, eating everything in its path. It was a force stronger than man, unpredictable in many ways, dangerous, fascinating. He often thought he'd like to be trained to identify and track arson, but he wasn't done with his paramedic skills, yet. He figured there was plenty of time, he wasn't even thirty.

The water beating down from the shower head was refreshing, left him feeling human again, softening the exhaustion of carrying around all his gear for hours—those oxygen tanks were heavy after a while. He dressed and trudged back to the kitchen to grab some food and a sports drink. Fluid replacement was one of the most important things the firemen had to remember. Dehydration was nobody's friend and in the heat of the fire with all of his gear on, it was a serious threat.

Finished with lunch, he decided to do a supply check on the rig he'd be using the next day. He was halfway through when James bellowed at him. "Hey, Danny, where are you?"

A moment later he stepped out of the back of the ambulance, clipboard in hand. "Yeah, what's up?" His eyes slid from his coworker to another man he didn't recognize and back to James.

"This dude's lookin' for ya." James wandered off.

Danny returned his attention to the dark-haired man. "What can I do for you?" He studied the stranger, trying to figure out what he was doing there.

"I hear you know Laura Dunaway really well."

Danny drew into himself a little, wary. What did this joker want? "Yeah. We grew up together."

"My name is Gavin McFadden." He stuck his hands in his pockets, obviously uneasy. "Is there somewhere we can sit?"

Danny's radar went off, telling him there was something wrong. His wariness increased, though he wasn't sure why. "I need to finish this inventory. Just tell me what you want."

Gavin paused for a moment, as if considering his words. "Do you have a sister named Janie?"

Suspicion joined Danny's other emotions. How could this guy know? And why did he care? If he was a friend of Janie's he should have just said it. And how did he know Laura anyway? The name Gavin wasn't familiar. Was he a reporter? One or two had tried contacting him after the accident, but Danny had ignored the phone. What would be the news angle now? "Yeah."

Gavin looked extremely uncomfortable, but he looked at Danny straight on. "There's really no way to say this, so I'm just gonna come out with it." He paused to take a fortifying breath. "Laura's alive. There was a mistake. She's had amnesia."

Hope followed by wrenching pain assaulted him and it was all Danny could do not to strike out at the jerk when the memory of Laura lying in the coffin popped into his mind. "Do you think this is a funny joke?" Danny's eyes narrowed as he wondered who sent the man to mess with him. "Get out of here."

He shook his head. "She's alive. You buried the wrong person."

"I saw her body, buddy. Do you really think I wouldn't know her? No matter how badly she was hurt, it's not like I wouldn't know my best friend." But he remembered all of the damage to her face and wondered if he would have recognized her without the mortician's artistic license. It was easy to dismiss, though, so he took a menacing step toward Gavin. "Get out."

Gavin moved back but didn't act as though he intended to leave. "Look, Danny, she's alive, and she needs to go home to her parents' house. You've known her for years; you'll know who should break the news to her parents. I can take her there myself, but I need some information first."

Danny stepped closer, hurt and anger pouring through him. "You leave those poor people alone. Don't you think they've been through enough? Do you have any clue how it's torn us all apart losing her?" He was able to contain the hitch of pain that nearly stopped his speech, but just barely.

Though his eyes showed his nervousness at Danny's aggressive movements, Gavin stood his ground, keeping his hands loose at his sides. "Since my friend—my brother—just found out that you buried his sister months ago and Laura isn't Adrianna, then yeah, I have an idea."

That made Danny pause. The dude was serious? "You actually believe this woman is Laura? You said she had amnesia. Did she suddenly remember everything?"

Gavin shook his head. "She had an appendectomy this morning. Adrianna already had an appendectomy years ago. It's not her. I poked around a little and realized she had to be Laura.""

Danny's brows winged up. "That was your *first* clue?" He still wasn't sure he believed, but he wanted it to be true so badly he couldn't walk away. Hope burgeoned in his chest and he fought to keep it under control.

Gavin gritted his teeth. "Look, she said she used to come to your place for a gingerbread house eating contest every year. You would make screaming noises for the gingerbread men when you ate them. I think she would have insisted on doing a gingerbread house this year except Megan's too busy and Laura's frankly dangerous with an oven."

Danny stopped and stared at Gavin as his questions dissolved. It took him a minute to reign in his emotions enough to talk. Then he chuckled without mirth. "You actually let her into the kitchen?"

An answering smile was all he needed.

It took seven calls and begging major favors for Danny to get the rest of his shift covered, along with his next one so he could spend time in Junction City for a few days with Laura and his family. He was glad his apartment was on the way to the hospital, since he still had to pack a bag.

Back on the road, he grabbed his cell phone and called Tia. She would be on her way to pick up Samantha from school by now. Luckily she answered on the second ring. "Hey, Tia."

"Hi, Danny. I heard about the house fire. Did your crew respond to it?"

"Yeah, it was pretty bad. The poor family lost everything." His mind was only half on the conversation, while the rest of his brain tried to figure out how to tell her what was going on.

"How heart breaking."

"Yeah, it can be." That was entirely true, though he'd leave off the part about how much he loved fires—no need to freak her out. He switched his mind back to the purpose of the call.

Tia spoke first, "Samantha's so excited about our plans tomorrow. She's hardly talked about anything else."

Danny bit back a groan. He *hated* letting people down. Tia would understand, but would Samantha? "Yeah, that's why I'm calling, actually. I have a problem."

Three seconds passed like rings of a gong before she responded. "What kind of problem? Did you pull another shift at work?"

He gripped the steering wheel harder. "No. I guess *problem* isn't the right word. Complication is more like it. You're not driving are you?" He didn't want her to cause an accident when he told her about Laura.

"No, I'm parked outside of the school, waiting for Samantha." Her voice was wary.

"Good." His gut felt tight, a ball of tension growing. "You remember me telling you how Laura and I had been friends since we were kids?"

"Of course."

"Well, this guy came to talk to me today. He said Laura *isn't* dead. Apparently there's been a mix-up and she's alive and been living in Paola, but she's in the hospital now after getting her appendix out, and she needs a ride home to her parents." He knew he wasn't explaining it well. He didn't know what to think about any of it, so how could he explain it?

"She let you all think she was dead this whole time? That doesn't sound like something a best friend would do. Come on, Danny, maybe the man was pulling your leg."

"I keep thinking that, but he was so certain. He said she has amnesia. She really hasn't known who she was until now." When he said it out loud, it sounded even more lame than it had when Gavin had told him.

"Do you think it's true?" Skepticism filled her voice.

He found himself nodding, even though she couldn't see him. "I think it might be. He told me something she's said about us growing up that only a few people know. And as for the amnesia, you're right that there's no way she would leave me and her parents thinking she was dead if she knew who she was. No way. So if it *is* her, then it has to be true." He wondered if he was rambling, but wasn't sure if he cared much at this point. He needed to get some of his thoughts out in the open. "I don't know. What if it isn't her? What if we get there and find out it's someone else? Her death has been haunting me, and now I find out she's not dead after all?"

"Are you okay?" Tia's voice was now pure comfort and concern.

He wished he knew. "Right now I'm running on adrenaline. When I see her I'll find out what's up. Then we'll go from there. This guy, Gavin, asked me to take her back home to Junction City."

There was a long pause before Tia spoke again, and her voice had cooled slightly. "You're not going to be back in time to take us out tomorrow, are you?"

"No, I'm really sorry. I won't be back until early Wednesday, or late the night before—Tell Samantha I'll make it up to you guys next week. I promise." He hated to cancel their date, but it wasn't his fault that things were going wrong.

The sound of a car door opening and closing, and Samantha's voice filtered through the background on Tia's end. "Of course," Tia said.

"Who is it Mommy?" Samantha's voice asked.

"Danny. He said he's not going to make it tomorrow. Something came up, sweetie."

"What? But he promised!"

Danny's gut clenched. He *hated* disappointing people. He wished he had time to wait until Samantha had gotten out of school so he could explain it all in person, but it wouldn't wait and he was already halfway to the hospital. He heard Tia's soft murmur, then Samantha's demand that she be allowed to talk to him.

A moment later her voice came onto the line. "Hi, Danny. What do you mean you can't take us?"

"Sorry, sweet pea. I have a problem." He searched for the right words, to ease the disappointment as much as possible.

"What kind of problem?"

"I have this friend who's sick and she needs me to pick her up from the hospital and take her home."

"But I thought you took sick people *to* the hospital, not from the hospital to their homes." Her voice was petulant and he could imagine her slouched in a pout, her free hand fisted and pounding her knee as he'd seen her do before.

Danny smiled at the image. "This is different. She's over the border in Kansas and she needs to get home to her parents in Junction City. She's been away from home a really long time."

Her voice turned to a full-out whine. "Why can't her parents come get her? I want to go to the movie."

"I know, sweet pea. I'm sorry. I promise we'll still do movie and dinner and everything next week when I get back." He felt like a jerk and wished things were different.

"When are you coming back?"

"Not until Wednesday. And then I'll have to work for a few days. It'll probably be next Saturday before we can go out."

"But, Danny, you promised!" Samantha's voice rose to a wail and he heard her sniffle.

"Honey, I'm really sorry." He grasped for any way to make her understand. "Hey, I want you to think of Casey. What would you do if she was sick?"

No sounds but sniffling came through the phone, so she was still listening.

"And what if she was so sick she needed you to help her, because no one else could. If you had to give up something you wanted to do so you could help her, would you help her anyway?"

Sniffle. "Yeah."

"I have to help my friend Laura. When I've helped her get home and straighten things around, I'll be back and we'll still get to have a fun time together. I'll explain everything to you then, and I'll make sure you get to meet her someday."

She heaved a deep, put upon sigh. "All right. I'll see you later." She didn't sound happy, but at least she wasn't throwing a tantrum anymore.

"Thanks, Samantha. Can you pass me back to your mom?"

"Yeah. Bye." Her voice was low and filled with disappointment, making guilt twist in his stomach.

"Bye, honey."

A moment passed before Tia's voice returned. "Sounds like you worked it out with her."

"I am really sorry about all of this. If I'd known—"

"That's why they call them emergencies, Danny." Her words were perfectly sensible, but her voice was clipped. "You can't schedule them into your week."

"Yeah. I guess so."

"Have a safe trip."

"I will. Take care of yourself, and the girls." He wanted to say more, but didn't know what to say. He wanted to tell her what he was feeling, except he wasn't sure he *knew* what he felt. A big part of him still thought this was going to turn out to be a wild goose chase.

"Of course. That's what I do."

"I'll call you tomorrow."

"Sure."

"Bye." Danny hung up feeling dissatisfied about the way it had all gone, and unable to figure out how to fix it.

Tia's grandmother lived in a tiny house in an old, dilapidated neighborhood in east Kansas City. She had raised two sons in the two-bedroom apartment while her husband worked strange hours as a bus driver for the city transit system. When he received a spinal injury in an accident at work, he was unable to return to his job, or any job full time again, and she'd gone to school and earned her CNA. Then she worked her tail off in a nursing home while she earned her RN certification. She had spent most of her life working in that nursing home, and had commented to Tia more than once that she feared she would work there until she had to move into it herself.

Thankfully Ron had been successful enough to pay off the little home she lived in and purchase her a decent car. When her social security benefits had kicked in, Glena was able to quit work and settle back on her 401K and government benefits. In addition to a couple of trips to her hometown in Alabama, she'd even taken a few trips to *exotic* locales like Florida and Louisiana.

Tia smiled to herself at the thought of her grandmother stretched out on the beach, trying to get a tan. It would never happen, though it was easy to see her under an enormous umbrella in a light sundress and lounging while she read. She had invited Tia to join her in Florida, had even offered to pay the plane fare a couple of years back, but Tia hadn't taken her up on the offer. It would have meant leaving the girls with Nichole for several days when Tristi was far too young to be left with someone else, and kicking in for a few expenses, which Tia couldn't manage financially.

She pushed the doorbell and smiled at the plastic flowers arranged in a vase beside the door. They were faded and nowhere near realistic, but they made Glena happy, so what could Tia say?

The door opened, exposing her grandmother's wrinkled smile and bright blue eyes. "Tia, I'm so glad you stopped by. Where are the girls?"

Tia entered at her grandma's behest. "At the neighbors'. I believe the older girls will be making gingerbread houses with graham crackers while the younger girls tip over stacks of blocks. I'll bring them next time, but I wanted to talk to you without a dozen interruptions for a change." The house always smelled of pine cleaner and had a warm, comfortable feel.

Glena's belly laugh—her laugh was as full out and heartfelt as everything else in her life—filled the room. "Well, I'm glad to see you, anyway. How are things at work?"

"They're going well. I've been thinking about putting together a cookbook. It's kind of overwhelming and exciting all at once."

"Good for you. How excitin'. I always knew you were the grandchild who would go somewhere, do somethin'. Right there in the hospital I could see it in you."

"You're sweet." Tia sank into the old gold sofa and accepted the tin of cookies Glena handed her.

"Not at all. I've always felt lucky to have you for my granddaughter." She bustled to the kitchen for drinks—as she always did when someone arrived. "Now, what else is goin' on in your life? Any hunky men?" She peered out through the doorway into the living area.

Tia smiled to herself and took a bite of the rosemary shortbread from the tin. She sighed in appreciation as the flavors hit her tongue. "Is this my recipe?"

"Of course, honey. Where else would I get a recipe like that?" Glena brought over a couple Cokes, handing one to Tia, who took it gratefully and popped the can open.

Glena settled into the chair across from her and opened her own can. "What was that smile? You have yourself a man, don't you? Come on, child, tell me everythin'."

Tia laughed. "I've been seeing someone. It's nothing serious." *Now. And after he ditched us, maybe never.* The thought made her uncomfortable, though, so she moved past it. "We're just enjoying each other's company. He's so unlike Lee in so many ways, but in the best ways, they're very alike." It surprised her to hear the words, as she hadn't allowed herself to think about how the men compared and contrasted, but she knew it was true.

"Is this someone you've met since the birthday party? Why haven't you been over here tellin' your old grandmother all about him before now?"

"Actually, we'd met before the dinner, but we didn't start seeing each other until after." She ran her finger around the rim of her soda can, a little confused by everything.

"Well why not? What's wrong with the man that he can't look and see my grandbaby is the best thing he'll ever find? I don't know if he's good enough if he didn't want to snatch you up the moment you met."

Tia sipped her soda and tamped back her smile. She should have come here sooner. Grandma always made her feel better. "I was having a bit of trouble breathing when I met him—and not because he's gorgeous and has a gentle touch, though both are true."

"Mmmhmm, that's what I'm talkin' about, girl, if they make you catch your breath, it's worth checkin' into. You been alone too long already."

Tia's objection was automatic. "It hasn't been that long since Lee died."

"You keep sayin' that, but time passes so fast. One minute it's here, and the next," Glena snapped her fingers for emphasis, "it's gone. Don't waste your time, honey, or you'll regret it."

Privately, Tia thought she was better off taking her time with this one. "I'll keep that in mind."

"So what you been up to other than gettin' yourself a young man—he is young, right? You're not seein' someone old enough to be your daddy?"

Tia laughed. "No, he's about my age, no worries there."

Glena wiped her forehead and shook off her hand as if she had been sweating over the answer. "That's good then, but what else is goin' on? Besides the man."

Tia nibbled on another cookie. "I've spent some time trying to figure out where I came from."

"I thought you already figured that out when you found Jesus, honey." When Tia didn't respond, Glena's mouth firmed. "You mean you've been lookin' into that blood-type fiasco. Your momma stepped out on your daddy. There ain't no other explanation. She always did have a wandering eye, even when they first met. I don't know what your daddy ever saw in her."

Tia played with the cookie, studying it for a moment. She would ignore the slurs on her mother—Glena had hated Mona for as long as Tia could remember. Since long before her parents' marriage had imploded. "Actually, there is one other explanation for the blood types."

"Tia, you don't want to go there."

"We did a DNA test. Mom, Dad and me. All three of us." She sipped her drink, hoping to get the lump in her throat to slide down, but it didn't help. She kept her eyes firmly focused on the cookie. "It turns out I'm not their biological daughter."

"Hogwash." Glena waved her hand, as if to bat the notion away. Tia looked up in surprise and saw her grandmother's red face. "I don't believe it," Glena said.

"It's true. I've been trying to wrap my mind around it, figure out what to do next, but I feel so overwhelmed. I even went to the newspaper office and looked up the births from the day I was born. Did you know there were ten girls all born within twenty-four hours of me? Ten? Do you have any idea how long it's going to take me to weed through all of them?" She'd spent so many hours already just covering four names, and she still wasn't sure about a couple of them.

"Why waste your time, child? Does it matter who your biological parents are? You have that sweet father of yours, and your mother will certainly keep meetin's from gettin' boring—she has a flare for drama." There was censure in her voice, and a bit of pleading.

Tia smiled at her grandma, though the last thing she felt was mirth. "I know you and Mom don't get on well."

"We haven't gotten on at all almost since the day I met her. The tramp." She crossed her arms over her chest and put on a stubborn expression.

"Grandma," Tia protested.

"I'm sorry it pains you to hear it, dear, but you know how she is."

There was no question about that. Tia sighed. Fighting about this wouldn't make anything better. "Yes, I know how she is."

"Now, you put all thoughts of search out of your head, and focus on the great life you have. Two adorable girls, a job you love, a cookbook in the works, and a hunk of man who you better be bringin' to meet me soon."

"Grandma!" Tia wasn't scandalized, Glena had always been outspoken. "If things look like they're going to keep going between us, I'll bring Danny by to meet you. No way am I going to have you pick at him to propose when we've only seen each other socially a few times." Okay, way more than a few by now, but she wasn't going to encourage her grandma.

"Well how long does it take you? Make your move, girl. Don't let him get away!"

Tia felt the laughter bubble up inside of her before it flowed out her mouth. She loved this woman—funny how much more happy and comfortable it was to visit with her was than with Mona.

Nineteen

It was almost five when Danny reached the hospital and found the floor where Laura was staying. He felt his feet slow as he approached the room. What if it wasn't her? What if, after all of this, it ended up being someone else entirely? He steeled himself for disappointment before rounding the open doorway and looking into the room.

The woman on the bed had the same brown hair, though considerably shorter than before, the same soft, open eyes. She turned her head and looked at him and a smile broke over her face. Something was different there, something in the face, besides the scars running along her brow. The smile, though, it was all Laura.

She grinned at him. "I should have known it would be you, if I'd remembered you."

Danny stood for only a moment staring at her, not sure if he believed what he saw, or what he heard—Laura's unmistakable voice. Then he took two long steps and scooped her into his arms, his throat clogging, his eyes watering and his heart bursting with relief. It was her. He buried his face in her silken hair, holding her tight. "I thought you were dead. I can't believe it. When that guy tracked me down at the fire department and said you were alive, I thought he was crazy. I can't believe it," he mumbled as he held her close.

"How could I possibly forget you?"

"Nothing's been the same since you died." He took another moment to study her. Close up, he could see she wore heavy makeup, which nearly covered some scars he had missed before. When he slid his fingers across her cheek, however, he could feel the bumps. "You look really great for a dead woman. Beautiful as always. I love your hair like this." He flicked a lock back and tried to figure out what else had changed. "I know what's different—you have a new nose. Cute." He tapped it with his finger. He preferred her old nose, but who was he to quibble when she was alive?

He saw her look over his shoulder at the door, and something altered in her face. The excitement shifted to longing. He glanced behind him and saw Gavin watching them, his brow furrowed. He looked at both of them, but didn't say anything, or return Laura's smile.

"Gavin, come in," she said.

She extricated herself from Danny's arms and he turned toward the doorway. "I guess you've met. Thank you. I think you picked exactly the right person to take me home."

"I'm glad." Gavin carried a suitcase, his other hand deep in his pocket.

"He didn't tell me how you know each other." Danny studied them both, watching their reactions.

Laura looked like she was trying to figure out how to explain. "He's um, a friend. I've been working for him for the past few weeks." She looked as though there was a whole lot more to things than she said. Her right eye twitched, a sure sign she'd left something out.

When she opened her mouth to try again, Gavin spoke first. "I was starting to think we worked for you, as efficient as you were at keeping us in line."

Danny laughed even while wondering what really lay between this man and Laura. Something decidedly more than friendship. "She does tend to be that way. I'm glad to see amnesia didn't change her too much."

"Laura's been a real asset to our business," Gavin said and Danny took the bag he held out, his curiosity growing by the second.

119

"As soon as she got home, Megan collected a few more things for you. She wanted me to bring them by. I know they're Adrianna's, but," he shrugged. "It's not like anyone else will need them." He mumbled the last bit, as though thinking better of it.

Laura reached out and took Gavin's hand. "Tell her and Jake thanks for everything, and please tell him I'm so sorry. I wish I'd had a chance to talk to him, but he's probably not ready yet."

Gavin nodded, then released her hand slowly. "He's pretty broken up. It's been an eventful couple of months, hasn't it?"

All of the joy was gone from Laura's eyes now. "Thanks for everything you've done. You've really helped me through. Take care of yourself and give Aiden a hug for me."

"I will. The office won't be the same without you." His eyes lingered a while before he turned toward Danny. "Take care of her. She tends to try to do too much at once." He looked back at Laura. There was a long moment of silence before he spoke. "Megan said to remind you to keep in touch."

She nodded slightly. "I will. Everyone's been so good to me. I can't tell you how much I appreciate it. Especially considering . . . everything."

The moment lengthened and Danny was about to interrupt the tense silence when Gavin asked, "Where're you going?"

Laura looked at Danny. He hadn't had a chance to tell her.

"Junction City. Our families live there. Her mom will be anxious to see her again. I sent my parents over there to break the news. They're just waiting for me to verify that this is Laura first." He tugged on her short-cropped hair, trying to lighten the mood. "It about killed me to stick to the speed limit on the way here."

"Oh, please! As if you ever went the speed limit!" Laura nudged him with her elbow.

"I'm hurt you could say such a thing." He put a hand over his stomach as if she had given him a mortal wound. Her nudge wouldn't have irritated a bug.

Laura just rolled her eyes and looked back at Gavin.

Gavin's mouth tightened and he nodded. "Good luck with everything. I hope it works out for you." With a half-hearted wave, he left.

After she watched the other man walk away, Danny saw the tears in Laura's eyes and pulled her into his arms, cradling her face against his chest. It reminded him of holding Tia while she cried—a completely different experience. "Hey, sweetie, it's okay. It's going to be okay." He rubbed a hand down her head and cupped her neck, letting her cry it all out. He let a tear or two of his own fall, then wiped them off before she could see. It was so good to have her back.

When she finished, Laura pulled away and laughed as she saw the big wet spot on his shirt. "You're going to need a towel after that one."

He'd been aware of the spot for some time. He smoothed the hair back from her face. "It'll dry. It's not like my clothes haven't soaked up your tears before."

"I've always been a baby, I know." She gave him a wobbly smile. "Thanks for loaning me your shoulder."

"It's my pleasure. Really, after thinking you were dead for almost three months, it's great to have you leak all over me." He moved away half-heartedly as she reached out and smacked his arm. "Now, perhaps we should head out. Have you been discharged?"

"I was waiting for you. They wouldn't let me out on my own, and since I had no idea where to go . . ."

"Come on." He shouldered her bags and led her out of the room. "So, about Gavin, you two seemed . . . chummy." His powers of understatement sometimes astounded him.

"Chummy? He barely spoke to me."

Danny sent her a look of disbelief. The walls practically vibrated with something special that ran between the two of them.

She explained, "We had a date last night, it was a lot of fun. We were supposed to go out again tomorrow, but I guess he's changed his mind."

"It didn't look that way." Was she trying to fool him, or did she honestly believe it? "You know me, I'm generally oblivious, and even I noticed something between you. He may not have said much, but those puppy dog looks he sent you spoke volumes. And when he came to tell me about you, he seemed pretty protective."

She flicked that possibility away. "Regardless, it's not like we could have a romantic relationship now. It'd be way too weird."

He didn't understand, but that was fodder for another conversation. There'd be plenty of time to grill her once they got in the car.

Tia put the kids to bed, then cleaned up in the apartment. Danny had said he and Laura were close friends. How close—exactly— was close? Carrie had insinuated it was quite a bit closer than he indicated. And why now when she'd finally met someone she wanted to get to know much better, did all of this come up? Had he and Laura been an item before? As if it weren't bad enough he had to break their date the next day, it was so he could spend time with another woman.

And was she being completely stupid? Did she have a right to be jealous? It had only been a few dates, and one, okay, two kisses that blew her mind. She had too much going on in her life to allow herself to stress over a man—one she'd barely started dating, anyway. A man she'd really started to trust.

She let out a huff of irritation. She hated it when she kept going over old ground. Determined to forget it for a little while, she sat back at the computer and began working her way through more searches on the five remaining women who could be her parents' daughter.

What did that make her—not a sister, not even a relative in any way, yet if Tia managed to narrow it down to the one woman who had been switched with her, then they would share something few other people would be able to claim. Would Tia want to share it with Claire, Lisa, Paula, Lois, or Rashelle? If Tia told them the truth, would they care? Would it be good for them? Bad? Would they love or hate Wes, would he hate her forever for searching? Should she let it go right now?

What if she checked and none of them looked like they could be the right woman? What if she even contacted them, and they all had tests done, and it was none of them? Would it mean she'd made a mistake with one of the other families she'd eliminated, or was she looking in the wrong place to begin with?

Changing gears, Tia began an internet search under the key words 'baby switching.' She found out there had been over 101 reported instances of switched infants in U.S. hospitals in the past twenty years. Then she learned the reported number was estimated to be far lower than the actual instances. She kept digging and tried some different key words. Eventually she came up with a bulletin board dedicated to support people who have been switched or had a family member switched.

Fascinated, she joined the group and began to read up.

Twenty

The weekend at home went well, Danny thought. Tia had been a tad cool on the phone, but it could have just been from distraction. It might not mean anything. He told himself this, but he had the funny feeling that he was going to have to grovel a bit to get back in her good graces. And she wouldn't be entirely out of line, seeing as how he cancelled their date, but surely she would understand when they talked it out.

Laura was surrounded by her family, avoiding the neighbors and limelight at all costs, but he knew it was only a matter of time until it became known she was alive, and then he expected the furor to begin.

Monday morning, after he knew her sister Sandra and her wild crew of animals masquerading as children would be gone, Danny swung by Laura's. During one of their many talks about the past few months, it had come out that her parents had sold her old beater of a car—something she'd bought used in high school, and he'd nursed through college and into adulthood for her. It was past time she replaced it anyway, so he figured it was a bonus that she had no choice.

He loped up the front walk, his long legs taking the steps in two strides. He didn't bother with the doorbell, but opened the door and called out, "Laura, you around?"

"Yes," she said from behind the door. "No need to yell."

Her voice actually made him jump. "Sorry." He shut the door behind him and glanced at her. "You look decent. Want to go for a ride? Or rather, want to go *get* a ride?"

"Today? I didn't think you meant before Saturday."

"The lots will be quieter on a weekday. Besides, I have to return to Kansas City for work tomorrow night. Time's a wasting, and if we don't get you a car before I go, you might not have a way to come visit me. Grab your coat."

Laura smiled and stood. "Give me a minute to put on some lipstick."

He was completely unsurprised by the request, since she was oddly addicted to wearing lipstick everywhere she went. This weekend was the first time he remembered seeing her without it in years. "You need lipstick to go car shopping? Are you sure you don't want me to wait while you paint your nails too?" He rolled his eyes at her. "Some things never change."

She threw a fake punch at his gut as she walked by, making him flinch back—she'd connected those punches more than once when they were kids, and she was no wimp. A laugh gurgled up from her throat. "Hold your horses. It won't take long."

Within a few minutes, she was back with the requisite lipstick. If she'd done more, he couldn't tell.

"I'm ready if you are," she said.

"Do you have your money and ID?"

She pulled a thin wallet from her coat pocket. "I'm traveling light. Mom said they tossed my purse because it was all ripped up and filthy from the accident. I'm lucky the things inside were still in good shape—and she couldn't bear to toss them yet."

They wandered through two lots before Laura found a car that seriously tempted her.

"It's an old Accord, like the last one we saw," Danny said, nudging her toward the year-old, black Infiniti shining next to it. She really had no taste in wheels.

"It's pearl colored, meaning it'll stand out from all the black and white cars in the parking lots. It also has seat warmers and a CD player." He could see the excitement gleaming in her eyes.

"The Infiniti has a CD player," Danny insisted. "And it gets good gas mileage."

Laura rolled her eyes. "It's virtually the same as the Accord—which, you'll note, has a moon roof, not too many miles on it, and since it's used, fits in my budget far better."

She had a point, but he was having fun pushing her buttons, so he continued. "It's not much less." He ran his hands over the shape of the car. "It's also not as cool-looking as this one. You need a ride that'll get you there with power. This baby will do that, and some!"

"Danny, you do realize I don't have a job at the moment, so I don't know if I'll even be moving close to you again—which means limited borrowing opportunities for you. If you want the Infiniti, buy it yourself." She shot him a pointed look, though there was amusement in her eyes.

He let out an exaggerated sigh. "You're such a spoilsport." Then he walked around her choice, tested the tires, and checked the exhaust pipe for soot. If she was going to buy it, at least he could make sure it was a decent car. No way he'd let her get stuck with a lemon—she'd had enough of that to last a lifetime.

A salesman whose nametag read "Craig" came over. "What can I do for you today?"

"Hey, can we take a test drive? She likes this one," Danny said.

They drove it out on the road and he took a turn at the wheel, then came back and popped the hood for a look. "When were the spark plugs changed last? What else have you done to the car? What kind of warrantees does it still have?" He grilled Craig for over half an hour.

Finally satisfied, he turned to Laura. "What do you think?"

She shrugged and made excuses, but he could see it in her eyes. She wanted it. They went in to talk prices and she haggled the salesman down more than Danny expected. He didn't remember her being so shrewd. Where had it come from? Eventually the salesman disappeared with the loan paperwork.

The wait seemed to last forever, but when they saw Craig again, he only apologized that things were taking so long.

"Not too shabby. When did you learn to haggle like that?" Danny asked when the door closed them into the small office again.

"I didn't have much to do in the hospital but lay there and stare at the TV. I saw it on some show. It worked pretty well." She crossed her ankles and her look turned mischievous. "So, you've been unusually closed-mouthed about what you've been up to since I died."

"My life really isn't all that exciting. It's just fighting fires, tearing apart cars, restarting hearts, and delivering babies. Boring stuff, really." He was pretty hyped about the baby.

"Delivering babies? It's a first for you, isn't it?"

"Yes. Though, I suppose the mother actually delivered the baby—it wasn't like I did much. By the time we reached her, the baby was already crowning. All I did was catch it as it popped out." He shook his head and remembered the look in the mother's eyes, the miracle of the tiny infant. "It was the most incredible run I've ever been on."

Laura's grinned. "Make you think maybe it's time you settled down and had one of your own?"

He knew what she meant, but pretended not to. "No way. Giving birth looks painful to me. I think I'll let women keep that job."

She sighed and shook her head. "Just like a man. So, is there a future wife in the picture? Have you and Ursula decided to tie the knot?"

"Ursula?" That threw him for a moment, until he remembered. Laura's memory was still patchy, even though a lot was coming back. "Hon, that was last spring, and we only went out twice. When you died, it was Carrie."

"Oh, all right then. Have you and Carrie gotten serious?"

He resettled in his chair, stretching his long legs to the side of the desk. There was a bit of sting still in the ending of the relationship—even if he was much happier with Tia. "Carrie was offended I was so torn over the loss of my best friend. She seemed to think I cared more for you than for her." He turned to look at her and caught the question in her eyes. She deserved a straight answer. "When I put your funeral ahead of her sister's wedding, and had the nerve to talk about you a lot the first bit, she figured she had to share me with you, even in your death. It wasn't what she wanted, so she broke up."

"Oh, I'm so sorry," Laura wasn't very good at holding back her grin. "Poor girl, to be so disillusioned."

"Poor me, to be so disillusioned. I thought she'd understand." A smile played around his lips and he looked into the distance and thought of Tia. "I think I might have found someone who will, however. Someone quite special. You'll have to meet her. I think you'll get along famously." His smile broadened even more and he met her eyes. "Actually, there are three very special females I'd like you to meet." He could keep their relative ages to himself for the time being.

"Three? In your grief over losing me, you've started juggling multiple women?" Laura didn't appear convinced, but shot him a disapproving look anyway. "Not smart, and not healthy either—and I don't mean as far as keeping track of them. Women can be dangerous when crossed."

He chuckled. "Don't I know it? But you'll have to visit real soon so you can check out jobs again, and I'll make sure you meet the girls."

The door opened and the salesman ushered in two blue-uniformed policemen.

"Laura Dunaway?" one asked.

"Yes, is something wrong?"

The first one, a tall, beefy guy, asked her a few questions, and when she answered them, smiled. "You're under arrest for identity fraud, which is a federal offense."

"You can't be serious. I'm Laura Dunaway." Her shock was plain on her face.

Danny looked at everyone around him and tried to figure out what was going on. They thought she was lying about who she was?

"Sure, lady, and I'm Elton John," the second one, a tall, thin, black man stated. He turned toward Danny. "And you are?"

Danny handed over his ID. This was not good. He worked with cops every day, and these guys looked primed for the collar. "She really is Laura. I've known her my whole life."

"Laura Dunaway is dead. At least, the one with the social security number she used is dead. I even ran her driver license in my system. That makes you an accessory. Turn around." He grabbed Danny by the shoulder and twisted him, latching onto his arms and cuffing him. Danny gritted his teeth and tried to explain, but his and Laura's protests fell on deaf ears.

They were taken straight to the jail and put in cells where they waited for hours to be booked. Danny could see the booking officer's desk from where he sat. Though she seemed busy most of the time processing the people who'd been brought in earlier, she also appeared to take her own sweet time—and plenty of coffee breaks. His irritation grew as he waited.

When Danny stood, he could see the clock from the edge of his window, so he knew hours had passed. Laura had to be in some serious pain by now—hours after she should have taken her next dose of meds for her surgery. He wondered how much longer they'd have to wait.

After a barely-edible dinner, he was surprised when the booking officer came to his cell first. "All right, your turn."

Danny knew their only chance at being released soon was in Laura getting a chance to prove she wasn't impersonating anyone. "Please, can you help my friend first? She's been waiting longer than me, and she was in surgery only a few days ago."

The officer gave him a look that questioned who he thought he was to be making demands, then shrugged. "Suit yourself. It's not going to make much difference."

Danny heard the two ladies go through the whole routine about tattoos and piercings, criminal history and the like. He didn't catch much of it, but some words filtered through to him as he tapped his fingers on the wall, recreating a beat he could hear only in his head. Finally the officer took Laura in for the fingerprint scan. He hoped the results were quick; they had to prove she really was Laura.

Twenty minutes later the officer led Laura back to her cell and they waited. Danny wondered what was going on—none of the other inmates had been taken back to holding. Was it a good sign? Had she realized it was really Laura? Finally the officer came back and let Laura out of her cell, then opened Danny's. "You're being released."

Relief blew through him as he stood from his bench.

When Danny joined her, Laura asked, "Is this going to show as an arrest on my record? I was working as a secretary in a high school. It could keep me from getting another job."

"I'm sure something can be worked out. Your booking won't be completed, so it shouldn't show as an arrest on either of your records. If worse came to worst you could request to have it expunged." She told Laura who to call the next day. "In the meantime, I don't usually do this, it's not procedure, but you can use my phone to call someone to come get you. Your cell phones probably won't work in here." She offered the receiver.

Laura looked at Danny. "Your dad?"

Danny imagined her parents' reactions after everything they'd gone through. They had probably gone ballistic, unable to reach their daughter for so many hours. Not looking forward to the call, he took the phone. "Definitely my dad."

After a bit of paperwork, Laura and Danny had their belongings back.

"The officer who brought me in said my car would be towed. Do you have any idea where it is?" Danny asked. He only had a day before he had to be back to work. He'd arranged to be off so much already, missing another day because his car had been impounded would not be good.

Then, the door to the sally port opened and the two arresting officers entered the room. They eyed Danny and Laura, but said nothing to them, greeting the booking officer curtly before heading down the hall.

"Let me find out," the booking officer said in reference to Danny's question. She picked up the phone and called someone. A moment later she wrote down contact information and gave it to Danny. One more issue to resolve before he headed back to Kansas City.

His father looked relieved when they greeted him in the foyer a while later. "Thank goodness you're all right." He hugged Laura. "Your parents called out the troops when you didn't return home. It's been hours." He scowled at Danny. "How on earth did you end up here?"

"It's a long story." Danny turned to the booking officer. "Thanks." He knew she could have been a whole lot nastier about everything.

The officer nodded, and returned to her post.

When they dropped Laura at her parents' front walk, Danny helped her from the back seat. "I'll be by sometime tomorrow." He could see the pain etched around her eyes. What had he been thinking taking her out so soon after surgery, anyway?

"I'm sorry about this mess," she said. "You were trying to help me out and I caused all kinds of problems."

"Think of the stories I'll have to tell at the fire station." He pushed a lock of hair out of her eyes. They were crinkled at the corners, a sure sign she needed her prescription pain killers.

She met his gaze. "You're really not mad at me?"

Like he had any reason to be. "At you? No. I'm frustrated and irritated about my day being wasted, being forced to eat nasty jail food, and that you're still hurting because you haven't had any painkillers in hours—don't deny it, I see the pain in your eyes. But it wasn't your fault." He put up a hand to stop her argument before she could start it. "I'll take up the towing fee with the police department before I leave town tomorrow. Get some rest."

He watched her parents rush down the sidewalk to get her. The poor people had been through too much already. No, it wasn't his fault, but he'd meant to watch out for her. He hadn't done such a great job.

Twenty-one

Danny pulled into the Dunaway's drive late the next afternoon. There was a big blue van with the letters KMXO painted on it, and a man with a large video camera standing outside.

Laura stood at the doorstep with a willowy blonde, but when she saw Danny, she said something and hurried over to him.

"You've got to help me out. This reporter wants to ask me questions about, well, I don't know exactly what question she wants to ask, but she knows about the mistake," she hissed at him when he came into range.

He was actually surprised the news hadn't broken before now. "Settle down. You knew there'd be interest in the story when it got out that Adrianna was the one who died in that accident. She was a celebrity of sorts. You had to expect this." Wanting to give her comfort, he slid an arm around her shoulder, turned, and guided her toward the house again.

"I expected something—I don't know what—but not this. I don't know if I want to do an interview." She bit her bottom lip, an old habit of hers that only showed up when she was really nervous.

He knew she'd never sought the limelight. "It'll be fine," he assured her. "You know how many people would give their eyeteeth to be in your shoes? Stay cool, answer the nice lady's questions, and it'll all work out." Seeing the distress on her face, he touched her chin. "I'll be here with you the whole time."

"I don't want to be on television."

"Do you want to give people heart attacks when you finally go

133

out in public? Care to be arrested for impersonating yourself—again?" Danny lifted his eyebrows and held her gaze.

"And who's this serious hunk?" the reporter asked when they drew near. "My name is Natalie Swamp with KMXO News." She extended her hand to him.

"This is my friend, Danny," Laura introduced. "I guess I can answer a few questions for you, if you'll answer a few for me."

"I might be able to do it." The blonde smiled brightly. "Do you mind if we go inside? It's awfully cold out here."

Laura forced a smile and nodded, though she muttered under her breath low so only Danny could hear, "I thought reporters would do anything for the story, even stand in subzero temperatures."

He snorted in response. This could be interesting.

Twenty-two

Tia picked over the apples for the next day's show. Samantha stood holding onto the grocery cart as instructed, gabbling on at a thousand words a minute. Tristi pounded her plastic toy against the shopping cart handle, demanding candy.

Shopping with the girls was one of the things Tia hated most. She missed the nights when she left Samantha with Lee and wandered the aisle for as long as she could, enjoying the peace and quiet. She could squeeze the bread and smell the pineapples at her leisure.

Reality now was much different. Samantha called to her from where she stood, holding tight to the shopping cart, as directed. "Mom, you said Danny's supposed to come back tomorrow. Can we go see him? I want to ask him about the shocking machine."

Danny. Tia had been trying not to think of the video feed from the news of him walking with his arm slung around Laura's shoulders. An hour after the segment, she still felt her gut clench. He'd blown her and her family off to be with Laura—like Carrie had said he would. She told herself she was being stupid, but jealousy and insecurity were definitely rearing their ugly heads. She hated when she did that, but couldn't help it.

"Well, well, if it isn't the castoff."

Tia turned to find Carrie standing there. The woman really did have a thing for making an entrance. "Hello. Carrie, isn't it?"

The beautiful brunette with the soulful eyes of an actress only smiled. "I suppose you learned where you fit in Danny's life quicker

135

than most of us do. What was it, a day, two, after I saw you together before he ditched you to be with *her?*"

Samantha brightened at the topic. "You know Danny? He's my friend. He's going to take me out on the fire truck again." She had released the shopping cart and skipped her way to them when she heard Danny's name come up.

"We're not serious, and I can accept that he has a life beyond me. I'm quite pleased Laura's back. I know he missed her a great deal." *Liar, liar, pants on fire.* She was glad Laura wasn't dead. The other woman had been nice when they ran into each other at the school when Tia had presented to a home ec class. But the way Danny talked about her, the way he ran off at the first moment to be with Laura, left Tia wondering if Carrie was more right than even Danny had realized. What if he was, even now, coming to understand that his feelings for his old buddy were much, much stronger than he'd thought?

"Very level-headed and mature of you," Carrie said. "Just wait until she starts showing up on your dates and butting into your relationship. He mooned around after her death like she was the love of his life, and he was continually choosing her over me when we dated. He has no sense of priorities when it comes to her. Your days are numbered." Carrie grabbed a bunch of bananas and turned away.

Tia tried to act unconcerned, but Carrie's venom only complemented the thoughts already running through her mind. What would happen when Danny came home? Was it even worth pursuing a relationship with him? Was the tenuous but interesting relationship they had started to share over?

Tia ordered Samantha back to the cart and finished picking out apples. She could sense which way the wind blew, and she refused to be second string to another woman.

Tia put Tristi to bed, then sat at the computer while Samantha went through the usual evening routine. Mona had left a frantic message on her phone asking for a call back. Tia couldn't deal with her mother, and she couldn't help herself. She pulled up the television station's website and clicked through to the story about Laura again, watching the section where she and Danny had walked down the drive, his arm across her shoulder. The story indirectly accused Laura of lying about the amnesia and derided her for thinking she could get away with such a fabrication. It also brought up the fact that the two of them had been arrested for fraud the previous day.

Tia had picked up a brief voice message from Danny saying the arrest was a mistake, that it was because they thought Laura was someone else pretending to be her, and that it was all straightened out. She was glad to hear that, but it still didn't explain how it happened. Maybe she should have returned his call, but she hadn't.

Tia noticed some of the comments below the video. In addition to the usual crazies who believed every word of the story, there were supporters.

"I don't believe a word of this story. Laura's a sweetheart. She and Danny were always such a sweet couple."

"I knew them in college, two peas in a pod all the way. About time they got together. I'm shocked about the fraud allegations, though. They much have changed a lot since then."

And Carrie's post: "Danny would do anything for Laura—always has and always will. They could be a regular Bonnie and Clyde."

Tia snorted at the comment. Bonnie and Clyde? Seriously, the woman needed to get a life. She did make some sense, though. Tia replayed the segment and watched the way Danny leaned over and said something to Laura as they walked. Then there was his arm around her shoulders, so tight and familiar. It was a very intimate scene.

Again she wondered how close they had really been.

"Mom, that's Danny!" Samantha said from Tia's elbow. "Who's he with?"

Tia jumped slightly in surprise. She hadn't realized Samantha was in the room. She clicked the video to pause it. How much should she say? "It's his friend Laura. The one he told you about, remember? They thought she was dead, and he found out she wasn't. That's why we didn't go to the movie last weekend. He was with her." She felt an ache growing in her chest, keeping up with her burgeoning confusion.

Samantha turned her earnest gaze to her mom. "But we're going next Saturday, right? He promised!"

Tia looked at the frozen shot of Danny and Laura together. Pain clogged her throat and she had to swallow it away. "I don't know, honey. We'll have to wait and see what happens." She stood and began ushering Samantha to bed. "He's pretty busy right now, though, so he probably won't have time to spend with us next Saturday."

"But he promised!" The complaint was a wail now.

"I know." And these small broken promises were already more than Tia could handle. What had she been thinking, letting herself get involved with him?

Her cell phone rang and without thinking, she answered it.

"Tia, it's about time you answered your phone," Mona said, sounding frantic. "I've been trying to reach you for hours. I can't believe that Danny has been seeing someone else and he was arrested!"

"It's not like you think, Mom. Calm down." So maybe it wasn't fraud, but Tia didn't know what to think about it.

"But he's a felon now. You can't let him anywhere near the girls, do you understand? You have to protect them! I knew there was something off about him."

"Mom, you totally misunderstand. The news blew it all out of proportion." Tia was too tired and emotional to deal with her mother's hysterics.

"You don't have a date with him this week, do you?"

"No, Mom. We don't have anything. I really ought to go now. I need to get Samantha in bed. I love you." *Even when I wish you would just go away.* The last thing she'd needed was another person making more of this than it was—Tia was doing a fine job of that all by herself, thank you very much.

"Love you, too."

Tia hung up and stood to check on Samantha. Maybe the whole situation would look better after a good night's sleep.

After driving half the night to return to his apartment, morning came way too early for Danny. As soon as he finished checking his rig at work, he went to the back room to try to sleep for a while. The pagers were busy, however, so by evening, he was beyond exhausted.

Though he was ready to drop, he wanted to talk to Tia, and hoped the vibes he'd been getting from her over the past few days were due to distraction. He dialed her number and smiled when Samantha answered the phone. "Hey, sweet pea, it's Danny. How're you doing?"

"Good." Her usual verve was noticeably absent.

"You don't sound like you're very good. What's wrong?"

She gave a loud and dramatic sigh. "Mom says you're not taking us to the movies on Saturday. She said you'll be too *busy*."

That made no sense—unless that was the excuse she was using with her daughter to explain why *she* was blowing *him* off. "When did she say that?"

"Last night. Don't you like us anymore?"

"Of course I do, Samantha. And I'll have to talk to your mom and find out what's going on with Saturday." He wished he could go over there, but her place was too far from the station and he was afraid he couldn't get to the scene in time if there was a call. "Can I talk to her?"

"Yeah. I'll get her. Mom!" In true six-year-old style, she'd screamed into the receiver.

Danny winced as he pulled his phone away from his ear. Then he wondered how many times he'd done the same to his parents' friends when he was a kid.

A moment passed, then finally Tia answered, "Hello, Danny."

"Hey, Tia. How are you doing?" Nerves assaulted him as he wondered what was going through her mind.

"Fine. Just fine." Her voice was flat and the kind meant to discourage conversation.

What was wrong with her? "I've missed you."

"Really? It sounds like you were kind of busy."

He paused for a moment. She was *really* mad. Was this over one broken date? "What's going on?" He'd left her the message explaining the news report. Did she think he'd lied about it?

"I'm trying to get dinner ready. Sorry, you called at a bad time."

His bad feeling got worse. When a woman was that polite it meant no good. "Are you sure? Because if there's something we need to discuss, I'd rather not put it off."

"Nope. Everything's fine."

It didn't feel fine to him, but there would be time to discuss it on their date to his Christmas party. "Okay. I'll be by to pick you up tomorrow night around six-thirty, if that works for you."

"What? You're not taking Laura?" Tia's voice was downright icy.

"Laura?" Suddenly it dawned on him. "Tia, Laura and I are *nothing* but friends. I know the news report came out sounding otherwise, but it's not true." He thought of the shot of him with his arm around Laura, but surely Tia knew how he felt about her. Hadn't he told her?

"You dropped everything, rescheduled your life, so you could be with her last weekend," Tia said.

It sounded a lot worse when she put it like that, but he expected she'd know him better by now. "She's my friend, Tia, and I thought she was *dead* for the past few months." He threw out his free hand in frustration. "Sue me if I wanted to make sure she was okay. She has nothing to do with my relationship with you."

"Of course not." She didn't sound the least convinced.

"Tia, it's not like that. Come on." How could he make her understand?

"I've got to go; Tristi dumped a bag of chips on the floor. And tomorrow night—something came up. Sorry." She ended the call.

Danny wanted to hit something. Their relationship had just started to get interesting. Why was she doing this? She wasn't Carrie—hadn't shown any indication she'd be as jealous and possessive. Had he totally misjudged her? Thoroughly irritated, he dialed Jason.

"Hey, Jase, it looks like I don't need you to cover for me tomorrow night after all. Thanks, though."

"What happened?"

"My date can't make it." *Or just plain won't.* He sure wasn't going alone, and since he wouldn't have a chance to track Tia down to talk to her until just before the date started, he might as well write it off. She may think their Saturday outing was off, but he had no intention of welshing on it. He'd take the time that day to straighten things out.

Danny held back a curse as he slid his phone into his pocket a moment later. She'd actually told Samantha he wasn't going to take them to the show. What was up with that? And how could he fix whatever was wrong?

He would never understand women.

Twenty-three

Tia hadn't heard from Danny since she'd broken off the date with him on Wednesday. She was disappointed—and realized part of her had hoped he would care enough about her to fight for their relationship. She knew that was completely messed up thinking, but couldn't help herself. Carrie must have been right; his tie to Laura was stronger than he'd ever acknowledged. She wanted to wish him luck, but she was hard pressed not to wish him to the devil instead.

She finished putting away the lunch dishes—hours after they'd finished eating—and tried not to regret blowing him off. Could their relationship have been salvaged? Was it worth the effort? It hurt that he'd let her go so easily.

"Mom, Danny's here." Samantha came streaking into the room and tugged on her shirt. "He said he'd be here to take us to the movie. He's here, like he said. Come open the door." She grinned and all but danced in excitement.

Tia felt her heart leap. Maybe he hadn't given up after all. And maybe, she reminded herself, he was just being nice to a little girl, and refused to let her down again. That thought was somewhat disheartening, but Tia decided not to hope for more until she had a chance to gauge his actions. She could deal with disappointment, after all. Samantha, on the other hand, wouldn't understand a sudden defection.

When she opened the door and found him standing on her doorstep, she caught her breath and wished she could have ignored him instead. He looked so good, his broad grin making his face irresistible, a bunch of wild flowers grasped in one hand. She reminded herself not to get her hopes up, even as she let him in.

"These are for you." He passed over the flowers.

She resisted the urge to sniff at them as she carried them back to the kitchen. "Thanks. They're beautiful."

"I know I didn't set a time to pick you ladies up," he said. "But when I checked show times, it looks like the one we want starts in forty-five minutes." He acted nonchalant as he reached into the cupboard and pulled out her vase.

Tia turned to the sink to add water, feeling the confusion and zing of electricity she so often felt in his presence. If he came only to sooth Samantha's feelings, she would deal with it, but it would have been easier not to see him again if that were the case. *On the other hand, these flowers say something different.* She played with the blooms a little as she slid them into the vase, then glanced over her shoulder at him.

He was looking at her, studying her. There was a wariness she'd never seen in his eyes before, but he smiled when he caught her gaze, making her heart flutter a little.

"Danny!" Samantha exclaimed when she finally got her turn. "I didn't think you were coming." She threw her arms around him.

"Of course I came. I said I would, didn't I?" He swung Samantha up on one hip and listened to her chatter about her week, turning his full attention on her.

"Danny, you didn't have to," Tia said.

He met her gaze, his expression firm. "I promised. Besides, I think we have a thing or two to clear up." He waited for a reply but after a moment, he continued, "How about if you grab Tristi and anything we'll need for the afternoon and we'll go?"

The thought crossed Tia's mind that she could have said no and told him to leave. But she was as glad to see him as Samantha had been, so she nodded and followed his suggestion.

The movie was fun, and dinner was both delicious and entertaining with Danny in their midst. He cleaned up spilled sodas and handed French fries to Tristi one at a time so she wouldn't toss the package on the floor. He smiled and laughed and cajoled them all, showing them some of the best holiday lights in town before taking them back home. It had been a wonderful afternoon and evening and Tia didn't know what to think anymore when he carried a sleeping Tristi in the house.

"I can take her," Tia said, reaching for her baby.

He met her gaze, held it, his expression saying he wasn't going to be dismissed so easily. "I'm sure you can. I've got her, though. Lead the way."

She nodded and took him into the girls' room. She grabbed Samantha's pajamas and sent her to the bathroom to change, then watched as Danny expertly changed Tristi's diaper, without waking her, and snuggled her down in the crib.

Samantha came back in and he read her a story and listened by the bedside as she said her prayers.

When they returned to the living room a few minutes later, Tia realized she was alone with him for the first time all evening. Things were suddenly awkward again. "Okay, you said we needed to talk," she started the subject, not wanting to prolong things.

"Yeah, but first things first." He leaned forward, slid a hand behind her head and drew her close for a kiss.

Her breath caught in surprise as his lips touched hers, soft but insistent. The next moment she found her hands resting on his well-muscled shoulders as she leaned closer, tipping her head for a better angle enjoying his touch. His cologne wafted between them, beckoning to her.

When his hands slid down to her waist, drawing her closer, she melted against him.

When he drew back, she had to catch her breath.

His thumb ran along her jaw, giving her chills. Their eyes met and his voice was husky when he spoke. "Tia, no matter what happens, I'm dating you, no one else. Believe me when I say Laura and I are nothing but friends, and neither of us wants to be more."

She wanted desperately to believe him, but needed reassurance. "Have you ever tried? Maybe you feel more for her than you think."

He smiled. "I think it's safe to say I know what I want." He kissed her briefly again. "If I were in love with her, don't you think I would have realized by now?"

Of course she'd thought that. Still, she pushed him. "She wasn't really dead."

His tone and expression turned solemn. "She was to me. You have no idea how much I missed her, but in all that time, I never once wished we had tried for a romantic relationship." He lifted Tia's chin so she had to look him in the eye. "You're the only one I'm interested in."

Tia's lungs felt tight with hope and nerves, "Carrie said you two were always together." She hadn't meant to bring up the conversation, but once the thought came, the words popped from her mouth.

His brow furrowed and his eyes hardened. "Carrie? What does Carrie have to do with this? When did you talk to her?"

"Tuesday in the grocery store." Tia felt like an idiot for bringing it up, but wasn't going to let him derail her thoughts. "She said you and Laura had a *special* relationship, and you mooned over her after the accident. She always felt like she was sharing you with Laura."

Danny's gaze didn't waver. "Carrie's a self-absorbed little woman who thinks the whole world revolves around her. She was angry with me because I skipped her sister's wedding to attend Laura's funeral. Then she was upset I didn't simply forget Laura existed the next day. If Laura had literally been my sister, instead of as good as, she would have been every bit as jealous about me putting the funeral first."

He touched her hair, combing it back from her face, his eyes never leaving hers. "You're not like Carrie."

So, what—she was a pushover? "If she was so bad, why were you dating her?" Tia pulled out of Danny's arms. Being that close to him made it difficult to think clearly.

He released her, reluctance in every move. "I probably wouldn't have been much longer. I needed someone who could support me the same way I supported her and accept my job for what it is." He shrugged one shoulder, as if this had been a hard realization. "I was never really good enough for her, and as much as I hate to admit it, she didn't matter enough for me to fight for our relationship."

Was that his MO? "And how is that different from our situation?"

He answered her by crowding close and kissing her again, though he kept his hands to himself. "You are well worth fighting for, and have the sense not to keep pushing me away over trivial things."

She nudged him away, narrowing her eyes. "Are you saying this was a trivial issue?" It hadn't felt like it.

"No." He slid his hands into his pockets, his gaze steady. "And it won't become blown out of proportion because I know we can work things out." He looked at the sofa. "Mind if we sit?"

She agreed and took the overstuffed chair, leaving him the sofa. She might have sat beside him, but his touches and kisses were a little too potent and she needed her wits about her.

"Two things you need to understand," he started when they were seated. "First, Laura's been my friend since the day when being friends with girls meant you kicked dirt on their tea parties and they wouldn't quit being competitive until their sand castle was bigger and better than yours." He leaned forward on his elbows. "That's not going to change. She's always going to be my friend, whether she moves back to the area or not. I hope you can be friends with her as well."

Tia wanted to be honest, even if she still had some reservations. "I liked Laura, from the brief meeting I had with her at the school last year." She had visited one of the consumer science classes and Laura had shown her to the classroom.

"Good. The second thing you need to remember is you and I have something special. It's headed somewhere important. I'm in no hurry to rush into something serious before you're ready, but I'm not going away, either." He stood, took her hand and sat on the arm of her overstuffed chair, their eyes riveted as his hand enveloped hers in comforting warmth. "I feel drawn to you. I haven't felt this way about anyone in a long time. While we're dating, I'm only seeing you, thinking about you. I hope you feel the same way."

Her heart pounded and it was hard to breathe. As romantic statement went, that ranked pretty high on her list. "It's not like I have guys pounding on my door for dates every night."

"I don't know why they're all so stupid." He ran a finger down her cheek. "A woman as talented and beautiful as you ought to be socked in with offers."

She laughed despite herself, charmed, and looked away. He was too sweet, too smooth. Could a guy like this be real? "You sure spin a nice line."

"It's no line, Tia."

When she looked in his eyes, she believed him. At least, she wanted to believe him. He'd taken her and the girls out for the afternoon like he'd promised, which definitely said something in his favor. "Are you sure Laura feels the same way you do? What if she wants more?"

He lips tipped up at the corners. "I'm like her brother. She doesn't want more."

"How do you know?"

"Would you like to talk with her? I can arrange it. Next time she's in the area we can get together. In fact, I'd like you to get to know each other better." He leaned down and brushed his lips across her temple.

Generally satisfied with his answers, she released her jealousy.

He followed the kiss on the temple with several others to her cheeks, chin and then lips, distracting her completely from the conversation for some time. When he pulled back, he returned to the sofa, and coaxed her down beside him. "Now, tell me how your research has been going."

Tia was still a little dazed and disoriented, and his change of subject took a moment of adjustment. He simply grinned as he waited for her mind to come back into focus. "You're a smug jerk," she told him, though she couldn't help but smile.

"I know. I can't help it." He tapped her chin with his fingertip. "Have you found anything interesting in your search since we talked about it last?"

His question helped bring her back to focus. "Yes. Did you know over a hundred babies have been reported as switched in the past two decades? It's unbelievable." Tia snuggled further into his arms and discussed the little progress she'd made before changing the subject to how his ambulance runs had gone over the previous few days.

Twenty-four

Back in the newspaper archives on Monday, Tia prayed at least one of the sets of parents she was still researching had taken the time to put a birth announcement in the paper. All five would be miraculously wonderful, but she wouldn't hold her breath.

She'd been there an hour before she found the first one, and another half an hour when she found the second. Though she paged through several more weeks of announcements, she didn't find any others. Still, it was time well spent, as she now had verification that the families she thought she'd connected to the hospital were in fact the right ones. She also had Facebook data on one, including pictures.

The whole time she tried to block out the verbal meanderings of the bubbly intern from her first visit.

Deciding she'd found everything there was, Tia flipped her notebook closed and put away the giant books.

"So what do you think about my idea for a show?" the intern asked.

"It sounds great. Unfortunately, I don't think the local stations make suggestions for new sitcoms." Tia tucked her notebook into her purse and slung it over her shoulder. "Thanks again for your time. I appreciate it."

Her phone started to ring before she even reached her car. She smiled as she saw Danny's number. He'd only had Saturday off, then gone right back to the firehouse to make up the shifts he'd traded for his trip home. She wondered why he didn't seem burned out on work after nearly a week straight.

"Hey, beautiful, how's the search going?" he greeted her.

"Terrific! I'm now sure that I have the right women for Lisa and Paula and based on pictures of her with her family, I'm ready to cross Paula off the list of possible switches. The woman posts everything on Facebook for the whole world to see, and she looks nothing like my parents, and vice versa."

"Great. That puts you down to four, doesn't it?"

"Yeah. The question is what to do next. I think I've reached the limit of what I can accomplish online." It had been a hard decision to make, but this had been her last idea.

"Then we'll check some other things. Any headway on how this happened in the first place?"

"None." She shrugged, hoping it would loosen up her shoulders. Between being hunched over the book and the intern's yammering, she was tense. "I'll have to contact the hospital, but whether they'll cooperate or not is another issue. Do they have lists of employees from then? Even if they have employee lists, it's highly unlikely they would have any way of finding out who worked that night. I don't even know where to start."

"I know a few people at the hospital," Danny said. "Let me ask some questions and see what I can find out."

Tia was touched, but didn't want to put him out. "Danny, I can't let you do that."

"Why not? I offered, I have contacts, and I want to help you."

"I feel like I need to do it." She reached her car and unlocked the door, opened it, and slid inside. Was she trying too hard to be independent? Nichole sometimes accused her of that.

"Then I'll wait until you can come with me. I'm off tomorrow. We could swing by in the morning, see who I can prod for information."

Though she was still tempted to say no, Tia decided she'd be a fool not to take his help. He might be able to find something she couldn't. "Okay, then. If I'm going to do it, it has to be between nine and ten-thirty. I'll be pushing the limit for getting to the station on time if it's any later."

"I'll swing by for you a little before nine, then. And if anything comes up and I'm running late, I'll let you know."

"Thanks, Danny. I appreciate it."

"You're welcome. See you tomorrow." He hung up.

Tia clicked end on her cell and tucked it back in her purse. Though she kept telling herself she needed to hold back a piece of herself, he was worming his way into her heart. She found she didn't mind after all.

Danny and Tia walked into the hospital shortly after nine and he led her through the entrance, around the corner and down the hall toward the ER. She smiled and pretended she was as comfortable as he was in the setting. He greeted a few people by name as they passed, but continued on through to the front desk where a statuesque woman in her late forties typed on a computer while she talked on the phone.

"I'm afraid I can't talk about a patient's condition. You'll have to speak with his doctor. No ma'am, the law prohibits me from giving out that information. The doctor's name is Ray Lacey. Yes, good luck." She sighed as she hung up the phone, then smiled when she saw Danny, turning on the charm. "Well, hello there, Tullis, how are you doing today? You're not in uniform this time."

"I'm here asking a favor." He turned and motioned to Tia. "This is my girlfriend, Tia Riverton, and she's looking for some really old information about employees. Tia, this is Dr. Clark. She runs the ER."

"Dr. Clark, it's nice to meet you." Tia tried not to be intimidated by the woman or the fact she and Danny seemed chummy. He had introduced Tia as his girlfriend. Is that what they decided they were?

She hadn't taken time to analyze it—or maybe she was trying not to think about it too hard.

"Same here." The doctor offered to shake her hand. "I love your cooking segment when I get a chance to see it. I don't know how much I can do for you, but I'm happy to help."

A man in scrubs approached and handed her papers, muttered something under his breath then continued on. A woman passed by and pulled a form from a nearby stacker.

Tia always liked hearing someone enjoyed her segment, which normally would have relaxed her, but the number of people close by made her uncomfortable. "Thanks. Is there a chance we could talk to you somewhere more private? It should only take a moment."

Dr. Clark laughed. "Yes. It is a bit crazy in here, isn't it?" She came out from behind the counter and led them down the hall to a corner with another counter, which had no staff. "Now, what can I do for you?"

Tia had grown more nervous by the second, and the reassurance she'd received from Danny's kiss before they'd entered the hospital had dissipated. She plunged forward. "This is going to sound completely crazy, but I was born here twenty-eight years ago—which I know had to have been long before you became a doctor. The thing is, we recently learned I'm not actually my parents' biological child. They always thought I was, but DNA tests prove otherwise."

Dr. Clark gave her a funny look. "You're saying your mom came in here, gave birth to some other child, and walked out with you instead?"

Tia nodded. "I've managed to track down information on the other families who had daughters born within twenty-four hours of me, and narrowed it down to a few possibilities, but even if I knew who my parents' biological daughter was, I don't know how this all happened."

"They put bracelets on the child while they're still with the parents—before the baby is even weighed and measured. For such a mix up to have occurred, the change would have had to be deliberate." Dr. Clark's eyes had narrowed and her arms crossed her chest in a guarded manner. "I hope you're not saying you think someone did that on purpose."

The woman's defensiveness made Tia uneasy. "I told you it would be hard to believe." She tried to modulate her voice to be as inoffensive as possible. "DNA doesn't lie, though. I believe once I left the hospital my parents would have noticed if their baby had been switched. The only reasonable possibility is that the change occurred while I was still in the hospital."

She hurried to explain when she saw disbelief on the woman's face. "I don't know who made the switch—it could have been anyone—but it makes sense that whoever it was had access to supplies like the bracelets—mine matches my mom's. I have them in my baby book and I've checked them. They would've had to have knowledge of other families, and access to the other babies in the nursery. It's unlikely they were some random stranger from the street."

A long moment of silence passed before Dr. Clark nodded. "I hate to think it, but it sounds like you're right. I can send you to the HR department. If there are any records about personnel from that time period, Nancy will have them." She took a pad of sticky notes and wrote on the top one, then handed it to Tia. "Her office is on the fourth floor, south wing. You'll know how to get there," she said this last to Danny.

"Yes." Danny shook her hand. "Thanks, I really appreciate it. And I'm sure you understand Tia wants to keep this quiet until she has the answers."

"Good. This could cause a major stink in the press if it came out." Dr. Clark straightened, looking weary. "I better get back. We've got a full load today. Good luck, and let me know what you learn."

"Will do," Danny told her.

They let the doctor return to her duties, and then Danny led Tia back through a twisted maze of corridors, up a bank of elevators, and down some more halls.

"How do you ever find your way around here?" Tia asked as they took a right at another intersection.

"After five years of coming here, you learn where things are. Besides, I studied maps a lot in my spare time when I first started running on the ambulance. Every hospital in the area is different and they can't always spare someone to walk us to the appropriate location." He gestured to a door at the end of the hallway. "And here we are."

Tia took a deep breath as Danny nudged her into the office. There were two desks plus a door leading into another room.

A young man at the front desk looked up as they walked in. "Hello, can I help you?"

Danny stepped up and greeted the man. "Yes, we wondered if Nancy's available to speak to us for a few minutes."

The man lifted his brows. "Let me see if she has some time." He stood and walked into the other room, stopping to speak to the woman in tones too low to understand from the reception area. She looked up, took a second to study Danny and Tia, then nodded and responded.

The man returned and gestured to the door. "She says to send you right in."

Tia was grateful for Danny's warm hand on her back as they entered the room. She was also glad when he shut the door behind them, so she didn't have to worry about eavesdroppers. "Hello, my name is Tia Riverton, and I have a question about your employee records from twenty-eight years ago." They shook hands and took seats when bidden, then Tia gave the same information to Nancy that she'd given to Dr. Clark.

"We use sophisticated methods to prevent baby switching, in addition to the banding done in the delivery room to prevent this very thing," Nancy told them.

"Yes, I'm aware of that, and as a parent, I'm very grateful for all of the safety measure you use. However, that hasn't stopped baby switching from happening, not even in this day and age. Half a dozen or so babies are switched in hospitals every year—and those are the ones we know about. Who knows how many more are happening without being caught."

Nancy's eyes narrowed suspiciously. "Where did you get those numbers?"

"They're available online from reliable sources. With some diligent research, I've even tracked down a national online support group for families whose babies have been switched. In almost every case the mom and babies were banded while they were in the delivery room together. Most switches have been total accidents, mine was deliberate. We don't want to cause trouble for the hospital, I'm not going to go to the news, or sue anyone. I just want some answers."

"I'm afraid I don't have records going so far back, so I can't help you." Nancy studied them from across her desk, her gaze wary and defensive. "I don't know how such a thing could have happened. While I'm not admitting that the hospital or its personnel could be involved in something like this, I am sorry you're struggling with the revelation, however, or wherever it happened. I wish you luck."

Tia felt her heart sink, though she hadn't really expected to get answers. "Isn't there anyone working here who might have been employed in the hospital back then? Maybe they'd remember who else was here."

Nancy shook her head. "I can't help you. I'm sorry."

Disappointed, Tia rose when Danny did and said goodbye. She didn't think the woman looked very sorry, but it was clearly pointless to push for more. Where would they go from here?

When they reached the privacy of the hallway, Danny took Tia's hand. "I might know someone who can give us something useful," he said after a moment.

Hope flared again. "Yeah?"

"It might be nothing, but one of the ladies in the cafeteria has been working foodservice here for twenty-five years. They were celebrating with a cake when I ate there once after we dropped off a patient. We can swing by to see if she's here, then see what we can get out of her."

Tia smiled. Right now she had nothing else to go on. She'd take what she could get. "That would be great. Thanks."

When they reached the cafeteria, Danny said the woman wasn't around. Tia tried to hide her disappointment, but he must have seen it because he squeezed her hand as they headed back to the entrance. "I'll keep an eye out for her. She may not have the answers you're looking for, anyway. This is just one possible avenue."

"I know. I feel like I keep hitting brick walls." Discouragement seemed to attack her from every side, lately. Would she ever find the answers?

He grinned and bumped her teasingly with his elbow. "Don't hit brick walls, they're bound to hurt you and I don't want to have to come patch you up."

"Very funny." She rolled her eyes at him as they walked out into the bright, if frigid sunlight. All of the questions made her head spin.

The spinning nearly took flight when Danny stopped at her car door, pulling her close for a leisurely kiss before nudging her into her seat and sending her home.

Twenty-five

Tia put her family search on hold after her visit to the hospital. Christmas was that weekend and though there were still a thousand and one things she needed to do, she and the girls took a break and headed to the fire station Wednesday afternoon.

She found Danny kicking back in a chair in the kitchen with a can of soda and a book. "Been slow?" she asked.

He looked up and grinned, opening his arms to accept a hug from Samantha as she threw herself at him. "Hey there, kiddo, how was school today?"

"We watched movies and had a party and exchanged presents and ate lots of junk food. It was fun and I got a Barbie."

"Very cool! You'll have to show me next time I'm over." He looked past Samantha and met Tia's gaze.

She shrugged. "Nothing new to report."

"We'll find another way." He set Samantha down and crossed the room to Tia, reaching for her. When she shied away, as she always did in front of the kids, he put a hand on her shoulder and held on, then turned to Samantha. "Hey, bug, do you have a problem with me kissing your mom?"

Samantha shook her head and giggled. A grin split her face.

"Good." He turned back to Tia and quirked his brows. "You heard her." Then he pulled her into his arms for a jolting, but all-too-brief kiss hello.

Since Samantha cheered at the kiss, Tia kept her few mild protestations to herself. She forgot them when his lips touched her

157

anyway. "Hey, there," she said when she had a chance to catch her breath. His deep blue eyes mesmerized her.

"Hey, yourself." He slid his hands down her arms to latch onto her fingers. "I wish I could come over for dinner and a movie tonight, but I'm working through Christmas."

"Holiday pay?" She wondered how long it would take her to say more than two words at a time.

"That *will* be nice, but more important, most of the other guys needed Christmas off to be with their kids." His eyes bore into her soul. "You mentioned you plan to stay in town, so I hoped I could get you to come here for a while, share your family with me."

She swallowed at the thought of spending the holiday with Danny. She was surprised at how much the image appealed to her. Finding she had her voice back, she gave him the rundown. "My parents are coming for presents and breakfast—which should make things chaotic and less-than-merry," she said this last under her breath so the girls wouldn't hear, but Danny still could. "Then we're going to Lee's mom's for a late lunch so the girls can play with their cousins and be spoiled by their other grandparents."

"That leaves the evening open to visit me, doesn't it?" His voice was just this side of husky, sending a thrill all the way to her toes.

"If you aren't out rescuing people from car accidents or from heartburn caused by too much Christmas dinner that the patient is sure must be a heart attack." The second scenario had come straight from his Thanksgiving runs.

"I'd like that." He looked into her eyes for a long moment and she thought he would kiss her again. Instead he seemed to pull himself back, released her and turned to Samantha. "You should see the new toy we got on the rig. It's so cool!"

Tia watched him take Samantha's hand and lead her to the ambulance with only a glance back over his shoulder. She wondered if Samantha was destined to become an EMT the second she reached eighteen. Watching her enthusiasm, Tia smiled at the inevitability.

Danny stood at the order desk at McDonald's, Tristi tucked up against him, laughing and babbling while he watched Tia and Laura talk. He'd arranged this meal for everyone to get together, the first of many, he hoped. He wanted to allay Tia's fears that she stood between him and Laura. Though she claimed it didn't bother her anymore, he knew on some level it did, and he wanted her to be comfortable with everything. Besides, they were both important to him, and he wanted them to be friends.

He picked up the tray of food he'd ordered for Laura and returned to the play area where they were eating while Samantha climbed through the plastic tunnels. "So, did you miss me?"

"You're interrupting our conversation," Laura said. "I was going to tell her about the water weenie incident."

He rolled his eyes as he set the tray in front of her. He *hoped* she was kidding. Why did women think they had to discuss every embarrassing choice a guy made as a kid whenever he dated someone new—or was it just Laura who was like that? "Then I'm right on time. There are disadvantages to letting you meet my girlfriend. I'm so happy to have you alive again, your penchant for stirring up old trouble slipped my mind." He'd gladly put up with her behavior since it meant she was alive to annoy him, but he wasn't sure enough about Tia's commitment to their relationship not to worry about her reaction.

Danny picked up a chicken nugget and handed it to Tristi, glad when she grabbed on and started chowing down. "So, did you manage to stop by the school and see your old coworkers?" he asked Laura. He sat across from them and settled the baby on his lap.

"Yeah, it nearly caused a riot—it made me late getting here. Some of the students saw me and came to investigate—everyone wanted to know if the news reports were true. Anyway, it took a lot longer to get away than I expected. They have, of course, filled my position." Her mouth formed a moue of disappointment before she moved on. "The district doesn't foresee anything else opening up soon." She ate some fries and took a sip of diet cola.

"So how's the process of becoming undead working out?" Danny picked up the nugget Tristi had dropped on the food tray and handed it back to her.

"It's coming. I almost have the paperwork together. Still, it'll be after the new year before the court rules that I'm alive. Then I'll have to contact everyone and send them the appropriate paperwork proving I'm only impersonating *myself* and not someone else. Sometime next summer I may even have it all straightened out." She looked at Tia. "It's been a mess, and bound to get worse. How are things at the station? You're still cooking for the noon news, I hear."

"Yeah. It's going well." Tia told her about the dishes she planned for upcoming segments. "Danny's always happy to help me test the recipes."

Laura laughed. "I bet! He's always had a bottomless pit. I think it got even worse when he became a firefighter."

"Hey, I'm a growing boy," he protested. He noticed how relaxed and easy Tia was with Laura and felt his shoulder drop a little in relief. It was going to be okay, even if he did end up the butt of their jokes.

Turning her gaze back to Tia, Laura nodded toward him. "He'll probably still be saying that when he's fifty and has a paunch."

Danny touched his stomach, offended she'd even suggest he'd ever get paunchy. No way he'd let it happen. "You're killing me here," he said when Laura laughed at him.

By the end of the hour all of them sat easily together. Tia seemed reassured, Laura was taken with little Tristi, and Samantha sparkled and shone in the attention slathered on her. Danny thought his world was nearly complete.

Tia had tried tracking down the doctor listed on her birth certificate—and learned he was dead. She wasn't having much luck with the nurses and other OB staff from that time, either. "I'm never going to get anywhere with this search if no one will talk to me," she told Danny as they snuggled in the living room after putting the girls to bed one night.

"Give it some time," he soothed. "I'll find the lady in the cafeteria soon, or I'll find someone else with the information you need."

"I hope so. I'm starting to think this whole thing's impossible." She rubbed her eyes and put her head on his shoulder. He had such nice, broad shoulders.

He slid a hand down her arm, then up again. "It's taken you twenty-eight years to get to this point. You don't have to find all the answers overnight." He caught a lock of her hair in his fingers and began playing with it. "Did I ever mention how much I love your hair? It's so bouncy, and gorgeous."

She laughed in surprise. "No, you never mentioned it before. Though I have noticed your strange tendency to play with it."

"I can't help myself; it begs to be touched." He tugged on it, then pressed a finger to the bottom of her chin, tipping her head toward him. "It's like my fascination with you—I don't think I'll ever grow out of it."

"Those are some pretty serious words, there." Tia felt warmed and tingly at the thought.

"Yes, they are." He stopped her next question with a kiss.

Twenty-six

Lights flashed and sirens filled the air as Danny grabbed the Broselow bag and checked to make sure they had a Broselow Pediatric Emergency Tape in it. They would be at the accident scene in less than two minutes and the reports coming in had adrenaline rushing through his veins, his mind whirling at top speed. Working on children always made him nervous.

Danny sent up a quick, silent prayer as the ambulance slowed at the scene and as soon as it stopped, he jumped out, trauma bag in one hand, Broselow in the other. "Where's the kid?" he asked the officer approaching the rig, and when directed, hurried to the place where the little girl lay fifteen feet from the edge of the road. The five-year-old had dark, almond-shaped eyes, and curly black hair. Her face contorted with pain and she whimpered as he knelt beside her.

"Hi, my name is Danny. What's yours?"

She didn't answer; just opened terrified eyes and cringed away from him.

"I'm a paramedic. Do you know what that means?" When she shook her head, he explained, then told her what he was doing as he began a full toe-to-head checkup, looking for breaks and bleeders. By the time he got to her head thirty seconds later, she had told him her name—Emily—but her face had gone ashen and she kept closing her eyes sleepily.

The icy wind whipped past them and through his heavy winter clothing as he knelt beside her. Someone had thrown an adult-sized coat around her, but Emily still shivered on the cold ground. He was pleased she didn't seem to have any significant external bleeding, but her femur appeared to be fractured, and she complained of pain in her stomach. Neither was a good sign, and she was going downhill fast.

"Get me a traction splint and a pedi backboard," he called when one of the firemen from his team came over. Chris waved that he understood and headed back to the rig at a jog.

Danny grabbed a bystander to hold Emily's head in alignment and put up a prayer of thanks when the C-collar he'd grabbed fit her. All the time he spoke with her, asking her questions, trying to keep her awake. Her pulse dropped so he could barely feel it at her wrist and he rushed to put in an IV and enlisted another bystander to hold the bag of saline.

He helped James splint the broken leg and pull traction to get it back into alignment and relieve the girl's pain. Finally they were ready to move her to the backboard. A glance at his watch told Danny the whole process hadn't taken as long as he thought, thank goodness, but with her shock and the cold, speed was the byword. The quicker they reached a trauma center, the better.

He wished her veins had been bigger. She needed more fluid as fast as possible. They loaded the little girl into the ambulance and he started prepping for the second IV. "Start a bolus," he called to James, "and get me some D-25." He may have been jumping the gun on the glucose, but when a kid her size started to decompensate, pushing sugar and fluids as fast as possible was imperative.

"Come on Emily, fight," he growled under his breath as the ambulance zoomed down the road to the hospital. He worried about internal bleeding, and he knew the pain had to be crippling from the broken leg, but her slow and shallow breathing made it so he couldn't administer morphine or fentanyl if he didn't want her to go into respiratory arrest. He double-checked her leg to see if she had broken a major vein there, but saw no evidence of swelling from blood loss. Her stomach, on the other hand, was growing hard and distended, which indicated internal bleeding.

Danny pushed the glucose into one vein while James continued to bolus fluids in the other, trying to rehydrate her as quickly as possible. The second set of vital signs looked somewhat better than the first, but were still far too weak.

Danny called into the ER, wedging the cell phone between his shoulder and ear as he counted Emily's breaths. He kept the conversation with the nurse on duty brief, then dropped the phone on the bench behind him and got out the intubation equipment. "Her breaths are too far apart. We're going to lose her." His heart raced and his hands shook, but he injected the medication that would keep her from gagging on the tube and slid the ET tube into her trachea as he'd done for so many patients in the past. "How's the bolus coming?"

"Almost done." Sweat dripped from James' brow. He glanced out the window and sighed. "We're here." The ambulance slowed and pulled into the entrance to the ER.

Reaching the ER didn't mean their work was over, however. The patient rooms were nearly full and Emily's injured mother hadn't arrived yet. The staff scrambled to keep up, so once they got her moved to the regular bed, Danny and James stayed, fighting to help the little girl as she continued to go downhill.

Back at the station an hour later, Danny showered, then headed for the kitchen. The internal bleeding and damage had been too serious. Though they'd rushed Emily to the operating room within five minutes of her arrival at the hospital, the little girl had died on the table before the paramedics had been able to finish their report.

Danny flopped into a chair and rubbed his face, trying to hold back the tears threatening to pour down his cheeks. He kept seeing Samantha's bright, laughing face in his mind, seeing it darken with pain, as she weakened before his eyes.

How did he deal with this? His heart ached and his eyes stung as the tears began to flow again. He'd thought he'd gotten them all out of his system in the shower, but he found it wasn't the case. He stood and walked out the back door into the cold night. He wanted nothing more than to hold Samantha close, feel her vibrant life in his arms, to remind himself she was okay, even if another family mourned the loss of their little girl.

Since he couldn't leave the station, he pulled out his phone and dialed Tia's number.

"Hello, Danny? What's going on?"

It was late to be calling, he knew. "I need to talk to someone about normal stuff. I suppose Samantha's in bed."

"Ages ago. Is she the one you called to talk to?" There was a hint of amusement in her voice.

"No, well, I wouldn't mind saying goodnight to her, but if she's in bed, that's fine. I'm more than happy to speak with you instead." He tried to make his words sound teasing, but wasn't sure he succeeded.

"I heard her giggling. She thinks she's being sneaky, reading under the covers, like she's pulling one over on me." Tia chuckled.

Danny smiled. He could see Samantha with her little princess flashlight, the covers over her head. The flashlight would be tucked between her shoulder and head as she turned pages in the book and giggled at funny drawings and lame puns. "I'm glad you're letting her stay up a little later than usual."

"Pretending like I don't know she's still up means she won't be in here in ten minutes complaining about how she can't sleep. At least she's in bed and quiet. More or less."

"You're an awesome mom." His feelings for her expanded in his chest, filling all of the empty holes. He couldn't imagine a future without her in it.

"Lazy is what I am. Now, what's eating at you?"

He smiled despite himself. She'd come to know him so well. "We had a bad run tonight. We lost a kid." *It'll haunt me for months.*

"I'm sorry. It must have been awful."

"I keep seeing Samantha's face." He paused, trying to hold back the emotions. He didn't want to crack again. "How would you feel about a breakfast visit tomorrow? I think I need to see her." He ran his hand over his mouth. "That probably doesn't make sense." She and Tristi had more than wormed their way into his heart. Along with their mom, they were quickly becoming the most important part of his life.

"No, it's fine. Come. Feel free to join us anytime. Really."

"Thanks." He fought down the lump in his throat, then decided a change of subject was necessary. "How's your search coming?"

"I've reached a dead end," Tia said. "I don't think I can do any more research on these other women by myself. I'm going to have to get a private detective."

"Can you afford it?" Danny had noticed how careful she was with her money. Either she didn't have much to spare, or she was extra frugal about how she spent what she had.

"My budget isn't limitless, but I think I can afford basic information. I'm hoping I can get what I need for a thousand or less, but I can double it if necessary."

"You've been researching PIs?"

"Yes, eighty an hour plus expenses seems to be the minimum rate. The thought makes me cringe."

"Let me check around and see if any of the guys knows some reliable, honest guys you can call."

"I'd appreciate it. I don't know where to start." She told him which cities she'd pinpointed, then changed the conversation to Tristi's first foray into crayon murals—which would come off with a little elbow grease, thanks to special crayons and advanced wall paint. The new artwork on the side of the sofa was another matter. This

166

discussion morphed into each of them sharing stories from their childhoods.

The pager tones called Danny away from the phone half an hour later and he ended the conversation to respond to a possible heart attack. Thanks to their talk, he felt ready to tackle the next challenge.

Twenty-seven

In the morning Danny stopped at the grocery store, then swung over to Tia's after work. The sun hadn't risen yet, but he couldn't handle the thought of returning home. Emily's face flashed behind his eyes every time he closed them. He'd spent the spare time between runs cleaning the rigs and doing extra maintenance, though it wasn't scheduled for a while yet. He couldn't settle down to sleep.

He carried a bucket of vanilla ice cream and a large can of peaches in a shopping bag when he knocked on Tia's front door.

"Danny!" She looked surprised and highly kissable in her pajamas with her hair still mussed from sleep. "I didn't expect you yet."

"I popped by the store for a few necessities, then came right over. How do your girls feel about pancakes?"

"They love them." She stepped out of the way, eyeing the ice cream bucket. "Do you always serve ice cream with breakfast?"

"Only when we have peaches on our pancakes." He shut the door behind him, then set down his purchases and pulled her close for a long, lingering kiss. If he could return home to a beautiful woman who had red tendrils tumbling down her back every morning, he thought his life would be about perfect. Then he paused and pushed the thought away. *Slow down, buddy.*

She wasn't ready to go there, and he needed to give her time to adjust to being a couple before he mentioned the M word. Though the progress in their relationship often seemed to drag, he knew slow and steady was the only way to win. And he very definitely wanted her to be a permanent part of his life.

When he pulled back, she smiled and studied him for a long moment, running her fingers along the light stubble of his chin. "You kiss me like that and I might give in to your demands of ice cream for breakfast."

"Oh, good." He leaned in and laid another one on her, only releasing her when Tristi's calls to her mom echoed down the hall. He picked up his purchases again. "You go take care of her and get ready for the day—though I have to say you look adorable in those pajamas. I'll get started on breakfast."

"I don't have any pancake mix," she warned him.

"I'd be shocked if you did. And I might be a little offended you think I need some. Scoot." He headed into the kitchen, grinning to himself. Oh, yes, he could stand to kiss her every morning.

When Samantha joined him in the kitchen twenty minutes later, Danny was pulling the peach topping from the stove. He already had a growing stack of pancakes on a plate beside him, and another three would join the others in a few minutes.

"Danny? What are you doing here?" Samantha asked. She sported a pair of fuzzy purple pajamas and an incredible example of bed-head.

Danny turned, relief and joy thrumming through him as he saw her sweet face. He snatched her up and pressed a noisy kiss to her cheek. "I'm making you breakfast. Did you have a good night?"

She wrapped her arms around him and held him tight. "Yes. I slept like an angel all night." She gave him a too-innocent smile.

He looked at her and lifted his brows in doubt. "I bet you stayed up late reading books by flashlight. Yes, I can see it there in your eyes. They give you away every time."

Her mouth dropped open. "How did you know?"

Danny leaned forward until they bumped foreheads, looking her in the eye. "You'd be surprised what I know." When she giggled, he grinned back at her, then deposited her on a chair at his side. He loved listening to her chatter, and the bright joyful noise was exactly what he needed to wipe away the pain and sorrow of the previous night.

They talked about diverse subjects, much of it nonsense as he cooked up the rest of the pancake batter, then he set the table while she ran to get her mom and sister, her footed pajamas slapping against the tiled floor until she reached the carpet.

"You really put ice cream on your pancakes?" Tia asked as she saw the stack he'd prepared for her.

"Try it." He nudged a plate toward her as she settled Tristi in the high chair.

"I want some!" Samantha chimed in.

"Good, because I have a plate here with your name on it." He stacked a couple on the plate, slathered the peach sauce on it and topped it with ice cream.

Tia's eyes rolled back in her head in obvious enjoyment as she took her first bite. "This is something you created in school, right? Or at the station?" She finished chewing and swallowed. "No way your mom made this for you."

"You'd be wrong about that." Danny slid Samantha her plate, then dished a small amount for Tristi, who would eat most of her food with her hands, and throw some of it on the floor if she was true to form. He knew her pajamas would be going straight to the laundry bin when she finished eating, anyway, so it wouldn't matter that much. "It was reserved for special occasions, like family reunions, Christmas, and camping out, but she's the one who came up with the idea."

"Your mom must be totally cool!" Samantha said after she swallowed her first bite. "It's yummy!"

Tristi grinned, peach topping sliding down her chin and another piece smashed in one hand.

Unable to stop smiling, Danny felt better than he had in twelve hours. A world with this much brightness in one room had to have plenty of other beautiful surprises waiting around the bend.

Twenty-eight

"Hey, let's grab some food while we're here," Danny said to James as they loaded the gurney back into the rig outside the St. Mark's ER. After nearly a month, he was still trying to find the old cafeteria worker he'd mentioned to Tia. He hoped she was still working there.

"You want to eat here?" James gave him a side-long look.

"It's handy, and they have awesome pie. You know you cave when it comes to their pie."

James considered for only a couple of seconds before grinning. "All right, hop in and we'll go around."

Five minutes later they'd pulled the ambulance to the other side of the building and were entering the cafeteria. Danny smiled in relief when he saw the white-haired lady standing at the cash register. Perfect—it was much harder to strike up a conversation with someone behind the food counter. It was mid-afternoon, and Danny's lunch was still hanging like a rock in his gut—never again was he going to the burger joint on Fourth—but he figured he could manage a piece of apple pie.

He hurried through the room, then took advantage of the lull in customers as he carried his snack to the cashier. "Hey," he greeted her. "Weren't you celebrating some kind of anniversary last time I saw you?"

She smiled as she rang in his purchase. "Twenty-five years I've been working here."

"Wow! I bet you've been here longer than anyone."

171

"Most anyone. There are a few still here from before my time, but they're getting fewer every day." She told him how much his pie was and he pulled out his wallet.

"Yeah? I was born here in February about twenty-eight years ago. Anyone from labor and delivery still working here?" He handed over a five.

"Why? You want to go thank them for helping you get out all right?"

He chuckled. "I helped deliver a baby a few months back. It was pretty incredible. Messy as all heck, but still incredible."

She gave a loud, braying laugh. "That it is. There's not much of anything worth having that doesn't require some mess, though."

"You got that right." He took back his change and pocketed it. "So, who is it that's been working here longer than you?"

"Dr. Angela Losee in obstetrics. She was probably still a nurse back then, but she's been here forever. There's a rad tech, Joseph Monroe, and one of the heart surgeons was a resident when I started here."

"That must be some incredible staying power." He picked up his tray and waved. "I'll see you later." He headed halfway across the room so he could make a call to Tia without being overheard.

Tia had warred with herself for more than a day about how she should handle her chat with Dr. Losee. Did she admit outright about why she was there? Did she make something up? Approach her through one of her charities—Google had indicated the good doctor was involved in several.

After staying up most of the night, though, Tia decided direct honesty was her best bet. At least, she hoped it was. She called the hospital and found out when the doctor would be getting off rounds for the day, then arranged for Danny to watch the kids for a few hours.

Thanks to the Internet, Tia knew what Dr. Losee looked like, so she was confident she would be able to recognize her on sight. As the shift-change neared, she approached the nurses' station and asked about the doctor.

"She's on rounds now. Can I help you with something?" the nurse behind the counter asked.

"Actually, I need to speak with her personally. I'm happy to wait until she swings back this direction. Do you mind if I scoot out of the way over there and wait?" Tia pointed to a corner within view of the counter.

The young man shook his head. "Sorry, but there's a waiting room down the hall. I'll let Dr. Losee know you want to speak with her, but I can't have you in the halls here, and it could be a while."

Tia wanted to protest, but she knew better than to alienate the staff. She nodded instead. "I'd really appreciate it if you made sure she knew I was here."

"What's your name?"

"Tia Riverton."

"Sure." The man turned his back on her, grabbed some pages from the printer, and snatched up a clipboard.

Tia forced a smile and headed for the waiting area. She found a seat with a good view of the hall so she wouldn't have to worry about missing the doctor if the nurse didn't send her over.

The wait was interminable. Though Dr. Losee was scheduled to get off at six, it was nearly eight when she finally came to the waiting room. She zeroed in on Tia right off—not surprising since she was the only one there. "You wanted to speak with me?"

Tia stood. "You're Dr. Losee?"

"Yes." She studied Tia. "You're not one of my patients."

"No. Or at least, if I once was, it's been a very long time." She gestured to the row of chairs. "I'd appreciate it if you can give me a few minutes to explain why I'm here. I know you've worked a long day already and must be ready to head home."

Dr. Losee sat with the air of one who hadn't been off her feet in hours. "It has been a full day, though no longer than usual. I think I might be getting too old for this." She smiled but weariness still etched her face.

Tia grabbed a nearby chair and maneuvered it across from Dr. Losee. "How many years have you worked in obstetrics?"

"I've been in labor and delivery for most of thirty-five years. I started out as a CNA when I was still in my twenties. Why do you ask?"

"And you've always been here at this hospital?"

"Yes." Her eyes narrowed and she seemed to grow suspicious.

Tia took a deep breath. "I was born here twenty-eight years ago." She briefly told about her recent discovery and the steps she'd taken to try to figure out what happened.

"And you think it was someone on staff here?"

Tia shrugged, trying to keep the conversation casual, not to spook the doctor. "I don't know. I needed somewhere to start, and this seemed to be a sensible place."

"So I'm one of your suspects." Dr. Losee's eyes narrow slightly and her face pinched.

"At this point, you're the only one I know for sure worked in this department during the time that I was born. I don't know who was here, how many people were in the department that night, or if it had nothing to do with hospital staff at all." Tia could tell she was losing ground—what little she had to begin with—and felt desperation rising inside her.

"Then why are you here?"

"Because I have to start somewhere, and you're the only one who might have some of the information that could lead me to answers."

"I had a daughter born that month," Dr. Losee told her. "She's a couple weeks older than you. I took the whole month of February, and most of March off, so I couldn't have anything to do with it."

"I'm glad to hear it." And she was. Tia liked the woman. "But you still might know something about the others who worked here at that time."

Wariness filled the doctor's gaze. "How do I know you won't use the information to harass someone?"

Tia hadn't thought about that, so she gave it a moment's thought. "I guess you can't know that for sure. All you can do is trust me, or not, when I say that I'm just looking for answers. I don't want to make anyone's life miserable. It's not like I'm unhappy with where I ended up, I just need to know what happened."

Dr. Losee didn't answer for a long moment as she rubbed a hand along the back of her neck. "I have a photo album I've kept from work, which includes pictures of my baby shower. I may be able to give you a few names. But I'm not sure I should, and I don't know where it is."

Hope filled Tia's chest for the first time in weeks. "I'll be glad for anything you can give me."

Dr. Losee stood. "I'll need to think about it. If I decide to help, I'll see if I can remember who was working here."

"I really appreciate it." Tia stood as well and returned the chair to its previous position. "Think how you would feel if it were your daughter who had been switched in the hospital. It was a life-altering experience, doctor."

"I'm sure it was."

Tia passed over a business card. "I've got my cell phone number written on the back, or you can reach me at the email address there. Thanks for your time."

"You're welcome."

Tia turned and walked out, feeling discouraged. Would the doctor really tell her anything? Could she, even if she wanted to? Tia didn't know, but she hoped something would come along soon.

"Any luck?" Danny asked Tia when she came into the house after her trip to the hospital. She'd been gone longer than expected and he'd nearly called to check up on her several times, but managed to hold back. He didn't want to be too pushy.

"I spoke with Dr. Losee, and she agreed to consider looking for names. I don't know if I wasted my time or not." She dumped her coat on the sofa beside the front door, looking tired.

"Did she sound positive though?" He pulled her into his arms, wishing he could do something to make this easier for her.

"Positive she thought I was a trouble maker." Tia rested her head on his chest, melting into his embrace. "If I had to say which side she was leaning toward, I'm afraid it would be to not help." She closed her eyes. "It's so discouraging."

He could feel her frustration, and deciding to distract her, nudged her head off his chest. "Let me take your mind off things for a while, then." His kiss seemed to do that almost instantly.

Twenty-nine

The first private eye report came back in late January. Rashelle Ibson Moon was married with an infant son. She and her husband lived in New York State, where she'd attended college. The PI verified that Rashelle was one of the other girls at the hospital with Tia. The pictures he sent also made it unlikely that she was the one for whom Tia searched. None of her features looked right, so Tia checked her off the list. If she had to go back to Rashelle later, she'd deal with it then.

Lisa Lowell's file showed up a few days later. Comparatively speaking, Lisa was practically next door in Jefferson City, Missouri. Less than three hours away. The photos of her were far more promising, even if they were taken from a distance. She owned a little gift shop and had only one part-time clerk working for her. Tia put Lisa at the top of her list.

Dates with Danny were getting more and more frequent, and Tia loved her time with him. Still, as the anniversary of Lee's death drew closer, she struggled with dreams of him, of his final battle. He had died the week before her twenty-fifth birthday, and then his gift had arrived in the mail, two days after the funeral. She looked up at the carving of a rose he'd picked out for her days before his death, and wondered how he would have felt about Danny.

Danny Tullis was one of the strongest men she knew. He was honest and hardworking, gentle with her and the kids, and willing to stick his neck out to help her. She'd seen the way he'd reacted after the accident where the little girl died. She knew he adored her daughters. And he'd dropped hints, with increasing frequency, that he was interested in something a little more permanent with Tia.

How could that be wrong?

She wasn't sure she was ready for it, though. He was talking serious future stuff here, stuff she'd already been through and embraced years earlier. And didn't he know she had too much on her plate already? Why did he have to come into her life right now, of all times?

Then again, he'd been a tremendous support. He'd helped find the doctor who'd worked at the hospital when she'd been there. He'd put out feelers and helped her find three of the four PIs she ended up engaging to find the other women. He'd been there as friend, confidant, and babysitter when Nichole wasn't available, cheering her up when she felt down, turning to her when he had a bad day at work. He was sharing her life in ways she didn't think she'd even shared them with Lee, if only because her husband had so seldom been around.

And Danny had fed her and the girls ice cream for breakfast. Really, could he be any more awesome? Samantha would say no, of course, but she was an idealistic kid with no clue of reality. Strangely, Tia was also starting to feel rather idealistic where Danny was concerned.

The doorbell rang and Tia put down the report from the private eye, a smile on her face.

The sun was setting when Tia pulled up at Wes's office. Her brother worked for a company that did online marketing and he managed to have regular business hours most of the time. His shift should be ending in a few minutes, so she parked her car and checked for his in the lot. Finding the electric blue Miata, Tia knew he was inside.

She had tried to track him down several times since Samantha's party, but it hadn't been easy to get him alone. Too many people had been around for Christmas and Thanksgiving. It made her think he must have been avoiding her, which only made her more determined to find him.

She pushed through the double doors into the muted blue reception area and smiled at the man sitting behind the front desk. "Hi, I'm Wes Parry's sister. Is he still in?"

"Yes. If you'd like to take a seat, I'll be happy to get him for you."

Tia sat, though she fidgeted constantly. When Wes came through the door several minutes later, he carried his coat and laptop bag. "I'm going to cut out ten minutes early," he told her as he shrugged on his coat. "Where are the girls?"

"Nichole has them. You care to grab some dinner?"

His brows lifted and he studied her. "Is this a conversation we can have in public?"

She stared back at him. "Are you expecting it to turn ugly?"

She saw his cheek bulge when he pushed his tongue against it. "Maybe I'm wrong, but I doubt you'd have tracked me down here, without your girls, if we weren't going to have a serious talk. Besides you have that look in your eye, the one that says you turned on the barbecue and I should prepare to be grilled."

"You're irritating, you know that?" She stood and adjusted her coat.

"I think you may have mentioned that completely mistaken opinion once or twice before." He put a hand on her shoulder and led her out to the parking lot. "Want to meet at my place? I'll order some Chinese to be delivered."

"Sounds good."

Fifteen minutes later she pulled into a visitor's parking spot at his condo. He met her at the door. "Come on in."

Tia removed her coat and draped it over a chair. She sat on the leather sofa and curled her feet beneath her. "So what are we ordering for dinner?"

"I did it on the way here. The food should arrive any minute." He pulled off his tie and laid it over his coat, then took a nearby chair. As if by mutual design, they discussed the girls and his job, but nothing of her search or the news about the cause of her parents' divorce.

The Chinese arrived and Tia loaded her plate. When Wes had done the same, she tiptoed into the main topic on her mind. "I have to say, you didn't appear terribly surprised by the reason Mom and Dad split up."

He grimaced. "No, I heard about it before everything was finalized. People in town seemed to know, and were eager to share the truth with me. I'm surprised you weren't aware before now."

"You knew then and didn't tell me?" The betrayal of that was strong. "Didn't you think I had a right to know?"

"Look. What good would it have done to tell you? You were only eleven! Did you *need* to know that about your mother? I wished I hadn't known. Strangely, people seemed to think it was their duty to make sure I was aware—after all, I was the grown up age of fourteen. Well past ready to hear the truth." Sarcasm dripped from his words.

Tia paused, considering for the first time how it must have felt for him. She now understood why he'd chosen to live with their father, instead of with their mom. He'd always been closer to their dad, which Tia had taken as the reason Wes had defected from their home when their parents split. Their mom's cheating would have been difficult for him to accept. "I can't believe I had no idea."

They both ate for several seconds before he changed the subject. "So Mom's been on a tear since the birthday party. She says she thinks the DNA tests are wrong."

Tia rolled her eyes. She filled him in on all the details. He'd heard some of them from Mona, but predictably, she'd twisted the facts to suit herself.

"So you're searching for the other woman?" he asked when she'd wound down.

"Yeah. I'm getting close. I'm still waiting on the last name to come back. Claire Hogan. Once the PI reports to me I should be ready to move forward." This was the place where things got dicey. It had taken a long time to decide to contact the other women, but she needed to be careful about it.

"And how many women are left on your list?"

"One for sure. I keep hoping Clair is going to come back half Asian or something so I'll be able to focus on Lisa."

"And once you know, then what?"

"Good question." She played with her noodles. "I'm going to have to make contact, but I'm still not sure who or how."

"Let me know how it goes. I'm curious about how it'll turn out." He shrugged when he caught her gaze. "I don't know how I feel about it. It's not like it makes that much of a difference to me. We're not kids and my life won't be turned upside down. I won't refuse to meet her if she's interested, but it's not going to change my life."

"I guess that makes sense." Considering how Mona had been acting, Tia had forgotten that she was the one who cared the most about how this turned out. Needing to change the subject, she settled back against the sofa and began telling him all of the funny things the girls had done recently.

Thirty

Lisa called goodbye to a customer and let her smile drop. She hadn't slept well the night before and could really use a nap. The shop wouldn't allow that, however, and her part-time clerk was off for the day. She walked to the stack of envelopes the mail lady had delivered a few minutes earlier and began to sort through them. Her mind was half on what she should wear on her date with Colby that night. After tossing the junk mail, she flipped back through the keep stack until she arrived at the white envelope again. She didn't recognize the name in the upper right-hand corner, but as the address was hand written, it was unlikely to be junk mail.

T. Riverton. Lisa flipped it over and opened it, pulling out one type-written sheet. She read the first paragraph and dropped into a nearby chair. This was obviously a mistake—there was no way she had been switched as a baby. She refolded it and pitched it in the garbage can, then sorted out the rest of the bills and filed them to be paid.

She looked up and greeted the next customer as they came into her boutique. More customers entered and she stayed busy, helping them find what they were looking for, putting out new merchandise and preparing statements for some of her better clients. The letter in the garbage stayed on her mind, though, lingering and creating doubt.

When she locked up that night she fished the letter from the garbage, reread it, then tossed it again. It had to be a sick joke, and she wasn't going to fall for it.

Danny gave one of the firefighters the go ahead after taking his vitals. The break had been sufficient; Mark could go back into the house fire. He wiped down the blood pressure cuff with a sanitizing wipe and smiled as the next man came to the ambulance doors. Structure fires held lots of dangers, and stress on the firefighters was one of them. After the crew members inside had emptied their air tanks, protocol required they come to the ambulance and be checked out before going back into the blaze.

"How's it looking in there?" Danny asked as he helped the guy from Station 3 strip off his jacket so the blood pressure cuff would fit.

"Bad. The house will be a total loss." He shook his head. "Looks like it started in one of the back rooms."

Danny nodded as he slid the oxygen sensor onto a finger of the man's left hand. "It was a beautiful house once." He glanced back out the window and saw a figure on the roof wielding an ax. "What's he doing up there?" Venting out the roof was a common practice, but the fire was too big and had been burning too long. There was no way the roof was safe at this point.

The man looked out the doorway and swore. "Fool."

"Did you get something to drink?" Danny turned the conversation, but kept an eye on the burning structure. A woman came in, her short-cropped hair plastered to her head, soot on her face. He switched the blood pressure cuff to her and gave her oxygen. Then a call came up and he swiveled his head to see nothing but flames where the man on the roof had been standing only moments before. His heart leaped as adrenaline pumped through him.

A few minutes later he cleared the firefighters from the ambulance so they could bring the man from the roof in. He'd fallen through, breaking his leg upon landing. Smoke inhalation and possible internal injuries made it all worse as the man gasped for breath. Another ambulance arrived, having been called to take over so the first crew could transport the firefighter to the hospital.

Danny hurriedly did an assessment on the man as they rushed to the trauma center.

Tia's mouth tightened as she listened to the news report. A firefighter was in critical condition after a roof caved in with him on it. She had spoken to Danny only minutes before she saw the report, so she knew he was well, but he had sugarcoated the man's condition. Tia wasn't sure if that was because of privacy laws, or to keep her from worrying, but she was plenty worried now.

She'd always known that Lee's job was dangerous. He was a soldier in a hostile country. Soldiers died. Firefighters weren't supposed to, though. Fires could be dangerous, yes, but it wasn't like anyone was shooting at them.

Now she realized things were not quite what she'd thought. That so easily could have been Danny. He could be the one in a hospital bed right now, fighting for his life. Could she live with that? With the fact that there was so much more risk than she ever realized?

When she started seeing visions of him getting hit by a car at an accident scene, she clicked off the television. She was *not* turning into her mother! There was no way she would jump at shadows or be unreasonable.

But the lingering fear wouldn't go away, no matter what she did.

Thirty-one

Claire grabbed the mail as she let herself into her apartment. Home sweet home: it was a dive. She ignored the water spots on the ceiling from a recent rain and pulled out the only envelope she didn't recognize. T. Riverton.

She stretched out on her love seat—a feat which could only be accomplished with much of her leg flopping over the arm on the far end. She read the note once, cocked her head and read again. Surely this Tia woman was crazy.

Then she thought about all of the times she'd felt out of sync with her world, her family. Could it be possible? She flipped on the TV and searched for the morning news. The answers wouldn't be there, but she watched anyway, not feeling her eyelids droop as they so often did after a night shift.

She looked at the clock and decided she'd give this Tia a call as soon as the hour was decent.

Tia spooned up the last of her oatmeal and set the bowl away in the dishwasher, hurrying to put the kitchen to rights. It seemed she did nothing but rush to try to catch up these days, and the late start due to lack of sleep last night wasn't helping. "Tristi!" Tia stopped in irritation and looked down at her daughter, who was covered in diaper rash cream from top to bottom. It was in her hair, rubbed into her clothes, and dotted the carpet around her.

After a slow count to ten, Tia scooped up her toddler and hauled her into the bathroom. That was one darling new outfit that would never be the same again. She stripped Tristi and plopped her into a bath, hoping this wouldn't make her late for work. Then the phone rang. Giving her daughter a stern look, Tia rushed to the other room to grab her cell and hurried right back. She didn't recognize the number of the incoming call. "Hello?"

"Hi, is this Tia?"

"Yes, can I help you?"

"My name is Claire. I got your letter this morning. I wondered if we could talk."

Tia's heart started to beat double-time, and she wished she could focus on the conversation, but Tristi was splashing water, and needed her hair washed, which was bound to be a pain. "I'd love to, but now is a really bad time for me." She poured a dollop of baby shampoo in her hand and started working it into Tristi's soft curls. "As mornings go, it's been rather nightmarish, actually."

"Oh, well, if this is a bad time . . . " Claire's disappointment was obvious.

"I'm really sorry. I've got my baby in the bath and I have to get to work. I should be available after one-thirty, if you'd like me to call you back later." This was her chance to finally get some answers. Maybe. She winced as Tristi splashed some more, and started to wail when Tia poured water over her foamy hair.

"That would work. This number's good for me."

"Great. Thanks."

Tristi slapped at her mom's arm and Tia, crouched at the side of the tub, wavered slightly. She reached out and grabbed the side of the tub.

Then watched her cell phone plop into the water.

She had a feeling this was going to be a very bad day.

Danny had a much smoother experience getting through the security blockade the second time he came to the news station. He sauntered across the floor and watched her feverishly chopping vegetables. She looked agitated, her red hair was pulled back in a ponytail and she lifted her hand to rub a flyaway piece away from her face with the back of her wrist.

"Hey. I've been trying to call you all morning," he said when she glanced up at him.

Her lips pursed. "Yeah, my phone's not working at the moment." She slid the onions off to the side and scooped them into a cup, measuring them.

He studied her carefully. This was about more than her phone not working. "Is your battery dead?"

"In a manner of speaking." She didn't look up at him. "Actually, I was giving Tristi a bath this morning and it fell into the tub."

He knew she bathed the girls at night, so could only assume a morning bath was the result of some catastrophe. It amused him, though he wasn't about to show it when she was upset—he didn't have a death wish. "What did she do that required a morning bath?"

She began slicing the green peppers with gusto. "Diaper cream. Everywhere. Her clothes are ruined."

Her eyes filled and a tear threatened to slip out. She blinked, then took a deep breath. "It's not been a banner day so far. Though, Claire called me, so that was good. Maybe. Of course I was in the middle of the bath so I couldn't talk. I should have let it go to voice mail. Who knows if my phone will ever work again."

Danny walked around the counter, took the knife from her hands, and pulled her into a hug. "Hey, it's all right. It's not the end of the world."

She buried her face in his shoulder, her voice coming out muffled. "No, it's just one more thing in a long line."

"I know." He held her tight and brushed his lips along her temple. "You're going through the wringer right now. Hold on, it'll get better." He nudged her face up and rubbed at the damp trail her tear had left behind. "And in the meantime, I'm here for you." He pressed a soft kiss to her mouth, wishing he could make it all better.

"I know. Thank you." But she didn't make eye contact with him, and pulled from his arms.

Danny let her go, but wondered if she was embarrassed to have broken down at work, or if she was upset with him again. Had he done something wrong? He watched her turn back to the counter and start chopping again. "So," he changed the subject, hoping it would perk her up, "I got a call from Laura last night. She and Gavin have decided to get married. They're thinking late April for the wedding." He reached out, and caught the tendril of hair that had escaped her elastic, tucking it behind her ear.

Her hands paused for a heartbeat before continuing on. "That's great. I hope things go well for them. Laura deserves some happiness after everything she's been through."

"I couldn't agree more." Danny studied Tia's body language and wondered what was going on inside her head. He'd thought he was starting to understand her, but was lost now.

When she finished her preparations, Tia borrowed his cell phone and looked up a number she'd scrawled across her notes for the day. "I was hoping to get a minute to call Claire back and explain," she said as she dialed. A moment later she frowned, then left a message, "Hey, Claire, this is Tia, sorry about the call this morning. I was bathing my toddler and dropped the phone in the water. I'll call again as soon as I get my phone replaced. Thanks." She ended the call and returned the phone. "Thanks, I appreciate you coming by," she said to Danny.

"Because you couldn't possibly have borrowed anyone else's phone," he joked.

Her lips curved up, but not into a full smile. "Thanks anyway. So how was work yesterday?"

Danny stayed with her until he was shooed back to the control room to watch the news, but he wondered why he bothered. She didn't seem to need or want his presence.

Claire was relieved when she heard why her phone call with Tia had ended so abruptly. At least she seemed to have a good excuse. Still, it was maddening waiting to hear from her again. Claire wanted answers, and she wasn't known for her patience. In her opinion, the secrets had been kept too long as it was. She wanted confirmation that there was a reason she didn't fit into her family.

"Claire, settle down," her fiancé, Carl, said when she puttered around the house all afternoon and evening. "I know you're anxious, but giving into your jitters isn't going to make it straighten out faster."

"Maybe I should go to Kansas City," she said. "I have a couple days off. We could get it all cleared up in no time." She moved toward the bedroom thinking she would pack a bag, anxious to do something.

He snagged her hand as she walked past and tugged her into his lap. "How about if I give you something else to think about?"

"Carl, I'm serious." She put a hand on his chest and pushed back, but he snaked an arm around her, not letting her get too far away.

"So am I." He tipped his head and studied her. "You promised to marry me, but then you refuse to make any wedding plans. How about if we firm up a few things. Like the date."

She saw the impatience in his eyes and knew she had been dangling him along. He deserved better. At the same time, she didn't feel ready to make final plans yet. Not now things might be changing.

Claire straightened his collar, which didn't need it despite the fact that he had undone the top two buttons of his shirt when he got home. His tie hung from the lamp on the end table. She knew he hated wearing them.

Carl had been so good to her, sweet, understanding and supportive through everything. When she'd had a tough day at work, he listened and consoled. When she had an argument with her mom—was she really Tia's mom?—he cajoled her into a better mood, distracted her with kisses and promises of a future together. He said she would be much wiser with their children. She liked the idea of raising children with him, of holding his hand as they moved into the future. But setting an exact date gave her the heebie-jeebies.

In response to his suggestion, she gave him a soft kiss, then pulled back, running a finger over his cheeks, following the contours. "I need to clear this up first."

He groaned, rolling his head back on the sofa. "You keep coming up with excuses for why we haven't set a date. So I give you a week and then you want another, then another, and another." He tipped his head back up and his eyes bored into hers, his pain clear. "Do you want to marry me or not?"

Claire closed her eyes, if only to block out the sight of his pain. He had been so patient. "Yes. I just . . . look I promise, as soon as I get this cleared up and know if this family really is mine, I'll set a date and we'll start making plans. As soon as I get answers."

He ran a thumb over her bottom lip and she shivered slightly at the rasp of his callous across the soft skin.

"You promise?"

"Pinky swear." She lifted her hand and held out her pinky as evidence.

He replaced his thumb with his mouth in acceptance of her terms.

It was almost two days before Tia called again. Claire had been nearly ready to get someone to cover for her, pile her things into the car and start driving—even if she didn't have Tia's home address. She'd done her homework and knew Tia worked at the television station. Someone there would know how to reach her.

Thankfully, she didn't have to resort to that. "I'm sorry I didn't get back to you sooner. I was hoping when my phone dried out for a day or so it might work again," Tia explained when she finally called.

"No such luck?" Claire asked.

"Nope, I had to pick up another one. Anyway, Dad agreed to pay for another DNA test. I can have the swabs sent straight to you, and you can return them to the lab through the mail."

Claire glanced at her calendar to see what her work schedule was going to be. "How long would it take for the kit to arrive?"

"The last one took three days. We have a weekend squeezed in there, so probably by Monday."

"Perfect. I'm off work Tuesday and Wednesday, and I'd like to meet you and your parents." She referred to them as Tia's even though she already thought of them as her own. She couldn't wait to learn all about them.

"You don't have to make the trip. It'll take half the day."

"That's okay. I admit I'm getting anxious for answers. If I hadn't heard from you in the next day or so, I might have shown up on your doorstep anyway."

Tia chuckled. "I understand your anxiety. This has been driving me crazy since October."

Claire wouldn't have used the word anxiety, as that insinuated she was worried or nervous. She was excited. "I don't know how you've managed then." She asked Tia a dozen questions about her family: Mona and Ron and their jobs, and Wes, the big brother Claire had always wanted but never had. She was dying to get to know them all. When she had the first set of answers—not nearly enough, but they would suffice for a few days—she made arrangements for the visit, then hung up.

Carl was munching a bowl of cereal by the kitchen sink. When she turned to face him, his expression wasn't nearly as excited as her own.

"You know things might not be quite as hearts and flowers as you'd like," he warned her. "Tia seems nice, and has told you a bunch about her family, but that doesn't mean they'll welcome you with open arms."

Claire scowled. "I know that." She didn't believe it, though. It might be awkward the first day or so, and the wait for the official word would take forever—even if she would know in less than two weeks. She picked up the bridal magazine she'd been flipping through when Tia called. It was one Carl had purchased as a nudging reminder weeks earlier—even though she didn't think a traditional dress was really in her future. She preferred to live outside the box. Since she'd promised to set a date in the next couple of weeks, she figured flipping through it for ideas wouldn't kill her, even if it made her chest seize with anxiety.

She heard Carl set the bowl on the countertop. He walked over and sat beside her. "I don't want to steal your excitement or ruin your happiness. I just don't want you to get so worked up when there's still a chance it might not be what you want it to be."

"You don't want me to belong to this other couple." It hurt that he was trying to take away her excitement. Why couldn't he be happy for her?

"That's not true." He set his hand on her arm, but she shook it off, stood and grabbed her jacket from the peg by the door. "I'm going for a walk." She checked to make sure she had her key, then took off. She could feel Carl's eyes on her back until the door closed between them.

Thirty-two

Tia continued to be standoffish through the week. Danny stopped in to see her whenever he wasn't at work, even coming for breakfast again, though he didn't break out the famed peaches and ice cream pancake topping. He noticed she didn't give him the cold shoulder outright, but held back part of herself.

At first he thought part of it was frustration about her phone falling in the bath, then he tried to excuse it as confusion about why Lisa hadn't responded to her letter.

Samantha seemed to be struggling, causing more trouble and picking on her sister more, and Mona never backed off.

But after a while, Danny realized there was something more serious going on. Something that had to do with him, specifically.

He dropped by Tia's place at the girls' bedtime, giving her a break as he read them stories and tucked them into bed. Then he came back out to the living room and watched her move anxiously around the kitchen. "What's going on, Tia?"

"I'm cleaning up."

He dropped his voice a few notes, allowing it to grow husky. "Tia."

She stopped wiping down the cupboard, standing there for a long moment before turning to face him. "What do you want?"

"I want to understand what's bothering you." He crossed to her, ran a finger along her cheek. "Something's been bothering you for more than a week. Can't you tell me what it is?" Her skin was cool and soft, and he watched her eyes close as his finger trailed along her jaw to her chin.

"I just have a lot on my mind." Her hands came up to his waist, settling there.

"Anything in particular that made you take a step back from us?" he asked.

She opened her eyes and looked at him, pain radiating from her. "I don't know what to do."

"About what?"

"Your job is dangerous."

He felt his brow furrow as his hand dropped from her chin. "Yeah, it can be sometimes. Most of the time it's perfectly safe, though."

"But firefighters get hurt, killed in fires. EMTs get hit at accident scenes, are exposed to pathogens, accidental needle sticks." She fisted her hands in his shirt.

"Woah, slow down." He pulled her close, wrapping his arms around her and urging her head against his chest. "Hey, it's not that bad. Most accidents are avoidable—and believe me when I say that I try to avoid anything dangerous."

"You *try*, huh?"

"Your line of work isn't without its dangers," he pointed out. "If it were, we would never have met."

"It's not the same."

"Sure it is. School teachers get beaten up, risk their health and eye sight with long hours of grading and test writing. Hospital staffs deal with abusive patients, virulent germs, truck drivers risk road accidents, back problems from lifting. Every job on this planet has its risks."

"Some are worse than others."

"True." He pressed a kiss to her head, wishing he could take away the pain and worry that plagued her.

"Would you quit your job if I asked you to?" she asked. "Find something safer?"

Shock rippled through him. He did not hear those words. He released her, pushed her back, and looked her in the eye. "Are you kidding me?"

Tears poured down her cheeks, and her face crumpled. "You have no idea how hard it was for me when Lee died." She wiped at her face, and moved away when Danny tried to touch her shoulder. "It was hard knowing I would have to have Tristi without him when he was half a world away. But then he died and I knew he'd never be back, that both my girls would grow up fatherless, that I would never have his love and support. It was more than I could stand."

"Honey, I'm sorry it was so bad for you. I can only imagine how worried you were about how you would make ends meet and how you've managed to handle all of this alone." He ached to touch her, but wasn't sure how she'd accept it. "You're so amazing to me."

"I'm not amazing. I'm scared and worried and never have enough day to get halfway through my to-do list. I can't imagine . . . " Her hands curled up at her sides. "You're important to me, Danny. More important than I thought possible. I don't know if I can handle getting any closer to you, knowing you could die out there, without going crazy."

He pulled her close again and rested his cheek on her head, tears stinging his own eyes. "It's not like that, Tia."

"It's exactly like that. Did you know the on-the-job death rate for firefighters is higher than for police? And it's almost as high for EMTs."

"Higher than for police? Hmm, I hadn't heard that. I suppose you looked it up?" He wasn't the least convinced that it was more dangerous than any other job if you took reasonable precautions.

"Of course."

"And what was the cause of all these deaths?"

She was quiet for a long moment. "More than half were heart attacks and strokes from stress on the job."

"Really?" That sounded fair. It was why they had to check all firefighters before they could go back into a structure fire. "And what about EMTs?"

She pulled back and looked at him in disgust. "Did you know ambulances are death traps? Seriously, more than two thirds of all deaths of EMTs were in ambulances and helicopters. You'd think they could put you in a safer vehicle."

He pressed the hair back from her face, then led her to the sofa and pulled her down beside him so he could wrap an arm around her shoulders. "I know. It's one of the things they warn us about all the time. Ambulances are top heavy, and it can be hard to do patient care if you're wearing your seat belt. We take every precaution possible to stay safe, honey. You have to believe that, and have faith that I'll come home in one piece."

"You make it sound so simple."

"It is simple. Not always easy, but simple." He urged her head up with his free hand and kissed her, lingering over it until he felt her muscles relax. "I can't quit my job, Tia. It's where I'm supposed to be." Pulling back, he met her gaze, knowing he had to clear the air. "And I don't think you'd want me if I could be so easily manipulated."

She pushed him away with both hands, clearly offended. "Are you calling me manipulative?"

He gave her a steady look and wished he'd picked a different word. Still, he wasn't going to back down. "If the shoe fits." He grabbed her hand as she stood and tried to move away. He tugged it and pulled her onto his lap. "Don't do that. Don't walk away when we're having a disagreement."

"Call it what it is. We're fighting." She held herself stiff, so she didn't lean against him, but she didn't try to stand, either.

"Maybe, but walking away isn't going to solve things."

"I don't know if anything can solve things."

His jaw tightened and he took a slow, measured breath before continuing, not wanting to react to the words and how much they hurt him, but choosing to act on the pain that caused her to say it. "Last fall a few heated words ended my relationship with Carrie, and I let her go, almost relieved to see the end of things. I'm not going to stand by and watch us fall apart. You're too important to me."

She stilled in his arms. "I'm too important to you? It sounds like it."

"Hey." He waited until she turned her head to face him. "I'm not saying that what you feel isn't important to me, that I'm not going to do everything in my power to stay safe, but I'm a paramedic firefighter. It's part of who I am—like cooking is part of who you are—even though you could get burns, poisoning, or another severe allergic reaction." He held her gaze. "It's what I studied for, and I love it. Don't make me choose between you and my career. Either way, I lose." He held her gaze for a long moment, then dug down and said the words that had been on the tip of his tongue for too long. "I love you, Tia."

Her breath caught and she stared as if she didn't believe him. "You love me? But we haven't known each other that long."

"Long enough. All I know is it would rip me apart to lose you. Please don't do this."

She tipped her forehead onto his shoulder. A long moment passed. "I like you the way you are. I don't want you to change. It just scares me."

He felt that knot of tension in his stomach release. "I know it does. I promise, if I ever develop a heart condition, I'll quit my job and become a greeter at Wal-Mart. If you develop another dangerous food allergy, you'll quit your cooking show and become a cashier somewhere."

She chuckled. "About equally likely, I take it?"

"The odds are slightly more likely that I'll develop a heart condition—in another forty years or so."

"Well, as long as we understand each other." She lifted her head and ended the conversation with a kiss.

Thirty-three

Tia was nervous. Claire was supposed to arrive any moment, and Tia was afraid things wouldn't go nearly as well as Claire expected. The woman had been oozing excitement every time they'd spoken—which had been daily since Tia got her phone running again.

The test kit had actually arrived on Saturday and Tia had gotten together with her dad to get his DNA sample that night.

Ron seemed to be dealing with everything fine. If she went more than a few days between calls or emails, he would contact her, check to see how she was doing. She appreciated his support, especially since Mona was being so difficult.

Because Mona was being . . . herself, Tia thought, they hadn't mentioned Claire's arrival, nor had Mona take the DNA test. If Ron matched, that would be enough proof and she would deal with it then.

Tia checked the pizza again through the oven window and noticed it hadn't browned noticeably in the past thirty seconds. She stood, telling herself not to be an idiot as she walked back to the living room. Samantha and Tristi were at Nichole's and they'd be staying there all evening. Danny and Wes would be by a little later, and she had made arrangements for Claire to meet Ron the next day.

The doorbell rang and Tia jumped slightly. She opened the front door to find a woman on the other side. Claire was shorter than Tia expected, around five-foot-three with straight black hair, an eyebrow piercing, and a visible butterfly tattoo on her upper right arm. Her smile was broad and her blue eyes danced with excitement. The heavy black eyeliner wasn't nearly as attention-getting as the black leather micro-mini skirt and black lacey tank top that peeked from beneath the woman's black marshmallow coat. Seeing all the exposed skin, Tia wondered if she wanted Danny to join them after all before pushing the thought away.

"You must be Tia," Claire said, her voice as bright as her smile.

"Yes, welcome, Claire, come on in." She gestured through the doorway and stepped back for the other woman to enter.

They went to the kitchen where Tia had prepared a green salad to go with dinner. "How was your trip?"

"It was fine, a little long, you know? I was tired when it was time to come here, even though I was totally excited, but one of those energy drinks totally took care of that. I'll probably be wired for hours now." She looked around the room. "Where are your girls?"

"At the neighbors'. I thought it would be better if we didn't have too many interruptions tonight." Tia pulled out four plates from the bone china set she'd inherited from Mona's mother—who could be Claire's grandma. She wondered, if the tests came back positive, should she pass the dishes to the rightful grandchild? The thought made her sad; she'd loved Nana so much. She brushed the subject aside. There would be time to consider those kinds of implications later, when Claire wasn't already talking as fast as a freight train.

"I totally understand. They aren't really my nieces, anyway, so how would you explain?" She studied the plates Tia set in front of her, a little disconcerted. "Are these family heirlooms?"

"They were a gift to me," Tia answered, not willing to explain. Claire seemed so ready to jump into things.

Claire looked almost relieved. "They're nice, I guess, but totally not my style." She folded her arms on the tabletop and leaned forward. "So you mentioned your boyfriend was coming tonight."

"Yes, he and Wes will be here soon." The doorbell rang and Tia smiled in relief. Claire appeared to feel no awkwardness at all, but Tia couldn't shake it. "That's probably one of them now."

She hurried to the door and let Wes in. "Hey, welcome. Claire's already here."

"Good. What about the firefighter?" Wes asked as he gave her a quick hug.

"Not yet. Any time now." Tia checked her watch, it wasn't quite six.

She followed Wes back to the kitchen where he introduced himself to Claire. Tia turned her attention to the oven, smiling when she saw a nice golden brown on the edges of the crust. She reached for her oven mitts as she listened to Claire and Wes go through the motions, asking the pleasant and polite questions you posed to someone the first time you met.

After Tia set the pizza pan on the cookie rack to cool for a few minutes, she turned and studied Wes and Claire. They didn't seem the least bit uncomfortable. Wes sat beside the woman who could be his sister, chatting amiably, asking questions about her work and her fiancé. Tia wasn't sure how she felt about the instant rapport. Could she really be replaced so easily?

She spent another minute looking for a resemblance between them—any resemblance. Not all siblings looked alike, she told herself, but there did seem to be a similarity around the eyes and nose. When Claire flashed a bright smile, Tia thought it looked much like Ron's, and her heart sank in her chest.

The doorbell rang, and Tia hurried to the living room, glad to get away. She knew she was being stupid. She'd been looking for the woman who could be Wes's true sister, so why was she suddenly feeling territorial?

She smiled as she opened the door for Danny, who brought a tub of ice cream with him. "Hey, honey." He scooped her close with his free arm and kissed her soundly.

When he released her, she looked at the ice cream. "We're not having pancakes tonight. I thought I told you it's pizza."

He chuckled and turned her back to the kitchen, his arm still around her shoulder. "Well I wouldn't want to try putting ice cream on pizza—that would be plain gross. Especially fudge ripple. I guess it'll have to be dessert instead."

He smiled and introduced himself to both Claire and Wes, and slid the ice cream into the freezer as if he belonged in that space, Tia's home, with her. She thought of his declaration of love and wondered if she would be able to make herself take that step and really let him in.

Though Claire had checked into a motel, she hung around after the guys left that night. Tia put the girls to bed and then returned to where Claire was flipping through the television stations with the remote.

"All set?" she asked.

"Yeah. That should guarantee us at least . . . " Tia pulled a likely number out of the air, "Three minutes before the first disruption. Ten if we're really lucky." She stood in the room entrance with her thumbs in her back pockets.

Claire chuckled. "The joys of motherhood."

"Would you like something to drink?" Tia asked. They'd spent the evening answering lots of questions for Claire, but Tia had a few of her own. "I make the world's best hot chocolate."

"Well, how could I turn down the world's best?"

Tia tipped her head toward the kitchen and watched Claire click the television off and rise to follow.

Tia got out cocoa, sugar and powdered milk and set them on the counter.

Claire stared at her. "You're going to make cocoa from scratch?"

"Yeah. I like it better than anything I can find prepackaged."

"I knew you were into cooking and stuff, but I've never met anyone who makes hot cocoa from scratch. Does your mom cook like you do?"

Tia laughed and reached for a sauce pan. "Not even close. I learned to cook to keep from starving—she prefers eating out, or heating something frozen. Her mom cooked pretty well, though. She's the one who taught me the basics. The rest I learned on my own." She measured in water to boil, then added sugar and cocoa.

Claire watched her for a long moment. "I don't know anyone like you. Our worlds are completely different."

"Yeah, they seem to be." Tia pulled out a wire whisk and mixed everything up. "So tell me about your family."

"I wondered when you'd get around to asking." Claire took the stool nearby and watched. "I have a sister, Marie, she's four years younger than me and my parents' favorite. She went to college and got a teaching certificate last spring. She works with disabled children."

"That's wonderful."

"Yeah." Claire's tone indicated there was major sibling rivalry there. "Everyone loves her."

"And you? Do the two of you get along?"

"Fine," Claire said with a shrug. "We have so little in common, and with four years between us, we didn't do any of the same things growing up. I mean," she grabbed the salt shaker from the counter and started fiddling with it, "we have nothing in common. She's the perfect daughter, and I'm a screw up. She did great in college and I barely made it through my CNA. I keep thinking of going back to school for more medical training, but I don't think I've got it in me. I hated school."

"And your parents? You haven't really talked about them." Tia had tried not to be curious about Claire's family, but couldn't help herself. The thought that these could be *her* parents was terrifying.

Claire shrugged one shoulder. "I've never really been good enough for them—but I didn't want to fit their mold." She looked back at Tia. "My parents hate the way I dress and do my hair and makeup. I think I went a little to the left because they expected me to hold right."

"Parents' expectations can be hard." Tia looked back at the mixture in her pan. "And their idiosyncrasies can be frustrating. My mom is a little . . . needy. And she worries over every little thing. That's how this all started, actually. I had a bad reaction to pine nuts for a dish I was developing for my show, and ended up in the hospital."

Claire's eyes grew round with surprise. "That must have been scary."

"Yeah. Mom decided I *must* get medic alert bracelets for the girls and myself in case we ever needed a blood transfusion or something." She gave a brief explanation about what happened from there— leaving out the bit about the infidelity. There would be time to mention that when they knew absolutely that Claire was related.

Before Claire left for her hotel that night, she did the cheek swab. Once she had driven off in her little blue clunker, Tia sealed the envelope and clipped it to her front door. She would take the package to the post office on her way to work.

Thirty-four

When Tia had a break between preparing for the noon segment and the filming, she called her dad to discuss the previous night's events.

"Hey, honey," he greeted her when he picked up his cell phone. "How did the meeting go with Claire?"

"Fine. She seems nice. A tad rough around the edges, with way too much energy, but that could have been nerves talking. Have you spoken with Wes this morning?"

"No. Did they get along all right?"

"Yes, just fine. You know Wes, he gets along with everyone." Better than she did anyway.

"So what's eating at you?" he asked.

Tia moved to a more private corner of the room and lowered her voice even more. "Maybe it's stupid, but it made me feel kind of unnecessary last night. She's so determined that she's the one that it actually made me feel like the third wheel."

"Do *you* think she's the one?"

"I don't know, honestly. There is a little resemblance with Wes, I guess, if I look for it, but it's not obvious. I kept finding things that didn't fit, rather than things that did." Tia leaned against the wall. "But then I wonder if that's because I didn't want her to be your daughter."

"Is there something wrong with her?"

Tia laughed. "No, not really, though as a heads up, she leans toward goth. Lots of black and a kind of cool looking butterfly tattoo on one shoulder—not that I care for tattoos, but anyway . . ." She was getting off topic. "Claire seems nice, and though she made it clear she didn't get on with her family, she didn't say they were jerks or anything, just that she didn't fit in. Honestly, I don't know that she'll fit into this one all that well either, but there'll be time to think about that when the results come back." She just had to keep reminding herself to be patient.

"Are you feeling threatened, honey? That she's trying to move in on your territory?"

It made Tia feel small to admit it, but she wasn't about to lie. "A bit, perhaps. I know that's stupid, but I guess I'm feeling a little lost right now."

"It's understandable, but she can't replace you honey. I kind of like the idea of having two daughters."

Tia chuckled again, her fears not screaming so loud anymore, then heard the notice that they would begin filming soon. "I gotta go. I feel better now. I'll see you in a few hours?"

"I wouldn't miss it."

The meet with Ron had gone well, though Tia could tell Claire felt sad about the way he held himself back a little. Tia felt bad about the other woman's hurt, but she wondered if her dad was trying to spare her own feelings, if he was uncomfortable with Claire or if he didn't want to get too close before he knew for sure if they were related.

When Claire left that evening, she gave Tia a hug. "You've been great. I really appreciate you letting me burst into your life like this. I like your family, your girls are adorable, and that is some hunk you're dating. You ought to snatch him up!"

Tia smiled when she thought about Danny. "I'll keep that in mind. Drive safe."

"I will. And I have the login information for the test results. Do you think we'll have them by the weekend?" She looked so hopeful.

"Probably not. Sorry. I'm guessing middle of next week. Call if you find out before me?" Tia asked.

"Yes, I'll be checking it often." Claire zipped her coat against the cold, covering her artfully ripped Led Zeplin T-shirt. "I'm glad I met you, either way. I want to keep in touch."

"We should do that." If the results came back positive, Tia had a feeling keeping in touch would be inevitable. "Good luck with that wedding date stuff."

"Thanks. If the results come Wednesday, I know Carl's going to insist on setting a date for the wedding by Friday. He's so anxious." She gave a little wave and disappeared into the tiny vehicle.

Tia was still filled with conflicting emotions as she watched Claire drive off. She hadn't heard from Lisa. Did that mean the letter hadn't arrived, or that she didn't think it worthwhile to respond?

Tia turned back to the house, tightening her coat against the chilling wind and headed up the walk. They would know in a week, maybe less. There would be plenty of time to worry about Lisa after the results came in.

Thirty-five

Danny pulled in front of Tia's grandma's house and tried to quell the nerves bouncing around in his stomach. He'd now met Wes, Ron, and even Mona—briefly—but Tia had been holding back on taking him to Glena's, which made this step seem much bigger than it should have.

"Calm down. It's fine. She's going to love you," Tia reassured him with a squeeze to his arm.

He flashed her a grin that said of course Glena would love him, but it was false bravado. "Me, nervous? Since when?" He got out and came around to open her door, then circled back around the car to let Samantha out—the girl was bouncing, her seatbelt already off, and anxious to be released from the car. Tia freed Tristi from her car seat and carried her.

Danny joined Tia at the sidewalk and she extended a hand. He took it, feeling comfort when she squeezed it. Samantha caught his hand on the other side, and he passed the squeeze along.

The tiny woman smiled brightly when she responded to their knock on the front door, looked him up and down, then waggled her eyebrows at Tia. "You sure know how to pick 'em!"

Tia flushed, but the comment immediately put Danny at ease and he offered Glena's his hand.

"Oh, child, don't you shake my hand. I expect a hug." She pulled him into a surprisingly strong hug. The scent of roses wafted from her skin.

After a round of hugs for everyone, Danny settled next to Tia on the sofa. When Tia got up to check on the casserole Glena said was still in the oven, Danny took Tristi and Glena turned her full attention his way.

"I been tryin' to get that girl to bring you by here for ages. Why you take so long to come see me?"

"You know Tia, always cautious. She probably didn't want to get my hopes up too much by introducing me around before now." Or create expectations in others that they would last. He kept that thought to himself, though, along with the hurt it caused. He wondered if she was comparing him to her husband, and falling short.

"And now you won't get your hopes up?" Glena took a sip of the ice tea she'd offered when they'd come in.

"Now I think she's finally decided she won't be able to shake me." He flashed her a grin and hoped he was right. "I could have told her that months ago."

"Good. You two getting' serious, then? You take her dancin' yet? That girl doesn't get near enough dancin'. I hope you gonna take good care of my sweet granddaughter." She shook a finger at him.

Dancing. The thought hadn't even occurred to him. Maybe it should have. "I sure hope to take care of her. She doesn't always make it easy, but I do what I can."

"She's a sweet girl. I couldn't have done better if I'd had a chance to pick her." Glena's eyes twinkled at him, sharing a joke.

"I did have a chance to pick her, and I happen to agree with you."

Tia walked in. "I sure hope you're not talking about me."

"Sorry, you leave the room, you take the risk of being talk about." He wrapped an arm behind her back after she sat, then he leaned in and brushed his lips across her cheek and her ear, teasingly.

She shivered, but didn't pull away. "Is that how it works?"

"You should know that by now. After your chat with Laura at the McDonald's, I have to say that turnabout is fair play." Tristi pulled on Danny's ear and giggled, and he turned his attention to her.

Though she knew it would easily be Wednesday, and possibly even Thursday before she heard anything, Claire started checking the website for results Tuesday. Every two hours while she was awake starting at five p.m., and once in the middle of the night because she couldn't help herself.

When she finally found the results posted on Thursday morning, she felt her stomach drop. No relation.

Tears rose to her eyes and she bit her lip in an attempt to focus her attention on something else, to keep the tears from falling.

Carl came up behind her, putting his hands on her shoulders. "Is that the results you've been waiting for?"

Claire turned in his arms and buried her face in his shirt. Yes and no, she thought. They were the results, but not at all what she'd hoped to see. "I guess I should have expected it," she said, her voice muffled against his chest.

He wrapped her in his warm embrace. "I'm sorry, honey. I know how much you wanted it."

"They were really nice to me." She hadn't been fully honest with Tia. Claire had said her parents were decent people, that they didn't get along because she couldn't stand the pressure. The truth they'd been mean and spiteful, picking on Claire for her lifestyle and appearance. She never saw them anymore, their dirty little secret. She'd so hoped for something better, even if she never grew close to Tia's family.

Carl held her while she sobbed into his chest. He was always there for her, supportive, loving. What had she been thinking, putting him off? She knew he'd always be there for her. So when she finished crying, had wiped her eyes with the tissue he provided, and wondered what it would take to get the eyeliner out of his shirt, she decided it was time to bite the bullet and commit to this man. For real this time.

She sniffed and looked into his face. "I told you we'd set a date when I had the results."

He pressed the spiky hair back from her eyes. "I'd like that, but we don't have to do it this second."

"No," she shook her head. "I've put it off long enough. You mentioned once that you thought we should just do it. I agree." She nodded decisively. "Tomorrow after you get off work. We can go do it then." She felt lightheaded for a moment, the terror of following through with her commitment taking over. She took a deep breath and felt the fear slide out again as she looked at him, at how happy he was.

"Don't you want a dress and stuff? You said you needed time to plan things."

She loved Carl, wanted to be with him always, so nothing would hold her back from making it all official. "What do I need if you're with me?"

A smile curved his lips and he pulled her in for a kiss.

Tia looked at the results online and felt nothing so much as relief, followed by a pang of sympathy for Claire, who had to be upset if she'd checked already. The woman had been so excited about the possibility of belonging to a different family.

Though she knew she ought to call Claire to make sure she'd seen the results, first Tia sent text messages to Wes, Ron and Danny to let them know. When the text had gone out and she'd heard back from them all, she picked up her phone and dialed.

It took a moment for the call to be answered, but when Claire came on the line, it was clear she knew it was Tia. "Hey, you must have checked the site."

Tia tried to decide what she heard in Claire's voice. "Yes. A few minutes ago. I guess you did too."

"Yes, it's been over an hour. I meant to call, but I was running late for work and I guess I wanted to take a moment to digest it all."

"I'm sorry. I know you wanted it to be true."

"Don't worry about it. Carl and I set a date. Actually, we're getting married this weekend. We just picked up a marriage license a few minutes ago; he's going to make arrangements and we'll just do it. I'm excited."

Surprised by the sudden decision, Tia tried not to sound like it. "Wow, are you inviting anyone?"

"No, but he's really all I need. I love him so much."

"I'm glad." And Tia meant it. Though she and Claire were incredibly different in so many ways, she wished the woman well, and hoped Claire found the happiness with Carl that her own family seemed to have denied her.

They ended the call with promises to keep in touch, but Tia wasn't sure if they really would. Only time would tell, she supposed. She turned her mind to Lisa and the fact that Tia would probably have to track the woman down in person if she wasn't going to answer the letter.

Thirty-six

Lisa ran the duster around a display of ceramic dogs at her store and wondered what she should do about dinner. The bell over the door rang and she turned with a smile toward the customer. A redhead entered, looking a little tentative. Business had been slow that day, and Lisa was determined to do something about it. "Hello, and welcome to Any Occasion. Is there anything special you're looking for today?"

The customer smiled tentatively, studied Lisa for a moment, and the smile turned more genuine, even a bit approving. "Actually, I'm looking for Lisa Lowell. You must be her."

"I am." Lisa extended a hand, and the woman took it. "What can I do for you?"

"My name is Tia Riverton. I sent you a letter a couple of weeks back."

Lisa dropped the grip a tad faster than was polite, but she had thought about the letter several times. It was complete nonsense, of course. She forced a little coolness into her voice. "Yes. I received your letter. I thought it must have been a mistake. You did mention there were other letters going out."

"*One* other letter," Tia clarified. "Claire contacted me the day she received hers. We've already checked paternity, and it wasn't her."

Lisa's stomach quivered, but she managed to keep her voice even. "Sorry to burst your bubble, but it isn't me, either."

212

"You were born at St. Mark's?" Tia followed with a date. Lisa's birth date.

"Yes, but I suppose you could have gotten that from anywhere."

"It took quite a bit of research, actually." Tia pulled out her driver license and presented it to Lisa. "We have the same birth date—so you know I'm not some crazy stalker."

Lisa checked the ID. Assuming it wasn't forged, and since nothing appeared to be off about it, at least there was a tiny grain of truth to the story. They *were* born the same day. "Sorry if I don't consider that proof."

"Then how about this instead?" Tia fumbled with the bag she wore over her shoulder and pulled out a 4x6 photo album.

As Tia flipped through it, Lisa noticed many of the pictures were undersized and had more than one per dustcover. She started to feel the grinding that always came to her stomach when her ulcer acted up. The stress of worrying about the letter, plus the slump in sales that always put her in a financial bind in the first part of the year were combining to make her sick.

Tia stopped at a page and turned the album so Lisa could see it better. "This is my mother, Mona, holding me when I was a few months old. She would have been a little younger than we are now."

The picture sent a shock through Lisa's system. The face was so much like her own that the resemblance couldn't be mistaken. She turned away, found a chair, and slumped into it. Her heart pounded and she heard the blood rushing in her ears. Feeling a little lightheaded, she leaned forward, putting her head between her knees so she wouldn't pass out. "It can't be true. It's a fake. You had it altered to look like me."

A pair of white sneakers appeared in Lisa's view and Tia touched her shoulder.

"Sorry, I didn't mean to shock you so much. I was hoping it would be you, just so the search would be over, but until I actually saw you up close, I didn't think it was possible."

"It's not possible. It can't be." Lisa's head began to clear and she tried sitting up again. Her vision swam a moment before coming to a stop and she touched her forehead. "You've got to be crazy."

Tia grabbed another chair and pulled it over. "I'm sorry. Maybe I was a little hasty in how I told you. This is so weird. I mean, I thought it was the other woman until a couple days ago. Or rather, she thought she was the one. She was so excited, and when she found out it wasn't her, I think she was really hurt." She shook her head. "I needed a few days to deal with everything when I found out too. It's crazy, after looking for all these months, I almost didn't believe that I'd ever find the truth."

Lisa held up a hand, hoping to quell the woman's nervous chatter. She couldn't think with all that talking, and right now, thinking was absolutely necessary. "Wait. Please."

"Sorry," Tia apologized again. "I'm not normally like this."

After a long moment of silence, and feeling a lot better, Lisa rose and walked to the counter where she had a picture of her mother. At least, she'd always believed Rose had been her mother. Now she didn't know what to think.

Rose had been a redhead too, before she'd gone gray. And though the resemblance between Rose and Tia wasn't nearly as strong as between Lisa and Mona, it was there. Lisa remembered the few pictures she'd had of her dad. It had been so many years since he'd died, there weren't many. Tia favored him.

The thought had Lisa groping for a chair again.

Another customer walked in and Lisa looked at Tia desperately. Tia popped up and greeted the buxom woman with the two children in tow. "Hello, and welcome to Any Occasion. Is there something special you're looking for today?"

"No, I'll just have a look around," the woman said.

Tia appeared relieved. Lisa was grateful she had taken the initiative, if only because it provided an extra few minutes to get her bearings.

The customer browsed, let her children run wild, and left without buying anything. By the time the store emptied again, Lisa felt more in control.

Tia turned back to her after having spent the previous ten minutes distracting the customer's children from anything breakable. "Caught your breath yet?" she asked.

"Maybe." Lisa sucked in a breath, then took charge of the conversation. "You need to realize I'm not happy about this, and I'm still not sure I believe it. I have a family of my own."

"I knew it was possible this wouldn't be welcome," Tia said. "While I was looking for you, I spent a lot of time considering whether I should bother you. When it came right down to it, I decided that despite the fact that I love the parents who raised me, I would want to know if our circumstances were reversed and you'd found out first. It doesn't make your family any less important to your history, or your future, it just opens a few possibilities."

Lisa moved behind the counter and pulled out her secret stash of chocolate truffles, taking one for herself, and offering one to Tia, who took it with alacrity. "My dad died when I was still really young."

Tia nodded. "I read that he'd passed away. I couldn't find his obituary, but there was a mention about it online. I wasn't sure when it happened."

"My mom's in a home. She has a genetic disease. Huntington's disease. You've probably heard of it. The symptoms started when she was forty-two, forty-three, but we didn't realize what it was at the time. Her father was probably the carrier; he died young, in Vietnam. Mom's been in a nursing home for a few years now. I couldn't take care of her anymore." The cost of the nursing home was mostly covered by Medicare, but there were a lot of expenses still falling on Lisa's shoulders. She felt tears prickling her eyes as she handed the photo to Tia.

Tia took it, studying the picture. "She's pretty. What does the disease do?"

215

"It depends on the person. With Mom it caused paranoia, hallucinations, moodiness. Facial ticks, her movements are jerky sometimes. Her dementia and confusion seem to be getting worse lately." Lisa explained. "The doctors believe she has several years left, and some days are better than others." She lifted her eyes to Tia's which were full of worry.

Lisa took back the photograph, studied it. "We didn't know about it until after dad had been gone for years. I have no idea if I might develop it someday." She stopped herself, realizing that if what Tia said was true, then there was no chance Lisa had the disease. It would be Tia's problem. She almost felt bad for the relief that poured through her. Seeing her mother suffer had been so difficult, but knowing it could happen to herself was one more thing she had to worry about. But not anymore.

"I haven't had the money to be tested, to see if I have enough copies to be affected. It's not covered by insurance—especially not what I can afford, but there's only a fifty-percent chance that you'll be a carrier, and even if you are, there's a slight chance that it might not present itself, though the symptoms tend to get worse with each generation, not better."

Tia covered her mouth with her hand and nodded. After a moment her hand slid down to her neck, her face was pale. "I have two daughters. They're everything to me."

"Do you have a husband?" Now she'd had time to regroup, she was curious about Tia.

"He was in the military and died in action. Before my youngest was born." A smile teased her mouth, though worry and sadness clouded her eyes. "I've been seeing a great man, however. Maybe. Someday."

"He must be special." Lisa grabbed the two chairs and ushered Tia back behind the counter as some more women entered the store.

Tia stayed the rest of the day, and they chatted about their families and lives. Lisa felt an incredible bond with Tia right off the bat, though she was more than a little nervous about the thought of actually meeting the parents and brother they would now share—if Lisa was interested.

And that was the crux, wasn't it? Was she actually interested? She didn't know.

After she locked up for the night, Lisa suggested they grab dinner down the street, and the two of them continued to talk through their meal.

When Tia insisted it was time she head home—she did have a three-hour drive still ahead of her—Lisa thought once she adjusted to the idea, she might be able to live with this new paradigm. Before she considered meeting Tia's family, however, Lisa decided she needed to discuss it with her mother.

Thirty-seven

It was nearly ten when Tia opened her front door. She felt wrung out from her meeting with Lisa, from the worry and tears that had plagued her all the way home. She'd tried to wipe away the smeared makeup before stepping inside and hoped the redness of her eyes didn't show as much as she thought. However, when Danny's bright smile melted into a look of concern, she knew she would have to explain.

"What happened? You said the meeting went well." Danny flipped off the TV with the remote in his hand, then set it down before crossing the room to her. He drew her into his arms, tipped her head back and studied her face.

"It did. Lisa's great. She's confused, upset, worried. Of course. But she's genuinely nice and I think she'll take the tests, want to meet everyone." Her stomach churned as she tried to put on a neutral expression.

He wasn't fooled. "So what's wrong—and don't tell me you're fine. Obviously, you're not."

A tear escaped and Tia buried her face in his chest. His arms tightened around her as she tried to force back the emotions pouring into her.

He waited for a couple of minutes, his patience infinitely longer than hers would have been, before he asked again. "What's wrong, Tia? Please tell me."

She felt her breath catch as she sucked in some air. "I'm sure Lisa's the one. She even looks like my parents, and I look like her

218

mom." Her voice cracked. "Her mom has Huntington Disease. I could have Huntington Disease. So could my babies. My girls, Danny, what'll I do if my girls get sick?" The fact that she was unlikely to live long enough to see them get sick was beside the point. She could barely speak as she fought for control. Hadn't she gotten all the tears and hysterics over with when she'd pulled to the side of the road two hours earlier?

"Hey, settle down. Shhhh." Danny made more soothing noises, but didn't tell her she was over-reacting, didn't give her false words about how it would be okay. He led her to the sofa, sat her down, got her tissues and a drink of water, then held and comforted her until she was ready to talk again.

"I've heard of Huntington's disease," he said when she was calm again. "But don't know much about it. What do you know?"

"She has dementia, paranoia, and is losing control of her body. The thought of being like that in another twenty years." She caught her breath, and centered herself. After a few seconds, she felt more in control again. "It scares me, Danny. I don't want to end up like that, especially not before I'm even fifty." *Too young. Too young.* The words kept reverberating through her mind. She was too young to be worrying about this.

"Are there tests you can have a doctor run?" Danny finally asked.

"Yes, but I don't know if I'll ever be able to afford one. Maybe if I got a job with insurance." Health insurance was a luxury she couldn't afford for herself, though she made sure the girls had some basic coverage.

"Let's not worry about the cost right now." He turned her to face him, kissed the wetness on her cheeks, then brushed his lips over hers. "Let's focus on the other stuff for a minute—the good stuff. You found Lisa. You think she's the one?"

"Yes." Tia pushed back the fear roaring through her and tried to focus on Danny's words. "She looks so much like my mom. Even some like my dad. And the picture of her mother . . . there's definitely a resemblance to me." Her voice hitched, but she pushed on. "We got along great, and I think she's nearly as confused and messed up about all of this as I am, but she's coping quickly. Or at least she looked like she was coping, but who knows? She said she'd think about the DNA tests. I wanted to give her a few days to come to grips with everything." She went on to talk about their afternoon together and things they'd discussed over dinner.

"Feel better?" He handed her another tissue so she could dab at the single tear on her right cheek.

"Yes, actually." Tia leaned her face against his shoulder, loved the warmth and the way he tightened his arm around her, pulling her closer. She would put the worry away for now, like he said. Tomorrow she could deal with it better. Hopefully it wouldn't haunt her dreams.

"I wish you would have let me go with you."

"I know, but it was a long day, and I appreciate you staying with the girls. I feel like I take advantage of Nichole sometimes. You've both been so good to me."

"I'm happy to help." His smile warmed and filled her chest.

"And how did the girls do?"

"Beautifully, of course." He tipped his head as if reconsidering his words. "Well, except for the incident in the kitchen. And the one in the bathroom. And I won't talk about what happened when I took them to the station for a while this afternoon."

Worried, Tia stared at Danny, but saw from his expression that he was teasing her. "No major wounds, no choking or need for CPR?" she asked.

"Nope. Totally good there. Nobody needed stitches or anything."

She allowed herself to smile. "Then I guess you handled everything fine." Feeling infinitely better than she had when she'd walked in, she lifted her face for a kiss. There would be time to worry about Rose's condition later. And she knew she would do a thorough job of worrying when Danny wasn't there to distract her, so she might as well take advantage of his presence for a while.

"How are you doing, darling?" Rose Lowell asked when Lisa stopped in to the nursing home to visit the next afternoon.

"Fine, Mom." She leaned over and kissed her mother's cheek. "How are you today? Been arm wrestling the guy who always takes your chair in the common room?"

Rose chuckled. "Only when I have to. I think he's sweet on me." She smiled and preened a little.

"I'm sure he is." Lisa sat in the straight-backed plastic chair the nursing home provided in each shared room. Her mother sat in the overstuffed lounger, a remote control in one hand and a mass-market romance in the other. She had read the book at least three times in the past few months—that Lisa knew of—but her dementia meant she didn't always remember.

"How are things going at that shop of yours? I know money gets tight this time of year," Rose said.

"Yes, it has been a little slow, but I saved carefully last year. I'll make it through, as fine as ever." Lisa wasn't actually sure it was true, but she would never admit it to her mom. If she ended up having to fold, Lisa would lie through her smile and say she got sick of running her own business. Thought she'd take a shot at working for a paycheck for a change. She knew Rose worried about her, and that stress complicated her own troubles. No need for Rose to have more to worry about.

"And have you met yourself a nice young man, then?"

Lisa squeezed her mother's hand. "I keep fighting them off with a stick. There's no extra time in my day for men." Her lack of free time was only too true. The plentiful attention from men was not.

This kind of back and forth banter continued for ten minutes or so as each dug for information on the other while trying to keep as much as possible about themselves secret. Lisa knew Rose had been struggling, and out of reality more than in the moment—Lisa had asked the nurse before she came in—so while she pretended to believe that all had been well with her mom, she studied Rose for any indication that things weren't what they seemed, and resolved to stop in more often. It wasn't as if she had a social life worth mentioning. The date with Chris a few weeks earlier had been a disaster she had no intention of repeating any time soon.

Finally, Lisa decided she ought to bring up the subject that had brought her in the first place. She could see Rose was starting to tire. "Mom, can you tell me about the day I was born?"

Rose looked surprised for a moment, then leaned forward in her chair and began. "It was a dark and stormy night." She had a twinkle in her eye. "Your father and I drove to the hospital, looking for a place to stay, the thunder roared, the lightning struck, and the headlights bounced on the wet pavement."

"Mom!" Lisa had heard the dramatized version of the story more than once, and knew it was actually a snowstorm, so there had been no lightning. This time she'd rather get it straight—if her mom was as coherent as she seemed to be. "The hospital. What can you tell me about when I was born? I popped out and then what?" As a woman who had never had a child, she preferred not to think about the vagaries of childbirth too closely. She'd heard many horror stories from women she knew. "Was I ever in the nursery instead of with you?"

"Fine, you're no fun today." Rose rested back in her chair again, a little put out. "They took you for blood tests and all of that, then to the nursery for a while. I am allergic to their usual anesthetic, so I was drugged pretty heavily from the C-section and wasn't ready to take care of you. Sometime before breakfast, they brought you back to me and you stayed with me for the rest of the time. Why?"

"Tell me what you remember," *and I'll hope I can believe what you say,* "and I'll explain." Tension gripped her shoulders and churned in her gut as her ulcer acted up. Would she learn something to corroborate Tia's theory?

"I slept some, but your father was in and out a lot, so I don't think they took you away again for more than a few minutes for diaper changes and such." Rose took her hand and gave it a squeeze, joy on her face. "You were such a beautiful baby."

Lisa had seen the pictures, but there weren't any taken at the moment after birth, as you so often saw. She wondered if she would have realized there was something wrong if there had been a picture of Tia. Probably not. Most babies look so much alike, and it wasn't as though she would have been searching for differences.

"Why do you ask?" Rose questioned after a moment of silence had passed between them.

"I had a visitor yesterday." Lisa wondered how to lead up to this. She'd been considering it ever since she'd said goodbye to Tia, but nothing made sense. "Her name is Tia Riverton."

Rose clasped her hands in front of her. "Wait, I know that name. You mean the woman who does the cooking segment on the noon news?"

"Yes. The same one." Lisa smiled. "She came into my shop yesterday."

"Did she buy much? Those celebrities always have so much money!"

Lisa doubted that was the case this time. "No, not much, though she picked up something for her daughter. Anyway, it turns out she and I were both born in St. Mark's on the same day."

"Really?" Rose was fascinated. "That's got to be some coincidence, you running into her out here."

She held her mom's gaze and shook her head. "It wasn't a coincidence."

"No? Why did she come?"

After a moment's consideration, Lisa decided to approach the subject at an oblique angle. "Have you ever noticed that she has that beautiful red hair, not quite your shade, but curly like yours?"

"It reminds me of when I was her age. Actually, she kind of looks like me, don't you think?" Rose asked smugly. She patted her gray curls, which still showed a few streaks of red. "I've often thought I looked a lot like that when I was her age. So young and pretty. Do you like my new hairdo? Vera permed it for me when she was in yesterday."

"Yes, I love the hair." Since it was Sunday, and Vera came on Mondays, Lisa knew her mother was confused. "Tia *is* pretty. And she does look like you." Lisa bit her lip, then plowed on. "But I think she looks more like Dad. Don't you agree?" She handed her mom a picture of Tia printed from the television station's website.

Rose didn't take it, didn't even look at it. Her tone cooled. "What are you saying?"

This was it. Lisa wet her lips in preparation to speak. "Tia sent me a letter a few weeks back. She said she had recently learned there was a baby switch at the hospital on the day we were born and she thought I might be the person switched with her. I didn't respond to the note—it was ridiculous, right? But she checked out the other woman, had a DNA test done and it wasn't her."

"You're my daughter." Rose's voice was strong and a little upset.

Lisa tried to placate, wondering if she had made a mistake in telling the truth. Would it make her mother's condition worse? "Yes, I am. I'm your daughter. But though I haven't had a DNA test yet, it looks like she might also be your daughter, only biologically instead."

"Why are you telling me this lie?" Rose's face grew red. "It's not true. You're my daughter. Don't you think I'd recognize my own baby?"

Lisa wondered if the response had been programmed into that generation. Tia had mentioned Mona said something similar when the news came out. "Look at this picture. And she showed me one of her mom, her name is Mona. She looked almost exactly like me at my age."

Rose slapped the picture out of Lisa's hand. "You don't want to be my daughter anymore? Is that it? Can't stand to have me as your mom?"

"No. You'll always be my mom, always and always. I love you." Tears overflowed Lisa's eyes and she had to bite back a sob. "I'm sorry I upset you. I don't have to meet them. Maybe she's wrong anyway, it's just ridiculous." She would have said anything to get her mom to calm down. These fits of temper always worsened Rose's condition, and the last thing Lisa wanted to do was make things worse.

"You don't love me anymore," Rose sniffed and wiped a tear.

"I do love you. I'm sorry, Mom. I'm sorry." Lisa bent over her lap, crying.

There was a long moment of silence before she felt her mother's hand on her shoulder. "You're a good girl. I'm sorry, honey. You know this is nonsense. We won't speak about it anymore."

Lisa cried for a moment longer as she tried to calm herself. It had all been so much—too much all at once. What had she been thinking bringing it up with her mother? She'd known what it would do. It would have been better if she'd introduced Tia as a friend, let them meet, but never told Rose the truth. Now it was too late.

Thirty-eight

Tia was home checking out dinner. Danny had agreed to meet her and the girls at her place this time, and he'd brought some pasta dish he'd invented. It looked interesting, she supposed, as she gave it another stir in the casserole pan. Tomato sauce, pasta, meat and olives had to be good, right?

Her phone rang and after Lisa introduced herself, she blurted out, "I spoke to my mom this afternoon."

"What did you tell her?" Tia's hand paused on the spoon, her breath catching.

"She's so upset. I shouldn't have told her." She filled Tia in on the details, or at least enough to get the picture.

Though it stung a little, Tia pushed it away for the moment. This wasn't about her. "My mom is still in denial about everything, so don't hold it against yours," Tia soothed. "Maybe she'll come around when she's had some time to adjust."

"She knew your name as soon as I mentioned it. Apparently she watches your show all the time."

"Yeah?" Tia felt a smile slide onto her face. Mona had caught the show a few times. She mentioned it to friends and acquaintances mostly as a claim to fame, but she wasn't interesting in the cooking segment itself. It felt kind of good knowing the woman who had most likely given birth to her enjoyed her segment. Tia wondered though, if Rose would refuse to watch it again, after the way she had reacted to the mere possibility that they were related.

226

"So how are you holding up?" she asked Lisa. "Have you thought more about the DNA test?"

"Yes. I'm still not sure that I want to meet your family, but I'd like to do the test, to be sure before I make any other decisions."

"That's a good idea. I'll have your part of the kit sent to you." Tia looked down when Tristi tugged on her pant leg.

"Hungry. Want eat."

Tia covered the microphone on the cell. "Good idea. How about you go get Danny and your sister?" She could hear Samantha's giggles along with the deeper rumble of Danny's laugh coming from the living room. From the sound of it, Samantha thought she was getting away with giving him monster tickles.

"I appreciate it," Lisa said from the other end of the line. "I'll keep in touch. I'll let you go now, I'm sure you're getting ready to eat soon, if I didn't interrupt your meal."

"You didn't interrupt, and thanks for calling." Tia said goodbye and ended the call as Danny came in, letting Tristi tug him by the hand. Tia leaned back against the counter. The thought of Huntington's disease hadn't been far from her mind since Lisa had mentioned it the previous day, but it didn't make her want to burst into tears anymore. Even the research she'd done hadn't freaked her out when she'd looked for more about the disease that afternoon.

"Who was that?"

"Lisa. She agreed to be tested."

He took her hand. "Good. How are you holding up?"

"Better. The call didn't make it worse, anyway. I think we're headed in the right direction." That was true. She made a decision to keep the positive parts of this in the forefront of her mind.

"Great." Danny leaned in and brushed his lips across her cheek. "Let's eat; I'm starved."

"Hey, that's my line!" Samantha said as she climbed into her chair.

Tia smiled and brought the casserole a la Danny to the table.

The test kit arrived. Ron went through the swabbing process yet again, and returned the kit. Tia didn't tell her dad or Wes about the Huntington's disease. There would be time for that when she had more information. Tia kept in touch with Lisa, and knew she was also trying to wait for answers before jumping to conclusions or thinking too far ahead.

Work and school and recipe testing continued on as before. A picture arrived in the mail from Claire and Carl's wedding—Carl wearing black pants and a tan dress shirt with the tails untucked, Claire in a white cocktail dress holding an enormous hot pink gerbera daisy instead of a bouquet. They looked as incredibly happy as Claire's emails proclaimed that they were.

The wait for the DNA results was interminable. Tia worked diligently on her recipes, saw Danny as much as possible—which meant visiting him at work a few times in addition to their dates—and exchanged emails with Lisa nearly daily.

Still, her search for more information about whomever might have switched them was crawling, when it moved at all. Tia had begun researching the doctor and staff. Unfortunately, she hit dead ends at every turn. The hospital administrator still refused to help out, so Tia headed back to the library. She learned the local newspapers were on microfiche, which would be far easier to handle than the cumbersome archive books, and was much more convenient.

She took an hour or two each morning starting with files dated a year before her birth, and moving two years past her birth looking for any article referencing someone who worked at St. Marks, especially in OB.

Very little came up, and what did turned out to be more dead ends.

Finally, after checking the testing website for three days, the DNA results came through. Ron was Lisa's biological father.

Tia picked up the phone while she stared at the screen. Her hands trembled as she dialed Lisa. The call went to voice mail, making Tia want to growl. "Hey, it's Tia, the results are in. We weren't wrong. Call me." She hung up and stared at the screen for a long moment. How did she feel about the results? She wasn't sure. It wasn't as if it was a surprise she hadn't been born to her parents, or that she hadn't been convinced that Lisa was their biological daughter, but actually seeing the results on the screen was disorienting.

This was really true. Lisa should have been raised by Mona and Ron. Tia should have been the one whose father died when she was young, whose mother was ill with a genetic disease that might have been passed along not only to Tia, but to her daughters as well. The thought had her stomach clenching with anxiety. She'd done some research on Huntington's disease. It was definitely not something she looked forward to experiencing, and all too soon, if she had gotten the gene.

She supposed she ought to wait for similar results between herself and Lisa's mom, but didn't see the point. This was enough for her.

The question was where to go from here.

Thirty-nine

Lisa received Tia's message as soon as she finished her phone call with a customer. Before the message ended, she was typing the lab's web address into her browser. Yes, she should have figured Tia's word was good, but she still had to see for herself.

Tia was right.

Lisa sat for a long moment, trying to figure out what that meant. What came next? Then the bell rang over the door, she looked up, put on an automatic smile and took care of the customers.

Through the final hour of work, end-of-day tasks, and the return trip home, Lisa's mind kept returning to the test results.

Her mom was already upset about the mere suggestion that there was a mix-up in the hospital. How would Lisa explain the test? And did it really matter? Besides the obvious point that she would never suffer from Rose's genetic disorder, that she wouldn't have to worry about passing it along to any children she might someday have, how did this affect Lisa? Did she want to get to know Tia's family? The two women had shared a number of memories over email while they waited and Lisa thought she might want to meet them, at least. Even if only out of curiosity.

By the time she arrived home, she knew she had to tell Rose. That night. Whatever else happened, her mom deserved to know. Lisa didn't know how to bring it up again.

She entered her apartment, dropped her keys in the ceramic dish by the front door, hung her purse on the hook behind the door, and slid her coat over it. She pulled her cell phone from her pocket, then called Tia back.

The phone rang twice before Tia answered, "Hey, Lisa. Did you get my message?"

"Yeah, I went online and checked it out for myself." She opened the refrigerator door and looked for something dinnerish. Half a carton of eggs, the last cup of milk, some butter, mayo and ketchup glared back at her. "I'm not really sure how I feel about it now that I know."

"I understand. I stared at the results for way longer than I needed to, trying to make myself believe they were true when I was tested. Have you told your mom yet?"

Lisa shifted the mayo to the side and found a small chunk of semi-dried cheddar. It would do. "Not yet. I'll have to soon. I have no idea what to say. She got upset when I talked about it before and," she paused, sucked in a breath in an effort to keep herself steady. "I can't stand the thought of hurting her."

"I know. I still have to tell my mom that we did the DNA test. She's not going to be happy. I mean, I think she'll adjust. You're in retail, after all, and she sure does love to shop." There was a smile in her voice, a teasing edge to it.

"And my mom always loved cooking." Lisa shredded the cheese into a bowl. "She despaired that I'd ever learn to do anything more complicated than spaghetti or scrambled eggs." She hadn't gotten much past that, so her mom's fears had come true.

"Then maybe she'll accept it pretty well after all," Tia joked. There was a pause, then she continued, "Danny's coming over in a few minutes. I'm going to have him watch the girls for a while so I can visit Dad. He didn't want the password for the website. Said he'd rather have me tell him right out then go crazy checking it himself."

"Maybe I should have done that too." Lisa set aside the cheese and cracked two eggs into a bowl. She really should do some shopping tonight. Sandwiches were easy to fix, but she was out of bread and a little variety was good. But that was for after she talked to her mom. "Do you feel as lost and confused as I do?"

"Oh, yeah. Does it sound bad to say that I'm glad if someone has to go through this with me, that it's you? Not that I would have wished this mess on you, but . . . "

Lisa understood but didn't want to think about it. She redirected the conversation. "Didn't you say there was another woman you thought it might be?"

"Yes, and Claire was nice, very nice, but . . . okay, honesty here, she was so excited about the possibility that it might be her, that I was a bit overwhelmed and a lot intimidated. And it made me wonder what her family was really like if she was so anxious to find a different one."

"I wish my family had been bigger; sisters and brothers and plenty of cousins around. I miss my dad. He and I were so close." Lisa had to swallow back the pain that still rose when she thought of her father. His death had been devastating.

"You'll have to tell me all about him. Samantha!" Tia sighed. "Sorry, my girls are going wild. I guess I need to corral them. Let me know how it goes with your mom and we'll see how you feel about it all in another day or two."

"Thanks." Lisa said goodbye and slid the food from the pan and onto a plate. She had no idea how she was going to tell her mom.

"Hi, Mom," Lisa entered her mother's room at the nursing home. "How are you feeling today?"

"Sweetheart! I'm fine. What brings you by tonight?"

"You." Lisa took the chair beside the bed. "I haven't been by for a few days."

Rose studied Lisa over her bifocals. "Something's on your mind. You're fidgeting with your purse strap."

Lisa stopped herself and set the purse on the floor. "You're right, of course." She licked her lips, which felt suddenly dry, and wished she'd brought along a drink.

"Well, that's better. Do you like my hair, Vera permed it when she was in a couple days ago."

This was sounding more than a little familiar. Not a good sign. "You remember me telling you Tia Riverton came to talk to me?"

"Tia Riverton?" She tapped her lips with a fingertip. "Is that the woman from the news cooking show?" Rose's lips puckered in thought. "When did that happen?"

"A couple of weeks ago. She came into the store." Lisa wet her lips. Rose didn't remember. What did she say? Could she stand going through all of that again?

"How nice." Her mother beamed at her. "I hope she spent a lot. Those TV people make so much money."

"She picked up something for her daughter." Though she wished it were different, Lisa decided to keep the truth to herself. The emotional turmoil of going through the disclosure of their biological relationship again was more than she could face. Since there was no guarantee Rose would remember this time, either, it would be easier to keep it a secret—even if it did make her heart hurt. "She's really nice. Maybe I'll bring her by to meet you some time."

"Oh, I'd like that, dear. Now," she set a hand on Lisa's arm, "tell me, are you dating anyone special?"

Lisa forced herself to smile and sat back in her seat to chat.

Spreading the news was far easier for Tia. Ron accepted the results with no fuss. "All right, let me know if she wants to meet me. I *am* kind of curious about her."

Wes's response was similar, though he showed a little more interest in meeting Lisa than Ron had. The big issue was telling Mona.

"What do you mean you found her?" Mona asked when Tia announced that she'd located Lisa. "How do you know it's her?"

Tia shifted her hot cocoa from one hand to the other on the tabletop of the coffee shop where she'd met her mom. "She did a DNA test with dad. She's the one."

Hurt filled Mona's face. "You didn't tell me? You didn't have me take the test? Why not? Am I not good enough?"

Though Tia had expected this to be a difficult meeting, she had hoped she was wrong. "I know how stressful it was for you when you took the DNA test for me, Mom. Since only one of you needed to match to be sure, I didn't want to put you through that again. Dad's nerves always were a little less fragile than yours." This was mostly just soothing nonsense, of course. Mona could handle anything. She was just a lot more difficult to deal with when upset.

"That's true. I am fragile." She dabbed a finger at each eye, as if catching imaginary tears before they could fall and ruin her makeup. "Though I wish you had told me about the tests, I suppose it was for the best. But tell me about this Lisa."

There was only so much Tia could say, largely because she didn't want to tell tales about Lisa without her permission. She filled in some of the basic details and discussed her impressions from their first meeting.

Mona listened attentively, then pulled out a paper from her purse. "Now, give me her phone number so I can call her. I have a million questions to ask and you don't seem to have any of the good answers. If she's my other daughter, then I need to get to know her."

Despite the demands, Tia refused to pass on Lisa's contact information. She wasn't going to let her mother push Lisa into meeting or talking if she wasn't ready. She promised to have Lisa contact Mona when she was ready.

A few days passed and Tia wished Lisa would contact her to let her know how things had gone with Rose.

Forty

The call to the home where a woman had been beaten made Danny nervous, as such calls often did. The police arrived on scene and went in first to verify that the home was safe, then the firefighters and paramedics went in with their equipment. Some of the guys grumbled that they had to wait to see the patient, especially since it sounded as if the injuries were serious, but Danny had no intention of flouting protocol. They couldn't help the patient if they had to fight off an attacker.

They found a woman in her forties with spiky apple-red hair, and multiple cuts and bruises on her face. Her eye was already swelling shut and she hugged her right arm to her, which had a disfigurement in the lower half, indicating a break. "Hey, my name is Danny, can you tell me where you hurt the worst?" he asked as he knelt by the woman's side.

"My arm, my stomach." She didn't mention her face, so the abdominal pain must have been severe.

Danny did a quick head-to-toe assessment, finding a flail chest indicating broken ribs on the right side, abdominal pain, though there was no swelling there yet, and bruises all along the woman's back and shoulders in addition to the things he saw when he first walked in. James started an IV while Danny did the assessment and one of the other guys took the woman's blood pressure on her lower leg, since they couldn't do anything with the broken arm. A fourth guy prepared splinting equipment and they got ready to load her on the gurney.

When Danny heard the back door open behind him, he turned away from the patient to see who it was. A tall, bald guy in his thirties, covered in tattoos and with a mean smile, grabbed Danny's shoulder and twisted him back. "What do you think you're doing? Get away from her." Then he pulled back his other arm and popped Danny in the face with his fist.

The patient screamed, one of the firefighters called out a warning a little too late, and pain blossomed on Danny's cheek.

The impact was like running into a brick wall and Danny saw his vision go dark for a moment before the light started to creep back. He felt the hand on his shoulder move away as some of the guys grabbed the attacker and pulled him off. There was noise and commotion, but when Danny's vision returned, he saw one officer sitting on the attacker and cuffing him, reciting the Miranda rights.

"You okay?" James asked from the other side of the patient. "You've got a gash."

Danny gingerly touched his cheek and his fingers came back wet with blood. He didn't think he'd pass out, so he brushed James' worry off. "I'll live. Let's get out to the rig."

In three minutes they had the patient loaded and headed for the ambulance. As Danny climbed into the back with the patient, he thought if Tia had been looking for an excuse to worry about him getting hurt on the job, this should do it for her. He'd been lucky the guy hadn't used a knife instead of his fist.

That was not a pleasant thought.

When they arrived at the hospital, the duty nurse took one look at Danny, grabbed his arm and led him to another exam room. "What happened to you?"

"I'm fine. I just ran into a guy's fist." Danny tried to smile her concern away, but it hurt the cut on his cheek.

"I figured that out. What were you doing fighting?"

"I wasn't fighting. I got sucker punched." He winced as the nurse used an alcohol wipe to dab at his cheek. It stung white hot. "Really,

I can clean that up back at the station."

"You could, but you won't. The guy must have been wearing a ring; you've got a cut on your cheek. It's going to need stitches."

"James mentioned it, but it didn't bleed much, so I didn't worry about it." He could feel the cheek swelling and his face still throbbed.

"Numbness is your friend right now." She grabbed a pen light and checked his eyes. "Concussion, if I'm not mistaken."

"Can't be. I'm fine." But now the adrenaline from the call was wearing off, he felt a tad woozy.

"You're not fine, Mr. Macho." She pursed her lips and shook her head. "Why is it the paramedics think they're invincible?"

Danny sighed. No way would the captain let him go back to work today.

When Stu stuck his head into the room and got the update from the nurse, he confirmed Danny's fears. "Take the rest of the shift off. James already called your girlfriend to pick you up."

Danny eyed the doctor as he entered, picked up the syringe with lidocaine in it to numb his cheek. "Great. Perfect. I love freaking her out." He closed his eyes as the doctor drew closer with the needle. It was one thing to put an IV in someone else's vein; it was something else entirely to have someone sticking one in your cheek. Still, he gritted his teeth and put up with the quick sting. It was nothing compared to what he would endure if Tia couldn't handle his injury.

Tia grimaced as she pulled to a stop in the hospital parking lot. James hadn't given her many details, just that Danny was going to be okay, but he was attacked on a call and was being treated. The thought that he could have been shot, could be dead or seriously injured had made her heart clench. She'd called Nichole to sit with the girls, who were already in bed.

She crossed the parking lot in long strides, anxious to see Danny for herself, to know he was all right. She couldn't imagine what her life would be like without him, how she would have coped these past months without his support and listening ear. This had been a revelation, though she'd been telling herself that the love she'd felt creeping closer wasn't that strong, that she could still back away.

Now she knew she couldn't.

The ER was busy, but the doctor Tia and Danny had spoken with months earlier stood at the counter.

"Hi," Tia came to a stop a few feet from the doctor. "I'm here to pick up Danny Tullis."

"Oh, yes. I remember you. Danny's in room four." She gestured down the hall. "Go on down. He should be ready to leave soon."

"Thanks." Tia turned, sucked in a breath to steel herself for anything and strode into the room.

Danny lay on the bed, a bruise growing on his cheek, a set of stitches taped up across the cheekbone. His eyes were closed, his face a bit paler than usual—or was that her imagination? She wasn't sure. Her fingers trembling, she reached out and slid her hand into his upturned palm.

His eyes flashed open and a smile spread across his face.

"Hey, there," she said, reassured by his smile. "James called me. He didn't tell me you'd have a shiner. Any other injuries?" She fought to keep her voice light and teasing, pushing back the worries that rose inside her when she thought of him getting hurt at work.

"Just my pride. The guy sucker punched me." He sounded far more put out that he hadn't seen it coming than over the fact that he was hurt.

She reached out, ran her thumb along his jaw, then leaned down and pressed a feather-light kiss to his bruise. "I'm told kissing things make them better."

"In that case, I hurt right here." He tapped his lips.

She smiled, bussed her mouth over his, and pulled back to look at him again, playing with his hair with her free hand.

"I actually hoped for a little more than that." He gave her an exaggerated look of disappointment.

"Well, if they hurt, I didn't want to make them worse."

"Your kiss helped; I think another one would make a big difference."

She laughed, loving this man more every minute. "You're such a guy."

"Guilty as charged." He took her hand from his hair and pressed a kiss to her palm.

Tingles spread up her spine and her heart flopped over. "How long until they cut you loose?"

"Should be soon."

A woman in green scrubs walked in. "Soon means now. If I can get a signature here," she handed a clipboard to Danny.

He took it, signed. "I didn't check myself into the ER, you know. Someone dragged me into here and whipped me into submission. I think I deserve a discount."

"Don't worry; the department is picking it up." She waved her free hand. "Wounded in the line of duty and all that."

He brightened. "Do I get paid disability?"

The woman laughed. "Dream on. Unless your concussion is *much* worse than we expect, you'll be good to go by the time your next shift starts. More or less."

"More or less?" Tia asked, concerned.

The nurse turned to Tia. "There are sometimes residual problems from concussion that last for months, but his isn't bad, so they would be mild and short-lived. Don't worry about it." She glanced back at Danny, though she continued to speak to Tia. "You can take Prince Charming home, now. He shouldn't be alone tonight. Someone needs to check on him every couple of hours."

That was problematic since Tia needed to get home to the girls. "Thanks, I'll see to it." *Somehow.*

Danny grabbed his jacket, which was slung over a chair in the corner. "Now there's an idea I can get behind."

"Me waking you up every two hours?"

"Me waking to your beautiful face." Now he was upright he took her shoulder and slid in for a real kiss hello, causing her to lean against him, just grateful he was okay. "Too bad we'll have to make alternate arrangements," he told her when he moved away.

"Yeah." They exited the hospital and climbed into her car.

"What do you want to do about your car?" she asked as she pulled onto the road. "It's still at work, right?"

"Yeah, but it'll keep overnight. I'll get someone to pick me up and take me back to the station tomorrow. Maybe after you get off work?"

Tia smiled. She'd like that. It seemed their lives were becoming ever-more intertwined. She wondered for a moment what it would be like to marry Danny, to make a family together, and she was comforted to find she could see it.

She took him to his apartment, fussed over him, made sure he had what he needed, lingered over several kisses, then promised to call every couple of hours to check on him.

Forty-one

It had been so long since Tia had visited Dr. Losee that she'd lost hope of hearing back, so her call was a surprise.

"Hi, this is Dr. Angela Losee." The doctor greeted after verifying with whom she spoke. "I've been thinking about what you said when you visited me and I just found the scrapbook I told you about. I thought you might like to see it."

Tia gave the cake batter bowl one last scrape and banged the spoon on the side of the cake pan. "Yes, I'd love to come by. When would be convenient?"

When she hung up a few minutes later, Tia called Nichole and made arrangements for the girls Wednesday evening. Maybe this was another dead end, but there must be something in that scrapbook, or the doctor wouldn't have bothered to call. She told herself this was true, hoped it was. She didn't think she could handle another dead end.

Dr. Losee lived in a three-story home over the border into Kansas. It didn't take long to find the home: brick, Victorian, though in this part of town, Tia doubted it was anywhere near a hundred year old, never mind from the 1800s. It had stained glass windows over the doors and half circles of stained-glass over the windows. A warm glow diffused through the colored curtains making the windows shine like jewels in the darkness. It was still too early for crocuses, but Tia imagined the bright buds would show soon in the flower beds.

The doctor opened the door seconds after Tia rang the bell, as if she'd been standing nearby, anxious. Her friendly smile reassured. "Hello, Tia. Come on in. Would you care for anything to drink?"

"No, thank you." Tia took the offered seat on the sofa and folded her hands on her lap so they wouldn't shake and she wouldn't fidget. "Thank you for calling. I had given up on hearing from you."

"I knew I had this scrapbook sitting around somewhere. It took a while to unearth. I've been busy." Dr. Losee sat beside her.

"I'm sure you have. I appreciate you keeping me in mind and working me into your schedule." *Get on with it, lady.* Tia didn't want to appear too anxious, to rush her hostess, especially when Dr. Losee was doing a favor, but she wanted the details so she could move on with anything that looked promising.

As if she read Tia's mind, Dr. Losee reached for a vinyl binder. "This is from my daughter's birth."

She began flipping past pictures of her growing belly. Then they came to a page of baby shower photos. "The girls at work threw a bash for me at the hospital. It was a total surprise when they caught me in the staff room after my shift." She began pointing to the women in the photos, giving their names, which were listed to the side and the department where they worked. "Lois Millward worked in OB for a few months. I think she had moved on to another department by the time you were born, but you could check. And Glena Parry only worked there part time; she filled in when there were holes in the schedule. I think she had another job somewhere else."

"Wait, Glena Parry?" Tia looked more closely at the picture and smiled when she saw the snapshot of the young woman. "She's my grandmother. I didn't know she worked at the hospital. She spent so many years at the nursing home. She only retired a few years ago. And she's enjoying her free time."

"That's nice. I liked your grandmother a lot. She had a tough time, what with her husband's death when she was still so young, and being a single mother."

Tia nodded. She understood what that was like, though she was much younger than her grandmother had been, and was starting to think maybe she was done being really alone. Perhaps, in the not-so-distant future, she might have someone coming home to her at the end of a work shift. The thought made her smile.

Dr. Losee moved on to the next woman on the page, and Tia scribbled down names as they went. They flipped through the rest of the book and she managed to add one or two more people she could look into.

"I appreciate you taking the time to speak with me," Tia said as she stood fifteen minutes after she arrived.

"You're welcome. I hope you find your answers." Dr. Losee offered her hand.

"Thanks." Tia shook with the doctor and let herself out. Her mind whirled. The doctor had provided updates on name changes and moves if she knew them, but it was pitifully little to go on. Maybe, Tia thought, she should go to her grandma and see what she remembered.

Glena welcomed Tia with open arms when she showed up on the doorstep a while later.

"Hi, Grandma. How are you doing this evening?" Tia asked, giving her grandma a big squeeze.

"Just fine, child. Come on in. I wasn't expectin' you tonight."

Tia stepped into the warm, cozy room. "I know. I've been out taking care of errands and was headed home. Your place was on the way, more or less." Less mostly. "And I thought I'd pop by to see how you are."

"I'm doin' fine." Glena sat in her customary brown lounger. "These old bones aren't as spry as they used to be."

"Are you kidding?" Tia teased. "You could dance circles around me."

Glena's laugh was deep and throaty. "How are things goin' for you?'

"We're doing well." She took a deep breath. The last time she'd brought the subject up, Glena hadn't been happy, but she needed the information. "Actually, I spoke with a doctor a few minutes ago. She said you knew each other when you did temp work at the hospital, Dr. Losee."

Glena paused for a moment, considering, then nodded. "Really? I remember her. Sweet woman. She has a daughter about your age."

Though Tia was nervous and a little upset that her grandma had been keeping this all a secret when she might have helped find the answers sooner, there was no point agitating Glena, so she tread carefully. "So she said. We looked at a scrapbook of her pregnancy and birth, her daughter's first year or so."

"That's nice, but why'd you go see her?"

Nervous, but not willing to back down when she finally had something to go on, Tia pushed on. "I've been wondering who else worked at the hospital when I was born. Specifically in labor and delivery."

"Honey," she shook her head, disapproval on her face. "Haven't I told you it's a waste of time?"

Glena's insistence on that point bothered Tia. She wasn't able to keep the irritation out of her voice. "Yes, and I suppose that's why you never mentioned that you did temp work there." She twisted her fingers in her lap. "Why didn't you say something? You know how important this is to me."

Glena waved her hand dismissively. "I didn't work there very long. Just a few months, and not very often, neither. It was one of those passin' things. I needed a little extra money for somethin' and the hospital needed some help. I barely remember it." She adjusted herself in the chair and crossed her ankles. "Now, you tell me how everythin' else is goin'. I want to hear all about those little girls of yours, and that hunky man you brought by. When you gonna marry that boy, anyway?"

Tia seethed over the omission, but after a moment she managed to rein in her disappointment and anger at Glena's response. She was an old woman and completely set in her ways. If she didn't want to talk about it, there was nothing Tia could do about it.

Tia decided she wasn't going to get anything useful out of her grandmother and set it aside for now. She kicked off her shoes so she could fold one leg under her in her chair. Might as well settle in for a nice chat. She'd try again in a few weeks if the information she'd learned that day didn't lead anywhere.

Forty-two

Soft music floated around Tia and Danny as they ate their meal at the restaurant. When he pulled her onto the small dance floor, Tia smiled, her head resting on Danny's chest, loving the feel of being in his arms as the romantic music circled around them. Her hand flexed in his and she tucked it between them. "This was a very good idea," she said.

"I'm glad you approve. When we popped by your grandma's the other day, she badgered me about taking you dancing. I should have thought of it myself." The music changed and the beat picked up. He released her waist and lifted their clasped hands, spinning her out, then tugging her back.

Tia laughed and returned to his arms smoothly. "Why didn't I know you could dance?"

"It's nothing special. Don't ask me to waltz. Did I mention that you look beautiful tonight?"

"You did. Three times." Not that she was complaining—she'd never had a night when she felt so feminine, so appreciated. If she'd ever felt like this with Lee, she'd forgotten. She pushed that thought out of her mind. Comparing the two men unproductive and unnecessary. "Thank you."

"You're welcome." He whirled them around the edges of the dance floor and pulled her near again. "You know, I was worried that you'd break up with me after my little incident at work."

She supposed she'd given him reason to think that. She bolstered her courage, she'd been holding things back from him—

holding herself back, and the time for that was over. "James didn't tell me what happened, just that you were hurt. It scared me, but thinking you could have been seriously injured had the opposite effect."

"Oh?"

Her face grew hot, but she met his eyes, determined to tell him how she felt. He'd said it ages ago, and she had been putting off reciprocating. "I kept thinking that I could lose you. I couldn't stand the thought of it." She lifted her hand from his shoulder and touched his cheek. Keeping his gaze. "I love you, Danny. I can't imagine living without you."

Danny stopped in the middle of the dance floor. He tipped her head up, a finger on her chin, and kissed her, his lips soft on hers, lingering as they stood still while others circled around them. "I love you, too."

Tia felt her blush deepen as another couple whirled past. She couldn't talk, her throat was thick from emotion and her eyes were nearly brimming with tears.

"I had this whole thing planned, but I can't imagine anytime better than this." One hand dipped into his pocket as he took her waist with his other hand, and moved them back into rhythm with the other dancers.

"Oh?" Her chest seemed to fill with excitement, love, and happiness. It amazed her that it didn't simply explode.

She felt something slide onto the ring finger of her left hand. Her breath caught and she looked at it in amazement. A diamond winked back at her even in the low lights.

"Marry me, Tia?"

Her chest clenched, but she had to ask, because it was never far from her thoughts. "You know I could turn into a demented vegetable in twenty years. Doesn't that bother you?"

"Bother me, yes. Change things, not at all. I'll take what I can get. Your first marriage should've taught you that life's too short. We need to enjoy it while we can, and I intend to spend the rest of my life with you, no matter the outcome." His lips brushed along her ear, his voice low, throaty, sent chills down her spine.

She bit her lip, torn between melting at his sweet, sweet words, and wanting to bring up one more point. The last point won. It had been weighing heavy on her mind since she met Lisa. "I don't know if I want any more children. If I might pass on the disease to them, I mean. It's bad enough that the girls might already be doomed to it." Her breath hitched as he pulled back and looked her in the eye.

They continued swaying, but his face became still as he studied her. "I won't pretend I like that idea. I want more children—your children, Tia. But as soon as the ink is dry on the marriage certificate my insurance will pay for you to have that test done to see if you inherited the disease. If you want. No need to worry about it before then, don't you think?"

His words should have brought her comfort, but she saw the disappointment in his eyes. "So you won't mind?"

He paused, but when he began to speak, she could tell he meant it. "I love you. If we need to adopt, we will. If we only have Tristi and Samantha, that's the way it'll be. Regardless, I know I want to be with *you*. So will you marry me?"

There was no hesitation this time. She pulled him close. "Yes."

A smile broke over his face. "Good."

They sealed it with a kiss.

Forty-three

Tia tucked the phone in the crook of her neck and continued folding clothes. "So I was thinking, what if we all met each other's family at once? I've mentioned a few things about your mom to my dad, and I know he'd like to meet her."

"It might make things easier," Lisa conceded. "I'd want you there when I met your family anyway, and vice versa. I haven't told my mom about the switch again. It'll just upset her for a second time, and she may not remember later anyway."

Sympathy welled inside Tia. "It must be so hard for you, watching her."

"It is." Lisa paused. "I hope this doesn't sound insensitive."

"Go ahead." Tia stacked the last of Tristi's T-shirts on her pile of clothes and stood to carry the pile to the girls' room.

Another moment passed. "It's still hard seeing my mom like this, seeing the slow deterioration, but am I awful if I admit that it's easier now, knowing I'm not going to be in her place in thirty years? I mean, I feel like I'm saying that at your expense, like I'm pointing my finger and saying 'ha, ha, it's not my problem anymore,' but that's really not what I mean."

Tia felt the worry curl in her stomach. It was always there now, the fear and uncertainty. "I know it's not. You should be relieved, though I'm warning you that my grandma is always making comments about how insane my mother's family is, so hey, if that's inheritable, you could be in for a bit of dementia anyway." She kept her voice light, even as she had to beat back the fear that always attacked when she thought of Rose's disease.

249

"That was totally insensitive of me. I am sorry," Lisa said.

"Don't worry about it. Actually, Danny has excellent insurance, and they'll pay for a DNA test to see if I'll develop Huntington's disease. We have to wait until after the wedding to add me to his insurance, but at least I'll know in a few months." She had waffled on this issue before deciding to do the test. What would it be like to know for sure that she had the disease? Could she face it? Knowing that she might develop it was bad enough. The relief of finding out that she *wouldn't* though, was worth it. She tucked the clothes into the dresser, separating each kind into their own stacks.

"I'm glad you'll find out for sure. I'm sorry about everything."

Tia wiped at the tear that escaped and worked to keep her voice even. "Don't worry about it. It's better to be prepared than to have it be a surprise. So, back to getting our families together. What day would be best for you?"

"With everyone's jobs, a Saturday or Sunday would be best. What do you think, the seventeenth?"

"Danny works that day, and I'd really like him to be there. Could we do it the next week?" Tia double-checked the calendar on the wall where he'd posted his schedule, at Samantha's request. Samantha was completely stoked about getting Danny as her dad.

"That should work. I'll spring Mom for the day. Are you sure having everyone meet at once is a good idea? What about Ron and Mona together at the same time?"

Tia laughed. "There is that, but if the weather's good we can meet at the park and they'll have a little space between them. "

"The park sounds great. Lunch time?"

They agreed on a tentative time and location between their two towns.

They were lucky, Tia thought as she got out of the car, and thanked Danny for opening the door for her. The temperature was comfortable, there was only a light breeze, and the playground was empty. They let the kids out of the back seat and directed them toward the playground equipment. "At least the weather's nice." She was anxious about the many ways the afternoon could go wrong and had to focus on the positives.

"Of course it is—I put in a request." Danny slid his arms around her waist and kissed her nose.

"Well, if you put in the request, obviously the weather is bound to be perfect." She hooked her hands around his neck, then tipped her left hand so the diamond in the ring caught the light and sparkled back at her. It still made her grin.

"Are you admiring my ability to pick out jewelry?" he asked.

"Yes. I still think Laura must have helped you choose the ring. How else could you have done so well?" It was an ongoing joke, though she believed he'd done the shopping solo. Either way, she couldn't complain.

"Laura helped me plan my big proposal moment—the one that didn't happen because you changed my plans." His grin said he didn't mind.

"Sure, blame me for your inability to wait. It *must* be my fault."

"I will." His face grew closer and she lifted her mouth for a kiss.

Before their lips met, however, the sound of tires on gravel and Wes's voice calling out to them, broke things up. "Gross! Can't you two get married already so you can start fighting like normal adults?"

The engine turned off and Tia peeked around Danny's shoulders to see Wes getting out from behind the wheel and Mona emerging on the other side. Wes still had a twisted view of marriage, a relic of his parents' breakup, and the unfortunate demise of his own brief foray into wedlock.

"You two are so cute together," Mona called.

Tia sighed and pulled out of Danny's embrace, but took his hand. She looked over and saw Samantha helping Tristi up the stairs on the playground so they could go down the little plastic slide.

Nerves ran through her as she thought of what was still to come that afternoon. Would things go smoothly or would it be a complete disaster?

The others arrived a couple of minutes later, Ron with Glena and Rose with Lisa. They talked for a moment while Danny opened the wheelchair for Rose. Lisa came over to introduce them.

"Mom, this is my friend Danny, and his fiancée, Tia."

Danny smiled at Lisa. "Good to meet you both."

Tia chuckled in embarrassment as she realized she should have done introductions already. Lisa hadn't met anyone else there. "Sorry, I'm falling behind in my duties." She introduced Tia and Danny.

"Don't worry about it," Lisa said. Then to Danny, "It's good to finally meet you."

"Same here."

"My, you're a tall one, aren't you?" Rose asked, staring up at Danny. "And handsome, too!"

Danny grinned at her. "I am pretty tall, yes. Do you need some help moving to the wheelchair?"

"Only a steadying hand, if you don't mind."

"No problem." Danny handled it like the pro he was, and in a moment had her seated comfortably in the chair. "Anything else you need or are you good to go?'

"I'm fine. Thank you."

Rose turned and studied Tia. "Now, you look so familiar, honey. Have we met?"

Her stomach felt like it might revolt, but Tia smiled at the woman who had given birth to her. "Not yet. My name's Tia. Lisa tells me you like to watch my cooking segment on the noon news."

"Oh, Tia Riverton! I can't believe I'm actually meeting you. I love watching you!" Rose took Tia's hand between hers, warmth and excitement radiating from her face. "You're such a beautiful girl. You remind me of myself at your age."

Tia smiled, charmed and relieved, though she still felt nervous and a little uncertain about the afternoon. "Thank you. Would you like to meet the rest of my family?"

"That would be nice. You did bring something delicious for lunch, didn't you? Where I live, we get lots of mashed potatoes and mushy vegetables." Rose pulled a face.

"Yes, I have some really yummy choices, nothing mushy in the bunch. Come on."

She turned and stopped short when she found Glena standing only a few feet behind her. "Grandma, let me introduce you to Lisa and Rose Lowell. Ladies, this is my grandmother, Glena Parry." Tia hugged her grandma. "How are you doing today?" she asked once pleasantries were exchanged.

"I'm fine, child, but I don't know why we had to take such a long drive to meet here." She tugged her shirt, smoothing the wrinkles.

"I wanted to have Lisa meet with us, and she lives in Columbia. This is a nice park, though, isn't it?" Tia put an arm around Glena's shoulders and started leading her back to the pavilion where Samantha still hung on Wes, and Tristi played a game of got-your-nose with her grandpa.

"How old are you, dear?" Rose asked Tia as they moved on.

"Twenty-eight," Tia said.

"Really? Did you know that Lisa is twenty-eight too? She's my February baby. I hoped to have her on Valentine's Day, but she insisted on arriving on the seventeenth."

Glena stopped and turned to look at Tia, then continued around to stare at Rose, and then at Lisa. Her eyes narrowed and she asked in a low, shaky voice. "I thought you gave up on this, Tia."

Tia pressed her lips together and guided her grandma away from the others, calling out that they should continue to the pavilion without her. "Grandma, I told you I had to have answers."

"Answers? Why? You have a good family, lovin' parents. Me! Even a sweet hunk of a man who loves you—why you have to go lookin' for somethin' that doesn't matter?"

"I needed to know." Tia stared at Glena. "I'm sorry you aren't happy about it, but that's the way it is." She bit her lip. "How did you guess?"

Glena's face was pale and her lips pressed firmly together as she sent the strangers distrustful looks. "That Lisa looks so much like your mother, and you and that woman . . . What's she doin' in a wheelchair, anyway?"

"She has Huntington's disease. It's given her dementia, and makes her a little unstable when she walks. Someone has to walk with her, an arm tucked in hers to keep her from stumbling, so Rose requested the chair today."

Glena's face blanched. "She's sick? Could you get it?"

Tia swallowed, then nodded. "It's genetic. There's a fifty-percent chance I'll have it too." As always, the mention of her possible future made her stomach tighten in a hard ball.

"That can't be true, if I'd known . . . the mother was healthy, it was supposed to be perfect." She mumbled this under her breath, rubbed her forehead and turned away. "Wasn't supposed to be like this."

Forty-four

Suddenly everything clicked for Tia. "Grandma, please tell me you aren't responsible for this." But there was the way she'd fought the search, keeping back the fact that she'd been working in the hospital. And didn't Mona say her grandmother had sat with her in the nursery for most of the time between the birth and when she'd been returned to the hospital room? Glena would have had ample opportunity, and as an employee, they would have trusted her. The tightness in her stomach grew worse and she felt a little nauseated.

When there was no response, Tia held onto Glena's upper arm and turned to face her. "Grandma." Her voice was pleading.

Glena's face grew angry and moved to the offense. "I had to do somethin'. I didn't want my son raisin' *her* daughter. Bad enough that she's crazy, worse yet that it wasn't even your father's child. And now you." She reached up, put her hands on each of Tia's cheeks. "You could be sick like that someday." She shook her head. "No. You must have found the wrong family."

Tia tried to separate everything her grandmother had said. It was almost as if she blamed herself that Tia might develop Huntington's diseases. As if she caused it, instead of it being the luck of genetics. And what was that about the baby? "Grandma, you thought Mom cheated on Dad and I wasn't his?"

"Well, she did cheat—it's what broke them up," Glena reminded her.

"Yes, but not until years and years later." Tia wondered if her mother had been lying about cheating earlier. "What made you think the baby wasn't Dad's?"

Glena's face twisted into a hate stronger than anything Tia had seen before. "I seen her cattin' around with another man. Eatin' lunch with him, the way he touched her hand, it was obvious there was something between them. A couple of months later she came up pregnant. I knew then her baby was his, not your father's. I couldn't let her get away with that, passing some other man's child off as my son's."

Shock had Tia moving back half a step. "Grandma! How could you do that? You had no right—"

"I had every right to protect my son." Glena slammed the end of her cane against the ground to emphasize her words, light flashing in her eyes. "I tried to talk to him, to tell him about you before you was born, but he didn't believe it. She turned him against me. She even tried to keep me from seeing you, but your dad wouldn't allow it. I was angry, so I made the switch. If he was going to have to raise another man's child, she shouldn't be allowed to raise her own daughter."

Tia had to sit down, lightheaded from everything she'd heard. She started moving toward a nearby bench, not sure if she even cared if Glena followed her. "But Grandma, how could you?"

Glena trailed along behind, keeping her voice low enough that the others wouldn't hear. "They left me alone with the babies. And a few minutes later they brought you in. I'd seen the parents while we waited for Mona to deliver. They were so strong and healthy and happy. I could see it, their love, like me and my Grant when we was young and in love. They looked so healthy and I knew their baby would be perfect. My son deserved something perfect considering who he was married to."

Tia stared at her grandma, wondering how she had hidden how deeply her hatred went for Mona. "So you made the decision and you changed the bracelets."

Glena nodded and sat slowly on the bench, wincing slightly as she settled. "I knew they were going on break and I'd have time. The two of you looked a lot alike then." She turned to Tia, her face imploring. "Are you sure you found the right family? You could be wrong." She sounded more hopeful than believing.

"No, I'm not wrong." Tia's shock started to wear off and she felt the disgust and anger rise inside her. "We did DNA tests. Lisa belongs in this family."

"But did you check your dad?" Glena's words shot out louder than before. "Or just that woman?"

"Yes." Tia clenched her teeth, and stood from the bench, too upset to sit anymore. "We did have Dad tested. In fact, we didn't have Mom tested at all. We only tested Dad against the girls. So guess what, she is Dad's little girl, and you kept him from knowing *his* child. What did you think you were doing, playing with all of our lives like that?"

Glena's face went even whiter.

A hand on her arm had Tia looking up into Danny's face and she wondered how much he'd heard. She hadn't exactly been quiet. Her emotions were getting away from her.

"Is everything okay?" he asked. "Can I do anything?"

"Grandma, she switched us." The words sounded foreign. How could it be true? Tia shook with anger and confusion.

He turned and stared at Glena. "What?"

Tia pressed her fingers into her temples, then rubbed her face. "We can't do this right now." She turned to Glena, who looked even worse than Tia felt.

"It's my fault," Glena mumbled. "I chose wrong. I shoulda chose different. So wrong. Thought I was right, but I wasn't. How could I been wrong? You're perfect, the best granddaughter I could want." She kept mumbling, but was no longer understandable.

Tia glanced over at Lisa, who seemed nervous, awkward as she spoke with Ron. Wes shot a few glances in their direction, obviously concerned, but not wanting to get in the middle of it.

"I have to go keep things together." Tia felt like her life had been turned upside down again. She looked at Danny hopefully.

"I'm sorry." He brushed a kiss on her forehead. "I'll stay here with Grandma. You go ease things with everyone else. It's okay, really." He pressed a warm palm to her cheek, offering comfort.

"Thanks." She didn't want to step away from him, wished she could curl up in his arms for a good hour or two, but she couldn't. Not right now. There would be time for that later. Now she had to get away from Glena and think about something else for a few minutes, though how she was supposed to do that in the middle of lunch with everyone else, she had no idea.

Tia returned to the rest of the group, still feeling overwhelmed. She moved through the motions of facilitating the conversation, got the food out and helped set up lunch. She saw Danny and Glena sitting with their backs to her, out of ear shot, and tried to wrap her mind around what she had learned.

When Tia returned to the group, Danny took Glena by the wrist and guided her to a nearby bench. She was still muttering nonsense and when he said her name, she looked up at him with confusion. "Grandma, are you okay?" Danny kept his hand on her wrist, felt her pulse beating against his fingers. Too fast. Even without counting, he knew it was too fast. He checked his watch and counted the beats. One-twenty-two. He couldn't believe this sweet old lady was responsible for everything Tia had gone through in the past few months, and he felt angry and defensive for her, but he worried about Glena too.

She still hadn't answered, so he spoke again. "Hey, I know this has been a bit of a shock, can you take a few deep breathes for me? Come on, in and out." He caught her eye and sucked in a long, deep breath as an example, then blew it out, glad to see her following suit. "Let's do that again." He prompted her through a few more good breaths. "Okay, what are you feeling?"

"I made the wrong choice. How could I have known?" the muttering continued.

Danny's breath caught as he watched her speak. The left side of her face wasn't moving in tandem with the right and her words were slurred. He pulled out his cell phone and dialed 911.

"Hey, Danny's waving at you," Wes said, nudging Tia.

She looked up and saw the worry on Danny's face. "I'll see what's going on." She left the group with a backward look at Lisa, but Wes took over the conversation, drawing Lisa in, and Ron seemed to be having a nice conversation with Rose. Maybe their families would work out all right after all. Not that she had any choice now, since her grandma interfered.

When Tia reached Danny, she realized he was speaking on a cell phone. "Yes, heart rate about one-twenty, sagging face and weak arm on the left side, confused."

Tia's eyes strayed to her grandmother, and she saw what Danny was talking about. Stroke, she thought. The sagging face told her it could be a stroke, but the thought was too frightening. All of her anger evaporated in an instant as worry took over. She knelt in front of Glena and took her hand. "Grandma, what's going on?"

More muttering, Glena looked right through her, then seemed to focus and gave a lopsided smile. "You're sho beautiful. I shaw the muver, knew you be bootiful too, love what you become. You make old lady proud." The words slurred, and were barely understandable.

"I love you, Grandma. Danny's getting you some help. We'll take good care of you." Everything tangled up inside Tia and she struggled to stay calm and focused.

The sound of footsteps had Tia turning and looking up into her father's concerned gaze. "What's going on?" he asked.

Danny hung up his cell phone and put it away. "I think your mom is having a stroke. I've called an ambulance."

"Don' need ambance," Glena protested.

Panic filled Ron's eyes. "Can't you do something for her?"

Danny didn't look up, focused on his patient instead. "Just monitor her until the ambulance arrives. They'll give her oxygen, get her to the hospital where they have clot busters available to help her." He touched Glena's cheek. "Grandma, take another deep breath for me, okay?"

She muttered some more, but then paused to breathe.

"Good." Danny nodded and glanced up at Ron. "If you catch strokes quickly, get them the medication, the recovery is much faster, and much more successful than it used to be. Sit down if you need to, but don't pass out on me or anything. I can't deal with two patients."

Tia noticed how awful her father looked and grabbed his arm, pulling him to the other side of his mother, and pushed him into the empty space on the bench. It wasn't very big, but it would do. "Come on, Dad, you need to breathe, too."

"Do you know anything about your mom's medications?" Danny asked. He alternately kept Ron and Glena busy answering questions until the ambulance turned the corner. Tia flagged them down, relieved her father was starting to look better, act more centered. She was glad she hadn't told him yet about his mother switching her and Lisa.

By the time the EMTs had the gurney out, everyone else from the group had gathered around Glena.

Danny looked at Tia, "Get everyone back out of the way." He turned to the ambulance crew and started giving them a rundown about her medications, surgeries and allergies, according to what Ron had told him.

Tia stood and snatched up Samantha as she cried and ran toward Glena. "Hey, kiddo, let's get out of the way, okay?" She turned to the rest of them. "Grandma's not feeling well. Danny thinks it might be a stroke, but they're going to take good care of her and get her to the hospital. Let's move back and let them have some room."

Mona turned to Lisa. "Heart problems, that's what you're going to have to deal with. My side of the family doesn't have heart problems. She always said my family was crazy, but look who's laughing now."

That irritated Tia. "*No one* is laughing, Mom, because this isn't funny." Tia gestured for everyone to move out of the way, but as soon as they had cleared out, she turned back to watch the proceedings. Danny helped strap Glena on, said a few last words to the closest crew member, then turned to Ron, who handed him a set of keys.

Danny walked back to them. "Ron's riding along. I'll bring his car out to the hospital in a minute." He pulled keys from his pocket and handed them to Tia. "You take my car."

Tia turned to Lisa. "I'm sorry you drove all this way to meet us."

"Don't worry about it. You're all going to the hospital?" Lisa set a hand on Tia's arm.

"I'm not," Mona said, folding her arms over her chest. "The woman hates me, and I'm not going to the hospital for her."

"Unless you want me to leave you behind," Wes interjected, "Yes, you are." He shifted his gaze back to Tia. "Let's load everything into the cars and head over. Once we hear something from the doctors we can grab a bite in the parking lot if we still have an appetite." He sifted his gaze to Lisa. "Will you come with us?"

Lisa looked at her mom, who appeared concerned, but not upset. "Yes. We'll come."

"The woman always hated me. Why should I sit in the waiting room?" Mona asked, her arms crossed in front of her.

"Because she matters to the rest of us, and she's the one who brought us all together," Tia said, then winced as she turned away, wondering if that was a little too explanatory. The anger and betrayal had been buried by concern for her grandma for now, but she'd have to deal with it again soon.

Danny pulled out his phone and looked up directions to the hospital from where they were. Wes wrote them down, then made copies to pass around while the women put the food back in the cars. As soon as he'd passed the directions on to Wes, Danny got into Ron's car and headed out.

Everyone else was only minutes behind him.

Forty-five

Tia found Ron and Danny in the waiting room when she arrived with the girls. Samantha ran to Danny, throwing her arms around his middle. "Will Grandma be okay?" She turned her face up to his, trust in her eyes.

He crouched to her level. "The doctors are doing everything they can for her. Don't worry, they'll take good care of her."

Tia appreciated that he hadn't lied to Samantha, though she didn't feel all that reassured. She watched him give Samantha a hug, then he stood and walked over to Tia, pulling her into a hug as well, Tristi sandwiched between them. "That not-worrying thing? It goes double for you," he said, then brushed his lips over her forehead. "Come, sit down. It'll be a while yet before they'll send someone out to give us an update."

Tia did as she was told, and the others joined them a few minutes later. Wes had apparently helped Lisa with her mom and the wheelchair, and entered the room pushing Rose. "Any word?" he asked.

"Not yet," Ron said.

"Are you sure we're not in the way?" Lisa asked.

"No, were glad to have you," Ron told her. "Come sit by me. We haven't had much chance to talk. Tell me about your dad. I need the distraction."

Tia smiled, watching them together. Danny pulled a couple chairs over to face Lisa and Ron, then gestured for Tia to sit in one of them. He settled in the other and Samantha crawled into his lap.

When he took Tia's hand, she thought she couldn't ask for more in a man.

The doctors came and went. Everyone walked out to the cars in shifts to put together plates of food, then returned to the waiting room to eat. Ron was allowed back to see his mother, and Mona complained and worried and fussed constantly. Tia was glad she hadn't bothered to ask about Rose's condition. She didn't think she was up to dealing with the hysterics that would have ensued if Mona realized Tia could end up like that someday.

Finally she and Danny were allowed in to see Glena, though she was totally out of it, so they didn't get to talk. It was just as well, since Tia had no idea what to say anyway. She was grateful for Danny's hand, for the silent support he'd been all day. They had opted for a short engagement, which made their wedding less than a month away. Barely.

After an hour, the doctor came in and told them they were transferring Glena to a larger facility in Kansas City.

Everyone gathered their things and returned the chairs to where they belonged.

"Do we get to go home now, Mom?" Samantha asked.

"Yeah. We can go home." Tia kissed her on the head and gathered the sippy cup Tristi had dropped on the floor beneath the chairs.

"Is Nana going to be okay?"

Tia felt that familiar ache in her chest. It was even worse trying to explain to Samantha than dealing with it herself. She took the seat, then pulled Samantha close so she leaned against Tia's knees. "I don't know, honey. Danny called for help really fast, and the doctors were able to get her good medicine right away, so hopefully she'll be fine, in a while. But Nana is getting old, so it's hard to know if she'll get all the way better. We'll have to wait and see."

Samantha pursed her lips, then nodded. "Okay. Let's go home now."

"All right, sweetheart."

Danny came back over, Tristi asleep in his arms. "We about ready?"

Tia stood, looked around the room again to make sure they hadn't left anything behind, then nodded. "Let's go say goodbye to Lisa and Rose." The whole day had been cut short, and Tia didn't feel like she had time to speak with Lisa, to ask Rose about her life, to really watch how things were going with Lisa's introduction to the family.

Wes was helping Rose into the passenger seat when Tia joined them. He picked up the wheelchair and took it around to the trunk.

"Thanks for everything," Lisa said.

"It's no problem. And Tia threatened not to make her cannoli for me again if I wasn't nice to you." Wes winked at Tia.

"You've gone above and beyond nice. So thanks," Lisa said. They stood looking at each other for a moment, as if uncertain what to do next.

"It was good meeting you. You'll have to join us again sometime, though I'm warning you that all of our get-togethers tend to be somewhat on the exciting side lately. You may wish you never heard of us," he said.

Lisa laughed. "I doubt that." She tucked her thumbs in the back pockets of her jeans.

He gave a little wave, then headed for his car where Mona was already waiting. "See ya, sis," he said to Tia as he left.

"See you later." Tia waited until he was out of the way, then gave Lisa a hug. "Thanks for meeting us, and again, I'm sorry this all happened."

"No, it's fine. It was interesting to see how your family worked together when there's trouble. Danny's so cool on his feet, too." She gave Tia's hand a squeeze. "I know you two are going to be happy together."

"Yeah, I can't argue with that." Tia wanted to tell her, right then and there about Glena, about how it had all happened, why it had happened, but she wasn't ready. She still wasn't sure how she felt about it.

"Keep in touch," Lisa said.

"I will." Tia walked to the passenger side of the car and leaned down to the opened window. "Rose, it was great to meet you. I hope I get to see you again soon sometime."

"I'm happy to meet you too, dear. Did I tell you how much you remind me of myself at your age?"

Tia laughed. "You did. I'm happy you think so. You're a great example for me." She touched the woman's hand, then straightened and waved goodbye before turning away. Tears pooled in her eyes, and she needed a moment to get herself back together. She looked at Danny buckling Tristi into her car seat and knew quiet wasn't going to happen anytime soon, but she'd get through it.

Tia stewed about everything she'd learned at the picnic, not ready to hash it out until she had a handle on it. When they finished putting the girls to bed after dinner Monday night, Danny slid his arm around her as they returned to the living room.

"So, you've had time to brood. Want to talk?"

Tia tipped her head against his shoulder. "I don't know. Will it help?"

"Maybe. You won't know if you don't try." He sat on the sofa and snuggled her close. "That was a big shock. I know you didn't expect it. Have you told anyone else?'

"No. I don't know *how* to tell anyone. Or even if I should. How could she do that to us, Danny? What was she thinking? I mean, I know what she said, but it just doesn't make sense." She rubbed her face with her palm.

"It can't be fixed, and no matter how much you might understand on some level why she wanted to get back at your mom, you'll never get what made her do something so extreme. The question is whether you can accept it and forgive her or not."

"I know." Tia had stopped by the previous evening, intentionally going while her father would be there so she wouldn't have to face Glena alone. She was conflicted: she still loved her grandmother, but couldn't forget what she'd done. "I just wish I could see things the way she did, for a minute, so I could let this go. And on the other hand, I never want to forgive her for doing this, for being so stupid."

"You know I love you?" He pressed his lips to her head.

"Of course." That went without saying.

"You know your parents love you?"

"Yes."

Danny took her hand in his, giving it a squeeze. "You don't have to forgive your grandma, but think about how you want to remember your relationship with her, because she won't be around forever."

Tia pressed her cheek to his shoulder, pain knifing through her. "I know."

Several days passed and Tia had stopped into the hospital to see her grandma three times, but she hadn't gotten the chance for a quiet chat alone. This time when she walked into the room, she slid into the chair beside the bed. No one else was around, and Glena appeared to be sleeping.

"Go ahead and say your say, child. I know you're angry."

The slightly slurred words made Tia jump, she didn't know how Glena could tell who had walked in. She still hadn't even slitted her eyes. "I don't know what I am. How could you do it, Grandma?"

"It was impulse. I held Lisa in my arms, rocked her, wondered about the man I seen Mona with. Knew your mother had been

267

cheating on my boy. It made me sick to think of your dad raising another man's baby and not knowin' it. I was angry, at Mona, at the baby for existing. I was alone for a while; I had the chance to take her daughter away and give her another, so I did it. I never regretted it for a moment. You've always made me proud."

That didn't help. It was hardly explanation. "You didn't think about what was best for me, for Lisa, to be raised in the families we were born to? You never wondered about Lisa, how she was doing? You realize the DNA tests were done with Dad, so she *is* his daughter. You gave her away out of spite."

Glena pursed her lips for a moment, as if trying to accept that she'd been wrong, at least about the baby's paternity. "I never thought about the other baby. I had you. I chose you. What more did I need?" She lifted her right hand and covered Tia's. "It's too late to be sorry, child, except for causing you worry."

Tia didn't know what to say to that. Glena was recovering well, but the doctor expected her to spend the rest of her life with a walker—and that was the best-case scenario. The stroke had done significant damage and it couldn't be completely undone. Though Tia didn't think God worked retribution like this, it seemed almost like a kind of twisted divine justice.

"I love you too, Grandma, but I don't understand how you could do it."

When there was no response, Tia wondered if Glena had fallen asleep. Her theory was confirmed when her grandmother took a deep breath and sighed. She squeezed Glena's hand and headed back to her car.

She hadn't told anyone besides Danny about Glena's secret. It would ruin her father's opinion of his mother, and give Mona more reason to hate her former mother-in-law. Wes could handle it, but didn't seem to care one way or the other. Tia decided someday, after Glena and Rose had passed on, she would share the truth with Lisa. Between now and then, Tia would try to forgive her grandma for interfering. She didn't expect it to be easy.

No matter the struggles she'd had in her family, the difficulties that had come her way, she was happy to have been raised by Ron and Mona. Having discussed this aspect with Lisa the previous night, she knew Lisa felt the same about her parents. Whatever the case, their lives were what they were, and that couldn't be changed. And maybe that was all right.

At least once she had time to adjust a little longer.

Epilogue

Tia breezed into the fire station on a Thursday afternoon in late June. The past several days had been rainy, so she enjoyed the beautiful weather—sunny and bright. Tristi and Samantha were both still in daycare, and she'd have to pick them up soon, but wanted to take a moment to chat with Danny without them around.

Lisa and her mom had made it to the wedding a few weeks back, and both seemed to be doing well. Glena was home again, as bright-eyed and positive as ever, but she would never walk alone, or drive a car again. Tia had stopped by to visit her a few days earlier. Their relationship would never return to what it once was, but Tia didn't have the heart to punish them both by wasting the few years Glena had left.

She found Danny mopping out the back of an ambulance. "Hey, there, stranger. Could you give me a lift?"

He looked up, grinning, then set down the mop handle and jumped from the back of the rig. "Why, do you need me to check your pulse?" He pulled her close and kissed her. "You still seem to be breathing," he said when he pulled away.

She laughed at the corny line, but threaded her arms around his neck. "I've been breathing for so long now that I don't even have to think about it anymore."

He chuckled. "That's a relief. You know I'm always happy to see you, Mrs. Tullis, but is there a particular reason you're here this fine afternoon?" He often called her that, as if reveling in the fact that she was his.

The new name always thrilled her a bit, so she grinned. "Well, Mr. *Tullis*, I thought you might like to know that I got the results back on those tests."

His grin widened even more, though Tia hadn't thought it possible. "Negative?"

"I do not have enough copies of the gene to cause Huntington's disease," she confirmed. She felt light today, filled with hope for the kind of future she'd always dreamed of. With Danny.

He sent out a hoot of happiness and spun them both around. "That's terrific news, and it leaves me with just one question."

"What's that?"

He lowered his head and spoke low so he wouldn't be overheard. "How soon do you think we could start trying for another little girl?"

Acknowledgments

As always, there are a host of people who helped me make this book a reality. A big thanks to my many critiquers who helped me catch problems with my story and build it into something better: Tristi Pinkston, Nichole Giles, Keith Fisher, Shirley Westenskow, Tammy Hansen, Delise Perkins, Mindy Holt and Annette Lyon. Any shortcomings that remain in this story are purely my own.

And a big thanks to my husband, Bill, who is always in my corner, always my biggest supporter and willing to step in for Web design, punctuation and grammar questions, and puts up with my insane schedule. I love you sweetie!

About the Author

Heather Justesen earned a BA in English Literature from Southern Utah University, where she met her husband, Bill. She worked in newspaper for several years, and they spent two years as foster parents. They now live in the little town where she grew up in Central Utah, run on their local ambulance as Advanced EMTs and raise a cat, two dogs, and a whole slew of chickens, geese, ducks, guineas, and a tom turkey, which is very vain. When she can squeeze in the time, she gardens and loves to bake. She also writes serial stories for BigWorldNetwork.com available in ebook and audio formats.

You can learn more about Heather on her blog: http://heatherjustesen.blogspot.com/

Or her website: http://www.heatherjustesen.com/

Or contact her via email at Heather@HeatherJustesen.com

www.ingramcontent.com/pod-product-compliance
Lightning Source LLC
Chambersburg PA
CBHW071128260626
47162CB00003B/702